It All Happened Like Clockwork . . .

It was great. And I had a ringside—well, above ringside, actually—seat. The whole building had been cleared out by now. The bomb threats did their job, so it was easy to move around from office to office, staring down at the streets filling with stalled cars and angry, scared people. . . . mixed in with the jagged edges of the business towers with all the dull, gleaming glass was a collection of filmy streams of smoke, slowly twisting and blowing in the breeze. Black smoke, white smoke, dirty, thick, ash-gray smoke all over the place, rising from the cars, stores, tenements, and fresh bomb craters I had created or caused to appear. It was a good feeling.

One Bang-up Job

GERALD LAURENCE

BERKLEY BOOKS, NEW YORK

ONE BANG-UP JOB

A Berkley Book/published by arrangement with
the author

PRINTING HISTORY
Berkley edition/February 1989

ISBN: 0-425-11390-6

A BERKLEY BOOK ® TM 757,375
Berkley Books are published by The Berkley Publishing Group,
200 Madison Avenue, New York, N.Y. 10016.
The name ''BERKLEY'' and the ''B'' logo
are trademarks belonging to Berkley Publishing Corporation.

PRINTED IN THE UNITED STATES OF AMERICA

10 9 8 7 6 5 4 3 2 1

One

"SEE THIS GUN?"

"How can I miss it? You're pointing it at me."

"At your stomach, to be precise."

"Yeah, I noticed." I noticed more than that. The gun was a snub-nosed, .38-caliber Smith and Wesson Chief Special. A very fine weapon. A little small for some of the smash-and-grabs I'd pulled off. A nice, big, blunderbuss type of thing is good for scaring the shit out of people. And it attracts more attention from witnesses too. One time I took out a whole corner of the Jewelry Mart without wearing a mask, and I found out later that the cops got great descriptions of the Webley and Scott Mark VI I'd used, but nothing good on me.

"You," he said, jerking the Smith and Wesson up a little.

"Me?"

"You're the bright boy who came up with the idea for the mass robberies, right?"

"What? I don't know what you're talking about."

"Don't give me that shit," he snapped. "How'd you like one in the belly right away?"

"I wouldn't." Who would? Jesus, I wish I had the Webley Mark VI right now. It was huge. Eleven and a half inches long. Nearly two and a half pounds. Heavy recoil, but it was worth the pain. You could shoot out a diesel-engine block with one. Although right now, even the Smith and Wesson looked big. I admired it from afar—about seven feet, the distance from me to the guy holding it.

"Now look," he said, smiling a little. "Let's be nice. You tell me about the plans for the robberies, and I'll be real careful where I shoot."

The gun muzzle made small arcs in the air, moving from my knees to my throat. I swallowed hard and shifted my body a little. I slowly pulled my feet a little farther back under my seat—a creaky old metal card-table chair. I had to get leverage for a fast leap from the chair to the light suspended from the ceiling. He didn't seem to notice my feet. He just stood there, leaning back against the wall, one foot up on another old metal folding chair.

"If—if you're going to shoot, anyway," I said, "where's the percentage in talking?"

He smiled again. "You ever been shot in the gut?"

"No."

"They tell me it's very, very painful. You bleed slow. Takes forever to die. You don't tell me what I want to know and I'll shoot you in the stomach. And we'll still have plenty of time to talk about the money. I mean, hell, I can shoot you somewhere else too. In the arm. In the elbow. Or the knees. Or your cock. And we'll still have plenty of time for you to tell me everything. You get me?"

"Yeah." He was enjoying himself. I looked scared. It was easy to do, and I figured he'd like it.

"You know," he was saying, glancing around the cramped, stuffy room, "the nice thing about coming here tonight is the peace and quiet. This is a nice little room. And right in the middle of the warehouse too. It's perfect. Right out on the pier, the sound of the ocean, everything on the wharf closed up—it's perfect. I could shoot you twenty, thirty times, nobody'd know."

"Yeah," I admitted. It was pretty stupid to come with him. How could I have misjudged it so badly? Shit, I was losing it. No, that wasn't true. Come on, give yourself a break, you've only been working eighteen hours a day for three weeks, trying to put this thing together. Too many arrangements, too many last-minute changes, too many jokers getting out of line . . . and too goddamn much acting. Jesus, that really takes it out of you. You're just worn-out. Besides, who the hell thought he'd try to put the muscle on me—the guy who was making everybody rich with the biggest robbery the world had ever seen?

"So," he said, "tell me about how you're doing it with the money."

"I—I don't know . . . 'doing it'?"

"You know what I mean, asshole," he snapped again. "What's the big deal with the money?"

"N-no deal—I mean, no big deal. . . ." I thought the quaver in my voice was done very well. "We've got guys going into the banks, grab what they can, come out, dump it into saddlebags on motorcycles, then everybody takes off in different directions." I moved my feet a little closer to the imaginary starting blocks under the creaky old chair. "The cycles take the money away from the action. It'll be wild, going on the sidewalks, in between cars, through people's front yards. Man, that's going to be something to see." I remember liking it a lot when I was one of the motorcycle drivers in a smash-and-grab I was re-

cruited for when I was seventeen. What a rush. "Uh,
anyway," I went on, "the guys who are on foot—you
know, the ones who took out the banks—they run
down into an alley or something and take off their
jumpsuits. They'll have regular clothes on underneath. Then they just blend into the crowds on the
street. Believe me, there'll be plenty of crowds."

"I bet," he said. Then he actually snorted. I didn't
think people really snorted anything except coke. Or
maybe when they snored. Jesus, what a clown. "So
where do they take the money?"

"All over the place." He moved the gun in little arcs
again. The metal glowed faintly yellow—it was one of
those bug light bulbs screwed into the single overhead
fixture. I got my feet into position and judged the
distance up to the yellow bulb.

"Quit stallin'!"

"All right. Yeah, okay, uh, I'll tell you," I stam-
mered at him. "Um, they head up toward Stinson
Beach."

"Then what?"

"Well, then they put the bags in the trash. You
know, those big dumpsters? Each cycle goes to a
different one on a route from the city proper to the
beach. Our guys come along in a big trash truck and
scoop it all up. Simple. You just have to know which
dumpsters, that's all."

"Stinson Beach."

"Yeah. That's where our guys are taking their
money. I don't know where the others are going."

"What d'you mean? What others?"

"All the others. Jesus, this thing's gotten so big, I
think half the city's ripping off the other half. You got
Foley's people, Henderson's Martinelli's, all sorts of
independent operations—shit, even some cops are in
on it now." I paused and watched as he frowned. He
had started thinking about it, but I was waiting for

that blank look, the one where the eyes aren't seeing
what's in front of your face because you're really
looking inward. Well, maybe he needs more encour-
agement. "Think about it," I told him. "How'd you
find out about it? You're probably just supposed to
fence a few of the hard goods, right? I mean, you're
not supposed to know about the Plan. If somebody's
let you in on it, then maybe lots of others are in on it
too. And, Jesus, with the cops involved, you just don't
know what's for real and what's a setup anymore, you
know?" I shrugged my shoulders, but that was just an
excuse for putting my hands at my sides. I wanted to
swing them upward when I took off for the light bulb.
He wasn't saying anything. I glanced at his eyes.
Bingo. Blank stare. I moved. Everything concentrated
on getting across a certain distance in the shortest
time possible. I aimed my head toward the light,
pushed off with both legs, and swiveled my arms over
my head like diving into a swimming pool. I smashed
both hands into the bulb, and it exploded into a
thousand tiny particles of glass dust.

"Hey!" he shouted.

The room was bathed in a faint yellow afterglow for
just an instant as I tried to picture just where he was in
the now black little room.

"Son of a bitch," he shouted, and fired wildly, then
twice more. Each time his torso was outlined in the
strobe of the muzzle flash.

I stayed low and reached out for the old metal chair.

"You asshole," he said. "You're gonna die slow."

I heard him moving along the wall toward the door,
stumbling a little in the darkness. I rose, holding the
chair by the very end of one leg, my palm clamped
around the rubber tip. I pivoted on one foot, swinging
the chair in a big overhand motion, bringing it down
right where I thought he was. The crunch of metal into
flesh and bone was very satisfying.

"Shit," he half screamed.

The gun bounced on the concrete floor and went off again. I think I heard the bullet slam into the wooden door. Maybe not. I was too busy swinging the chair again, this time in a sidearm motion. He must have moved away from the door because I only caught him with part of the chair. I heard fabric rip, and then he was on top of me and we went down in a heap of jabbing, clawing, scratching fingers and arms. I brought my legs up between us and lashed out at him. I struck stomach, chest, shoulder, head. The angle was right, so I kept on pumping at him with my feet, left-right left-right, until he didn't move any more.

I felt around for the gun, couldn't find it, and pawed my way over to the faint crack of light around the door. Once it was open I got the gun, dragged its sorry owner into the light, and went through his pockets.

Wallet, keys, pocket comb, pack of cigarettes, lighter, extra ammo for the gun, and a small notebook filled with mostly blank paper. One of the few notes was the address of the warehouse we were in.

I shook him awake.

He said something that sounded like "Mmrumph."

"Your turn," I said.

"Wha?"

"Your turn to talk."

"Go to hell."

"Sure. But not now. Who told you about the Plan?"

"Ah, screw you."

"You ever been shot in the gut? They tell me it's very, very painful. Something about bleeding for a long time." I put the barrel of the Smith and Wesson against his protruding pot and pushed. Hard. "Shall we try it and see?"

"N-no, wait. Don't, don't shoot. I wasn't really going to shoot you."

"Yeah."

"No, I wasn't. Just scare you. You know, scare you to find out about the money. That's all."

"Who was it told you about it?"

"Yeah, sure. It was, uh, Weisberg. Tommy Weisberg. He told me."

"Bullshit." Tommy was the guy I'd been working with on this thing. We had done the protection game together, then the hot-car operation, and then the dope "importing," each time getting a little closer to the big scores. Every operation was bigger and took more planning. He and I sweated blood over this Plan, nurtured it, worked it until it was perfect, and then we put together the biggest conglomeration of criminals you'd ever seen, mostly with guts and a prayer and a ton of work.

Then, last week, he disappeared. Gone. I smelled a kiss-off from one of the big guys—Foley, Henderson, or Martinelli—and I almost skipped. But nothing happened. Not to me or to any of my guys. It was weird. I was still working eighteen hours a day, but now I wasn't getting much sleep the other six.

Two days ago Tommy was fished out of a waste-disposal tank, his body full of little holes, .38-caliber holes.

I jumped to conclusions and pulled the trigger. The shot wasn't as loud as I expected. I guess his bulk muffled the pistol's report. It wasn't the best shooting I'd ever done, but it wasn't the worst, either. Killing that girl coke runner was worse than this. She hadn't shot at me. I probably should have just pistol-whipped him and gotten him to talk that way, but like I say, I was tired lately.

The shock of it sank in and he began yelling. "Oh, God—no!" Then the pain hit and he ground his teeth together.

"I bet you didn't give Tommy much of a chance."

"It wasn't me!"

"Yeah. For example, I'll bet when you first shot him, you didn't think to call an ambulance for him. But I might be persuaded to call one for you."

"Yes!" he hissed.

"Tell me what you know. And tell me who else knows."

"Call," he pleaded.

"First talk, then call." I can be pretty cold to people who shoot my friends. And who threaten to shoot me.

In between gasps for air and cries for help, he told me everything he knew about the Plan—my plan to rob most of the city of San Francisco.

TWO

My boss, F. J. Milo of Milo Security, was making his standard introduction of me to a new client.

"And in here is our agency within an agency, a firm we call Dauntless Investigations, headed by our own Dauntless investigator, Natalie Dauntless Fisher. Nat, I'd like you to meet Walter Falkes."

He led into my office a middle-aged man who reeked of money and recent discomfort.

"How do you do," I said.

"Yes, I—" he began, then turned to F. J. "Frederick, I don't think this is quite what is required."

"Now, now, Walt. You just sit down over there, and Natalie will convince you she's the right man for the job."

We all smiled at that one. Me with tolerance. F. J. with satisfaction. Walter, well, let's just say his smile was halfway between weak and grim.

"I'll leave you two now," F. J. said, and he did, closing the door after him.

Walter and I stood there for a few seconds. I went to

the window and twisted shut the metal blinds, which automatically turned on the hidden tape recorder.

"So, shall I tell you what you're thinking about me?" I asked him.

"Well, I don't know . . ."

"You've got a serious problem on your hands. There's an element of danger. So you think that someone built along the lines of Humphrey Bogart, or maybe an all-pro linebacker, would be better for this job."

I walked up to him, smiling all the way, patted him on the lapel, straightened his tie, removed his overcoat from his forearm, and went to hang it on the wooden stand in the corner.

"Look," I told him, "I didn't get this far in this business by being soft. Not in the head or anywhere else. You want tough, I can give you tough. Excluding the use of blunt instruments, I've got twenty-three methods for killing people within easy reach on that desk. Twenty-four if you count burning them to death with the lighter."

"Well, I don't know . . ."

"You want stealth, I can give you stealth. Here's your wallet back. I removed it when I took your overcoat."

He looked amazed. That little carnival sideshow stunt usually has that effect on people.

"And if you want some straight talking, here it is: Put your ass in that chair and let's discuss your problem. We don't even know if brawn is even necessary yet. Okay?"

"Oh. Yes, all right."

He sat. I sat.

"I will say this, miss, ah . . . miss? Mrs.?"

"It's Miss Fisher, but Natalie is fine."

"All right, then. Natalie. I'll give you this, you got me to sit down, and I wasn't going to do that when I came in. So, um, where should I begin?"

"The beginning's always a safe bet."

"*What?*"

"*Sorry. Being flippant is a bad habit. What happened that made you go to the police?*"

"*How did you know I've been to the police?*"

"*I didn't. It just figured, that's all. You look as if you have some standing in the community. And I'll bet that made you think you would get some response with the cops. But they don't want to do anything the way you'd like to see it done. This is all guesswork and it may be impressive, but it's not getting us anywhere.*"

"*Yes, well, the thing is, I found a body in a building I own over on Pier Sixty.*"

"*What kind of body?*"

"*A dead one.*"

"*Yeah, I figured as much. I mean, male, female, black, white, shot, stabbed—what?*"

"*Oh, yes, I see. Well, it was a man, a Caucasian, um, about forty-five years old. He'd been shot in the stomach and in the head. The cops—I mean, the police— said he had been shot in the stomach first, then later on in the head.*"

"*Do you know who he was?*"

"*He didn't have any identification on him, but one of the detectives said he recognized the man as a fence, a man who purchases stolen merchandise.*"

"*That's what fences do,*" I said. "*Was there a name?*"

"*Yes, but I . . . let's see, it was something odd, like T. Bowen, or possibly even T. Bone.*"

"*If it was T. Bone as in Trombone, then whoever shot him did us all a favor. Thomas Roman 'Trombone' Bone was not one of our more upstanding citizens. Most crooks try to find something legit to use as a front. Bone used fencing as his front.*"

"*And you know this Bone person?*"

"*Know of him,*" I said. "*Never met him. Okay, you found a body and called the police. What's the problem?*"

"Well, you see, they—the police—seem to be, oh, I don't know," he began. "They're . . . well, they're just so slow."

"Slow."

"Yes. Well, methodical, I guess they'd call it. But they took forever to get started on the case, and now they don't seem too interested in solving this killing and letting us get on with our lives."

"I see," I said. But I didn't. So I waited.

"I mean, this inactivity may be normal, but I just wish they'd get on with it," he said irritably.

"Um hmmmm," I said. And waited some more.

"Well, I just don't see why they can't either pin it on someone or close the case soon. That's all." He folded his arms.

"How soon?" I asked.

"What?"

"Today is Tuesday," I said. "In how many days would you want them to be closing the case?"

"Well," he said, looking troubled, "by Thursday."

"Thursday."

"Well, yes," he said.

"Why?"

"What?"

"Why should the case be closed by Thursday? What happens Friday?"

"Well, I'm selling the place. The warehouse."

"So?"

"So the police coming around could . . . I don't know, affect the price I'll get."

"And you can't sell it later?" I asked.

"No, I think I'll get the best price right now. Look, this isn't getting us anywhere. Perhaps I should go."

"Just a second," I said. "Let me see if I have this straight. You would like it if you could use your warehouse on Friday without fear of the police showing up? Is that about the size of it?"

His eyes blazed.

"Because if that's what this is all about, perhaps it can be arranged. A medical quarantine should take care of it. Post a few signs, get a few documents, post a couple of lookouts wearing the right uniforms and driving the right county vehicles, and you're in business."

He looked relieved. "You can do that?" he asked.

"Don't see why not. Where can I reach you? I'll work out the details and the fee with F. J., and someone will come see you with the contract, get your signature, make it all final, that sort of thing."

He gave me his card after writing his home address and phone number on the back. He smiled. I smiled. We shook hands. He left beaming. I went to my desk, switched off the hidden recorder, and switched on the cassette player. Paul Winter's *Canyon*. Soothing sounds to wait for the boss by.

"What the hell was that?" F. J. said, sticking his head in the door.

"Interesting, ain't it?" I asked. "You listened in?"

"You bet I did. What kind of a stunt is he pulling? And is he pulling it on us? And what is this quarantine jazz? That's out of the question."

"You say that now"—I smiled at him—"but you'll feel a lot different if Thursday rolls around and we haven't figured out what this game is all about. Something strange is going to happen in that warehouse this Friday, and I intend to be around to find out what it is. Besides, this gig is probably good for a five-figure fee."

He thought that over, then said, "Just how would you go about getting quarantine signs, anyway?"

Three

FRIDAY. JESUS, I didn't think it would ever get here. A million things to do. Reassure the nervous nellies. Give the go to the smash-and-grab leaders. Get the last-minute payouts organized. Buy three more motorcycles to replace some that didn't show up. Several guys chickened out. Had to recruit some new ones. Jesus, they're getting younger all the time. Then there were the two jokers standing in front of me right now, demanding more money.

"See, we know this is big, real big, you know?" the small one said. Small, like about six-two, two-twenty. "An' the thing is, we think we're an important part of it. I mean, if we don't roll our rigs, you got cops coming off the freeways, right?"

"Right," I said.

"An' what we're doin' is dangerous, you know?"

"I know."

"A man could get trapped in the cab. Or maybe the gas tank blows. Could happen, right?"

"Could happen."

Silence.

"Fuck this," the big one said. "He ain't getting it. Look, we want a thousand more each. Five hundred now, five hundred on Saturday. You got it?"

"Oh, I got it," I said. "Now, here's something for you to get." I reached out with a fist right at the big one's nose. He arched back, and quickly. I half crouched and slammed him in the gut. He made an *ooof* sound, but by then I had pivoted, whistling an uppercut at the small one, coming at me from the side. I was hoping to hit his chin but settled for catching his cheek with two of my knuckles. Neither blow did much damage to them, but they had been forced to backstep, giving me a chance to reach into my pocket and bring the can of mace out where they could see it. They stopped just as they were about to rush me.

"Hey, ease up on that," the small one said.

"*You* ease up unless you want a case of the dry heaves."

"Yeah, sure." They slowly came out of their attack stances.

"Now, just listen. Do you two numbnuts think it's me alone you're dealing with on this thing?"

They glanced at each other.

"Who else?"

"Oh, lots of people, but a man named Martinelli is the one you'll recognize."

The effect on them was fun to watch.

"The Man's in on this? Bullshit."

"Bullshit," I said back, louder. "You ever have a Friday with an open run before? You ever get orders to pick up a nonunion rig and run it empty through the middle of the city? And those orders came through your union, right? Nobody came up to you on the side with this offer. Which means the guys at the top know all about it."

They looked at each other again. All the tension drained out of them.

"Now," I said, "do I tell your guys that you're holding us up for more money?"

Silence.

"Aw, shit."

"Well put."

They turned and left me. I lifted the mace canister around and brought it up to my mouth. Gave the knob at the top a push and shot some into my mouth. Economy-size breath spray. I laughed. Another acting job. The other thing that was funny about the scene with the two truck-driver goons was that their boss, Martinelli, was in on it, but I had no idea how to contact him. When I explained the plan to him, Foley, and Henderson, that was the first and last time I saw any of them, outside of a crime report on the evening news. Our meeting was in the home of some well-respected local businessman who was conveniently out of town. It was a nice big place, big enough to hold the city's crime lords and lieutenants and bodyguards. Jesus, the bodyguards—there must have been fifty of them.

Tommy said I'd better make a good speech or they'd just use us for target practice. I told him not to worry about all the goons with the guns, that the three big boys obviously were interested in our deal or they wouldn't have agreed to meet like this. "Besides," I said, "each of them probably brought lots of firepower just to impress the others."

"Yeah," Tommy said, "I guess so. But be real convincing, anyway, okay?"

"Sure."

And I was.

"Gentlemen, you've seen our preparations for this thing, and I think you'll have to admit we've got it figured pretty good. We need just five percent of your truckers, three percent of your union boys, and one percent of your trash-truck drivers. With that we can pull off the biggest bust of all time."

"And if you don't get 'em?"

Foley. He didn't waste words. I looked at him, smiled, and said, "Well, Mr. Foley, I think you know the answer to that one." I glanced at the other two crime czars. "I think you all do." I paused a second. "We'll just go ahead with the plan. I mean, it's too late to stop now, anyway. And we'll pull it off too. You know that the odds are about one in four on a smash-and-grab in this town, but the odds go way up in your favor if the cops are busy with something else at the time of your job. And we intend to make sure the cops are *very* busy.

"But the thing is, it'll all be so much better if you and your people are in on it and prepared. It'll be something to talk about in the future, something to be proud of.

"What we're talking about here is the zapping of an entire city. The place will be shut down. No cops able to move, no feds able to move, nobody able to prevent anything. Nobody able to chase anybody. Panic. Smoke, sirens, alarms. And in that confusion, gentlemen, lies opportunity. If there's anything you want to pull off that would ordinarily attract too much attention, this will be the time to do it. If there's anything you need to fix that normally would be impossible, this will be the time to do it.

"We've already got every punk kid on the street willing to punch in a fire alarm—hell, even the grade schools will have kids pushing the alarms. We've got most of the hookers, most of the numbers people, *all* of the second-story men. . . . Then there's the phone teams. The guys who run the boiler-room phone-sales operations are having their people make calls to the cops all during this time, just to further tie up the lines. I've got ham-radio operators filling the airwaves with prerecorded garbage, CB owners leaving their units on even if they aren't talking with anybody . . . I'm telling you, nobody will be communicating anything with anybody in this city from noon to four P.M. on Friday.

"Okay, then, we've got the squads who will be hitting the banks, the jewelry stores, the racetrack, and so on. It's a well-trained operation. I know—I trained 'em. They know what to do, how to do it, and the escape and pickup of the money and merchandise is all worked out."

"That bothers me." Martinelli this time. "Why should they turn the money and stuff in? Why won't they keep it?"

"Some of them will. But most won't, or at least most of them won't keep all of it. They know that a lot of money in banks is marked, and they won't know how to separate it from the clean stuff. And they know that jewels have to be broken out of their settings and recut. They're just not set up to handle that kind of thing."

"Ach, most of 'em won't give a damn about that. You got a real problem with this part of your plan."

"Well," I said, smiling, "that's one reason why I want you three gentlemen in on it. See, that will solve the whole problem of people complying with instructions. I mean, what do you do with people who go against your orders?" They glanced at one another for a second. "You see what I mean, gentlemen? With you in on it, the percentage of people following the plan goes way up. People just don't like to cross you. For just that reason, I'm keeping the money-pickup teams separate from the smash-and-grab teams, so no one will know if they're dealing with someone who's reporting back to me directly. Or reporting back to one of you."

"And what happens to the money and jewels?"

"We have drops all over the place. Some are actually outside the county, although most of them are right here in town, just out beyond where we'll have the most traffic tie-ups. It's all based on the routes of the big trash trucks. We'll be using a couple of them for the pickup on the regular Saturday runs."

"How are people paid for their part in it?"

"Well, here's another part where having you in on it makes things go a lot smoother. Your men can be paid off through your own organizations. The men just get a little extra—or a lot extra, depending on their contribution—in their pay envelopes. Just like giving a bonus. Some of the others I have taken care of with fairly crude methods: tearing some hundred-dollar bills down the middle, giving them half, and keeping the other half in an envelope with their initials on it—that sort of thing. Others I'll pay off afterward . . . depends on the level of trust, or the amount of leverage I've got with them in the first place."

"And what do we get out of it?" Foley spoke up this time.

"Right. What's in this for us?" Martinelli.

Henderson just nodded. I wondered if he knew what I was about to say.

"And if you're thinking of offering anything less than eighty percent, forget it." Foley.

"Don't be piggy about it," Martinelli said. "We agreed on seventy before we came in here." Martinelli was a stickler for details sometimes.

"I changed my mind. You mad about an extra ten percent?"

"I said we *agreed* on seventy. That's what's important. We agree on eighty, fine. We agree on seventy, fine. Don't go agreeing to one thing, then changing to another thing."

I could see this thing getting out of hand, so I tried to get their attention: "Gentlemen, if we—"

"Oh, listen to Mr. High-and-Mighty, here. 'We agree, we agree.' We talked it over and we batted around some figures. Now that I've heard the plan, I don't like the sound of the payout, so I changed to eighty percent."

"And I suppose you think you speak for the two of us?"

"I speak for me, and me is agreeing to eighty. If *you* want to settle for seventy—"

"Gentlemen! If you—"

"Don't give me that crap! We'll *all* decide, or the whole thing's off."

"Oh, just like that, eh, Mr. Big Shot?"

I glanced at the bodyguards and didn't like what I saw. Several of them had their hands inside their coats, eyes wide and darting from Foley to Martinelli and back again. I still wondered why Henderson was so quiet. I had wanted to make my next point very dramatically. Shit, I'd even rehearsed it. But with the possible outbreak of a gangland war right under my nose, I just blurted it out: "Hell, you guys can have all of it."

It took a second for it to sink in.

"What?"

"You're nuts."

"Now, wait—just wait and listen a minute. The reason I can say that is that I'll make out fine with my own scores. You think I'm not going to take advantage of this thing? I've got one team of people reporting only to me. We have two rather special targets in mind—two places that you three gentlemen don't have a stake in, I'd like to add—and I'm going to be more than satisfied with what I get from them.

"Besides, I kind of hoped you'd appreciate the

planning and work that went into this thing, and maybe you'll have a place for me and Tommy after it's all over."

They wanted to know the two places, just like Tommy and I figured they would, and I played coy and cute for a few minutes, just like we planned. But basically I was just making it look like they were having to drag it out of me. Oh, I was very reluctant about it. I looked down. I looked up. I shuffled my feet. They raised their voices, threatened to pull out of the whole thing unless I told them, etc., etc.

So I told them. No big deal. I wanted the jewelry exchange and the bond-market trading center. They obviously didn't think there was too much percentage in either place, so they weren't interested in them. Just like we figured.

After the confrontation I just stood there, looking a bit dazed. They just sat there, wondering what they had just agreed to. But I knew they felt good about the last part of the presentation. They felt they had pushed me to the wall on two things—one, getting me to name my two special targets, and two, more importantly, arranging to give themselves the lion's share of the profits. After all that they could look one another in the eye and say they were tough sons of bitches.

So they ended up giving me the name of one of their lieutenants to use for coordination. They wanted to be left out of all the details, which was fine with me and Tommy. All we really wanted was their agreement not to get in our way on the deal. If we got some help, so much the better, but we just needed them to let us go ahead with it, and we got that and more.

After that the whole thing just exploded in size. Now, every time I turned around, somebody else had come into the picture. Some were shady types. Some were businessmen. Some were cops. And everybody knew somebody who knew somebody else. The way it was set up, the attitude was "the bigger, the better." But I had a queasy feeling that somewhere in the city two groups of men were going to try knocking over the same bank at the same time. That would produce jurisdictional disputes. Which would produce bullets. Which would produce dead bodies. Which would produce a gangland war. Which meant I wanted to be long gone by Saturday.

Which meant I would be missing payday. I would only do that if I could get my share of things right away. That might leave a lot of people very, very upset with me, but such is life.

I made one last check on the warehouse. The quarantine signs that Falkes told me about were still in place. The men that the female dick had hired were still doing their thing, keeping people away from the place. I got to hand it to Falkes, finding that chick. When he described her, I thought he was putting me on. Then I saw her when she brought him the papers. Built. Real sure of herself. Sharp, too, to come up with the quarantine bit. No getting around it, she was one bang-up job.

Right now I wanted to see my plan in action. I went to the Transamerica Building and busted in on a very surprised executive on one of the top floors.

"Hey, you can't go in there!" a secretary yelled.

"Watch me."

"Just what do you mean, breaking into people's offices?" she demanded.

"I mean business," I said, grinning at her.

The guy looking up at us from across a desk as big as my car was getting ready to pull a first-class indignant number until I told him Foley had sent me. Foley deals in many things. Narcotics. Girls. Boys. Gambling. This guy was a high-stakes bettor whose luck had been running a little thin.

"Oh, uh, well," he said.

"Yup." I smiled at him. "Oh, uh, well. I couldn't have said it better myself."

"What do you want?" he asked.

"Privacy," I said, glancing at the anxious and disapproving face at the door with me.

"Ah, um, that will be all, Jane, thank you."

"Are you certain, Mr. Andrews?"

"Yes, um, thank you."

She hesitated with her hand on the doorknob.

"Bye." I smiled at her.

She left us.

"Now look . . ." he began.

"That's what I'm here for."

"What?"

"To look," I told him. "Great view." I walked over to one of the windows.

"I don't think—"

"You don't have to. Just fetch me some binoculars, and we'll enjoy the show."

"The show?"

"The big score. The plan. The Friday fake-out." I looked at him. "Today's the day for the fireworks. And you can do your bit to help." I stopped smiling. "Get me a pair of binoculars. Now."

He left and came back with a magnificent twelve-power zoom model. Guys in office buildings often have stuff like this.

"Great," I told him. "Now make a call. You might as well be the first." I checked my watch. Eleven forty-five. "A little early, but what the hell."

"Me?"

"You."

"Where should I call?"

"Get the number of the local police department."

He called Information.

"That's fifty cents these days," I said. "Must be nice to have money to burn. Now call the cops."

"What should I say?"

I told him. He dialed.

"Hello," he said woodenly, "I want to report a man with a gun in the lobby of the Transamerica Building. Oh, my God, he's started shooting." He hung up quickly.

"Very impressive performance," I told him.

I raised the binoculars and watched a beautiful city dissolve into chaos.

I was only able to see part of the whole plan, of course, but it was impressive just the same. That's not bragging. I'd worked damn long and hard to make this the most important robbery ever. This was going to be a part of history. This thing was big. Real big. The secret to pulling it off was breaking it up into lots of little parts. Like training the teams to hit the banks and stores. It just took time, a notebook, and the willingness to sit around day after day, week after week, doing it. Then having the balls to go out and tell a bunch of slobs how to act and when to act. And then having the guts to bust anybody who thought about going their own way. It was tough. But, man, what a payoff. And now that the deal was finally going down, I could see how the hundreds of little parts were all coming together nicely.

I swung my binoculars around to the telephone power station on the near side of the Civic Center. My guys had paid a visit to the building's upper structure just yesterday. It went up right on schedule, a beautiful little charge that sent just enough explosive into the line connections to sever them at the base. Zap— no phone service for nearly a quarter of the business district.

Another important phone source for the downtown

area had required a more deliberate attack. Right
now, four guys dressed in black—a nice, theatrical
touch, don't you think?—were shooting their way
into the building, making their way to the generator
and switching it off, *then back on again,* over and
over, blowing out the whole station's power supply
because the emergency backup generator was automatically powered up but had to be manually powered down prior to a resurgence by the main
generator. My guys ignored the warning buzzers and
watched the electricity eat up the core of the machin-
ery. I'll bet it was fun to see. Wish I could have been
there. Snap, crackle, pop—and no more Ma Bell or
Pac Bell or Gen Tel or whatever the hell the phones
are called these days.

There were lots of other scenes I wish I could have
witnessed. Strangely enough, it was some of the old
muscle stuff that I most yearned for: tossing a brick
through a plate-glass window . . . using a sledgeham-
mer on the "please-do-not-lean-on-the-glass" counter-
tops of a big jewelry store . . . setting a few parked
cars on fire, then releasing their brakes to let them
weave their way down the long hills . . . or even the
stupid joy of smashing the cover on a school fire
alarm.

Right now all these beautiful little destruction der-
bies were taking place all over the city as my big
Friday freak-out went down. It was pay-back-the-Man
day for some people. The day when you could fuck up
whatever authority figure you most hated at the
moment. You don't like the cops? Fine. Make a phone
call reporting a shooting that didn't take place. Hate
your employer? Great. Call in a bomb threat and take
the afternoon off. Got a beef against the city for
tearing up the streets near your apartment? Swell. Call
City Hall from a pay phone and leave it off the hook to
tie up the lines. Just a simple citizen's protest action,

no more than a prank, really. A way to strike back. Lots of people *are* mad as hell, and that's how we got hundreds of normally law-abiding people to participate in our Friday freak-out, working right along with the grifters, con artists, hookers, numbers runners, and every smash-and-grab home boy from Novato to Half Moon Bay.

It was great. And I had a ringside—well, above ringside, actually—seat. The whole Transamerica Building had been cleared out by now. The bomb threats did their job, so it was easy to move around from office to office, staring down at the streets filling with stalled cars and angry, scared people. I put down the binoculars at one point and looked straight out the window, level with the floor I was on. The skyline of the city had a strange silhouette. Added to the curve of the hills with all the white-fronted houses—mixed in with the jagged edges of the business towers with all the dull, gleaming glass—was a collection of filmy streams of smoke, slowly twisting and blowing in the breeze. Black smoke, white smoke, dirty, thick, ash-gray smoke all over the place, rising from the cars, stores, tenements, and fresh bomb craters I had created or caused to appear. It was a good feeling.

Four

At first I thought there wouldn't be a way to watch the warehouse on Friday. There were empty lots and railroad tracks around the front of the pier that supported the warehouse. Besides, it wasn't the sort of neighborhood a girl likes to parade around in. Then F. J.'s fondness for electronic gadgets got the better of him.

"Why not put a video camera inside the warehouse?" he said.

"Please do," I told him.

"Is that some sort of challenge?"

"Take it as one if you wish."

"Okay, my fine female hawkshaw, I'll get a wide-angle lens on a closed-circuit setup that'll show you everything. You'll be able to watch from that transient hotel across those empty lots. It'll serve you right to sit with the bedbugs."

I'll say this for F. J., when he puts his mind to something, it gets his full attention. He made good on

his boast ("It ain't braggin' if you can do it," he said,
quoting one of his sports heroes) and got a neat little
camera with a fast lens mounted way up in the rafters
of the place.

All I had to do was pack my standard stakeout
kit—picnic lunch, thermos of coffee, binoculars with
tripod, and Walkman with cassettes—and add it to the
other electronic gear I needed for this job. I lugged
the television monitor into the dingy hotel room, gave
the place the once-over with bug spray, then went back
to the car for the police radio receiver and the walkie-
talkie, which would keep me in touch with the "officers" I'd hired to guard the front of the warehouse and
enforce the quarantine I'd imposed on the whole pier.

On my third trip into the hotel it struck me that the
way these things work in the movies is always a lot
easier. They get to have about four tons of stuff at their
disposal, and they never have to lift a finger to get it. I
use one tenth of the stuff they use, and I've got to
muscle it all over the place. And then it still may not
wind up where I want it when I really need it.

I settled into the boring job of watching a boring,
lifeless television monitor. I had Michael Hedges's
Aerial Boundaries on the Walkman—that's one of his
solo guitar albums, not the ones with the vocals—but I
also had the police channel tuned in, just for the heck of
it. It slowly crept up on me that something was wrong.

The police broadcasts had been as per usual. Terse.
Dull. In a monotone. Full of code and jargon. My mind
barely registered the translations: domestic disturbance
in the Fillmore district; purse snatching on Market
Street; fender bender on Bush at Pine.

Then it hit me. No breaking and entering. No
assault. No grand theft. No robberies.

In short, no normal criminal activity. Weird. I picked
up the dirt-caked phone and called the office. It was
eleven-thirty.

Sadie answered. "Milo Security."

"Hi, Sadie. It's Nat."

"Ooh, how's it going?"

Sadie always got excited about fieldwork.

"Things are quiet. Just like in the cowboys-and-Indians pictures, when someone says, 'Yeah, too quiet.' Sadie, do me a favor. Let some of the guys know that most crime seems to have stopped in the city. See if anybody can find out what's going on. Is it the phase of the moon or something?"

"All right. I'll see what I can do. Call you back. Bye."

Sadie was great. We were always throwing some sort of oddball request at her, and she more often than not came through.

About fifteen minutes went by, and then the police channel crackled with the report of a shooting in a downtown area building. From the cross streets, it had to be the Transamerica. Then a bomb threat at the same location. Hmmm. Crazies on the loose.

Suddenly the police cross talk got hot and heavy. Burglaries, break-ins, rapes, fires, rioting, bomb threats galore. Every kind of misdemeanor and felony that could possibly be imagined was being reported all at once.

After about ten minutes of this, the cop chatter, normally so unemotional, was getting very nonprofessional. Instead of "This is One R Twenty-four, now proceeding East on Chestnut," we got something else entirely: "How the hell do we get through this mess? We got five, six cars on fire in the goddamn street."

"Proceed south, I mean north, on Leavenworth to Houston, then east on Houston to Columbus."

"If we could do that, we could fly. No way are cars getting through here. You better have some fire trucks take care of this."

"Negative. All fire stations have answered alarms."

"All of 'em? What the hell's going on?"

*What the hell, indeed. The same story was being
repeated all over the city. Eventually the language lost
all formalities.*

"Hey, Muriel, we need backup units out here,
dammit."

"Keep your pants on, you ain't the only cop who's
hard up for help."

*You know things are in a bad way when the people at
Dispatch blow their cool. The walkie-talkie squawked
at me just as the phone began ringing.*

"Come in, Dauntless. This is Wright. Over."

"Hang on, Wright. Gotta get the phone." *I lifted the
receiver with my other hand.* "Hello? Sadie?"

"Hi, Nat. Well, all is not quiet anymore."

"Tell me about it. No, don't. Hang on, I've got
Wright on the box. Fisher to Wright. Over."

"We got company here. Over."

"Putting you both down a sec," *I said into both
handsets. I leaned over to the window and peered
through my binoculars. I saw a bunch of men in police
uniforms, one of whom was talking heatedly to Wright.
I grabbed the phone.* "Sadie, unless you've got something great, let's hang up."

"A-okay?" *she said.*

"You bet." *That was our signal. If I had said
"A-okay" back to her . . . well, actually, I don't know
what would happen because I've never tried it, but
knowing Sadie, she'd have had about three thousand
state troopers mobilized and descending on the place.*

*I put down the receiver and grabbed the walkie-
talkie.* "Come in Wright. This is Fisher. Over."

"Yeah, Dauntless, we got a problem here. These
gentlemen, who say they're cops, want to claim the
premises. They have no warrant, no ID, and if that's a
cop car, I'm a roller skate. We'll go either way on this
one: quit the scene or stay and fight with 'em. You call
it. Over."

"Aw, hell, Wright, I'd dearly love to watch you squash a couple of them, but I think you should call it a day. Go collect your money from F. J. Oh, and thanks, guys. Over and out."

"Thanks back at you, darlin'. Over and out yourself."

Wright was fun to work with. He was about the size of a small horse but he had the brains of a Rhodes scholar, which he was until a wanderlust hit him and took him away from his studies to the college of the street. No finer judge of human character walked the earth. He regularly picked up a small fortune advising F. J.'s lawyer friends on who to have on a jury, who to believe during sworn testimony, and sometimes even who to defend.

I watched through the binoculars as Wright waved the intruders toward the building. He then took our own two rented guards to our own pseudo-county vehicle. Ah, the world is full o' sham.

Nothing much happened at the warehouse for a couple of hours, but the sound of anger and confusion poured out of the police radio channels practically nonstop. I flicked on the portable radio the hotel management had thoughtfully welded to the nightstand, just to find out how the local deejays were taking the events of the day.

The rock station was still cranking out the hits, but in between each song came breathless announcements of looting and burning, each one ending with a plea for all of us to just cool out.

The country station was also still playing music, but there were a few comments every now and then about a mess of trouble going on in town, with particular emphasis on the fact that truckers were finding it difficult to make their scheduled routes.

The pop station had suspended their regular playlist in favor of "live, on-the-spot reports," which obvious-

ly were phoned in by people who were blocks away from the scene of any action whatsoever.

The talk/info station had gone on what they called a "full news alert" to bring us such great reporting as this: ". . . already blazing out of control here in the streets. The shock of seeing their cars set on fire right in front of their stores and commercial establishments has put many people into shock. Let's go to one of them. Sir, could you tell me your name?"

"Ralph. Why you want to know?"

"We're on the air live. KNFO for Info—the All-Information Station. Isn't this a tragedy?"

"I guess so."

"What did you feel when you first saw your car had been set on fire?"

"This isn't my car."

And so on. I rolled the knob over to the network news channel and got some facts.

". . . of the overturned trailer trucks blocking most of the major access routes. The junction of 101 and 80 is completely closed to traffic. Route 280, that's the Southern/Embarcadero Freeway, is a solid mass of autos—only one lane in either direction is moving. Normally, under these conditions, we would advise the use of alternate routes, but a series of car fires and bonfires in the middle of many streets has, for all practical purposes, closed most alternate routes. If you are in your office, we recommend staying there. If you are in your home, we suggest walking only as far as your corner market. Wherever you are, you aren't likely to be leaving by motor vehicle. Jess?"

"Thank you, Shelly. What about BART? Is that affected at all?"

"BART has not been touched by the sabotage, Jess, but there is one problem with using BART to get into the city: you can't go anywhere except on foot, and the stations are so completely jammed with people trying to get out of the city that the manual override is being used on the doors of the cars—they aren't letting passengers on or off during the regularly scheduled stops. It's a mess no matter where you are."

"All right, thank you for that report. We have just received word from the commissioner of police that several more banks have reported holdups in many of their branch locations. Fifteen more branches have been hit by the teams of gunmen, bringing the total number of bank robberies to sixty-one. The method of the thieves never varies—men wearing identical dark blue jumpsuits and ski masks run into the bank; one leaps up on a table or counter and holds a shotgun or automatic weapon on the customers and employees, while the others quickly clean out the tellers' cages. They pay no attention to the alarms, and it seems no one else does, either, because, as you know, if you're anywhere near the city, alarms, gongs, buzzers, and bells are giving many people a headache today. Back in a moment."

So that's what that ringing sound was. I turned off the little radio, went to the window, and leaned out. Coming from everywhere was a tinny, vibrating cacophony—a silly symphony of bells floating on the offshore breeze.

I went back to my perch. The "cops" were still outside the warehouse. The police radio was still a litany of civic impotence. The news was still sketchy on the who and the why part of today's activities, although they had beaucoup facts on all the what, the where, and the when.

This is the part about stakeouts I like best in the movies: the waiting. They just pull a nice, slow dissolve to indicate the passage of time. I, of course, have to live through it.

I was pouring coffee out of the thermos when the first

motorcycle rolled up to the warehouse. This caused some consternation among the group of blue-clad goons. The driver didn't seem too happy, either. Lots of gestures toward the door of the warehouse and back toward the city. Two more motorcycles arrived. More unhappiness. More gestures. Several people went over to the warehouse and tried the doors, first the human-size one, then the sliding one for trucks. Since both were padlocked, this was more a gesture of impatience than a practical application of energy.

Things were just about to get interesting when who should drive up to the warehouse but Walter Falkes. His car had several dents, and the side facing me showed the result of passing too close to something that was burning. The warehouse owner, my client, joined the unhappy brigade of gesturers, and once again I watched grown men using a great deal of body English to express their dissatisfaction with the world.

Eventually they went inside, leaving one fake cop by the door. I watched on the monitor as Falkes checked a big clipboard, then reached into a metal box for what looked like stacks of money.

Five

"THIS IS GOING to be great," I said happily. "Just watch."

"Great if you like crime, maybe."

"If you like master-planned crimes," I corrected. We were talking together in the Transamerica Building. Just me and Robert, a building security guard I bumped into while I was going from office to office, watching the robbery plan unfold. "Here," I told him, holding the binoculars out. "Go to the window and take a look." He did so, slowly and a bit warily. I stayed where I was, back by a desk. I didn't want to rattle him. "Look at the banks down on Montgomery."

"Montgomery?"

"Hell, look at any bank on any street on Nob Hill."

"You can't see all that from here."

"Don't be so literal. You can find a bank down there. Just look."

He used the binoculars to scan the streets below. He stopped scanning and grunted to let me know.

I said, "Okay, in about five minutes, give or take a few, you'll see four men in blue jumpsuits come up to the front of each bank."

"You mean, overalls?"

"Yeah, overalls. It doesn't matter what bank you're looking at, because my men will be hitting all of them."

"Hey," he said, still peering through the lenses.

"Hey?"

"Ah, I see some men comin' up to the bank."

I looked at my watch and said, "Close enough for criminal work."

"What?"

"Nothing, Robert, nothing. Now just watch. The men will wait out in front of the bank. Remember what I told you about the trucks—they've been tipped over on the highways and major intersections, which is why the streets are all blocked."

"And there're fires," he said.

"Right. Cars in the streets have been set on fire."

"You guys set all those fires?"

"No, we just set off a few, and it caught on, you might say. It became the hot thing to do."

"You a funny man," he said, shaking his head sadly.

"Yeah, I'm a funny man. Watch the bank, Robert." He stared at me for a few seconds, then slowly brought the binoculars back up to his eyes. "Also, the phone lines are jammed, or they're knocked out of order. You probably noticed that the phones are dead in this building."

"Don't know about that," he said.

I picked up the receiver on the desk in front of me. There was silence on the line. "Dead." I punched into the various lines on the multiline receptionist's phone. "Dead, dead, dead."

"That make you happy?"

"Yes, Robert, that makes me happy. No phones, no phone calls to the police."

"I thought you said you called the police yourself . . . ?"

"Lots of us did. Bomb threats, reports of shootings, rape, armed robbery . . . you name it, we did it. It was the bomb threats that emptied out this building."

"Just so you could be alone?"

I smiled at the thought. "That would have been a good idea. No, I just wanted as much confusion in the city as possible. Now there are thousands of people out on the street, which makes it even more difficult for any vehicles to get through to my guys. Look at 'em down there—they should be pulling on ski masks and going into the bank about now."

"Ain't moving."

"They will, they will."

"There they go."

"What'd I tell you? It should only take around three minutes to clean out the branch."

"Streets so crowded, how're you guys going to get away?"

"That's simple, Robert. They aren't."

"Say what?"

"Under those jump—overalls, they're wearing regular clothes. When they're done with the bank, they just take off the overalls and blend into the crowd. No need to get away."

"What about the money?"

"The money will be on motorcycles."

"Don't see no motorcycles."

"You will, Robert. Just another minute or so. Do you see anybody on a motorcycle yet?"

"Naw. Wait, there's one across the street."

"Yeah, banks are a popular place for men on motorcycles right about now."

"What?"

"Nothing."

"Your guys are comin' out of the bank."

"Yeah," I said, glancing at my watch, "that's about right. They'll have the money in those plastic garbage sacks they're holding."

"Yup. Each guy's got one. They're taking off in every direction."

"What? Those assholes—they're supposed to be met by the motorcycle."

"Yeah, he's there, but only one guy is putting his garbage into the trunk."

"The trunk?" I walked over to where Robert was standing, near the window. He took a step back and stared at me. "I'd just like a look through the binoculars, Robert, my man. Okay with you?" I smiled at him.

"Oh. Yeah, sure." He held them out to me.

"Thanks." I took the lenses and began panning the scene down below. I only caught a glimpse of two of the men. One was just finishing doing what he was supposed to be doing—stuffing the plastic sack into the saddlebag on the motorcycle that had come up to the front of the bank just as the men ran out of it. The other bozo was running up the street with a bag in one hand. It bounced off his thigh after every couple of steps.

"Stupid little shit," I said. "He isn't even getting rid of the ski mask and jumpsuit. Jesus, what an asshole."

"Enough of your guys do like that, you won't get the amount of money you say you'll get."

"Yeah. That's true. Instead of ten million, I might only get five. That's the breaks."

"Ain't no ten million in the banks. Not with the tellers. You won't take more'n a couple hundred grand. Minus your expenses. And from what you say, you're going to be paying some heavy expenses on this gig."

"You're sharp, Robert. Expenses have been a bitch. But profits are going to be very high."

"No way."

"You're forgetting about the military transfer of funds." His face clouded for a moment, then comprehension came. Henderson and Martinelli had caught on to what I was aiming for about two days after I told them about the Plan. Foley let me know he knew about two days after that. They were telling me about the luck we had going for us on this job. I was amazed at the news. "Wow," I said, "that's fucking great." Yeah. Just like Tommy and I planned it. For the first time the military divisions stationed around the Bay area were placing their payroll funds through the commercial banks. It was part of what some Department of Defense guy called "the intermingling of enlisted personnel with indigenous civilian populations for the bettering of community/service relations." Or something like that, anyway.

I looked at Robert, standing there awkwardly in his Surety Security Guards uniform. "Robert, my man, don't worry about our profits. We'll do just fine from this 'gig,' as you call it. Besides, you don't think it's just the banks we're hitting?"

"What else? Markets?"

"Sure." I nodded. "Grocery stores, liquor stores, jewelry stores, department stores, gas stations, five-and-dimes. Hell, for all I know, Boy Scout troops are hitting on the Camp Fire Girls. There's lots of people in this great land of ours who are hungry for some of life's quick pleasures. Every kind of deal that couldn't normally go down while out in the open is taking place right now—in broad daylight. Right out in plain sight. Even guys that aren't in on it are helping us out by knocking over places we'd never think to hit, like houses and apartments, or mailboxes and parked cars. Shit, I'll bet somebody's robbing the cashiers at the hospitals and hitting the poor boxes at the churches."

"Shit."

"But my guys are only hitting the big-ticket items. Like at your favorite betting establishments, both legal and illegal."

"That don't make it right."

"Right? Jesus, Robert. It's more right than stealing from a hospital. We're making history here. Anyway, the profit picture is going to be really good. With my guys fanning out to drop-off points all over the city—and since I've got a way of collecting the stuff even through the roadblocks—I'll be clearing several million."

"How'd you do it all, man?"

I smiled. "A lot of planning, Robert. A lot of planning and a lot of work. Getting to the big boys didn't hurt."

"The big boys?"

"Sure. The guys who already control the action in this town. You know who. The ones who have so much legit action that they could forget about the crooked stuff and still do great. They're in this for the big score. They'd get it, too, unless . . ."

"Unless what?"

"Forget it. Not important. Look at the city." I waved my hand at the windows, and we both went back to watching the show. He got nervous after a while and said he'd better leave.

"People will wonder what I'm still doing up here," he said.

"Yeah, okay. Beat it. Thanks for the use of your view." He walked slowly across the carpeted floor. "Robert?" He stopped, his hand on the office door. "If you've ever had the urge to knock off a liquor store, today's the day. Know what I mean?" He nodded, taking it very seriously. I winked at him and he took off.

I turned back to the view. It wasn't as exciting anymore. Telling Robert about it had been a kick, a real rush, but now there was a kind of numbness that was building up inside. I thought about the big boys coming out of this thing with next to nothing. Could I pull it off? Would I go through with the second plan Tommy and I had worked out? Who's kidding who?— of course I would go through with it. Christ, I had to. Sticking around would mean the end. Too many people knew who I was.

I wandered through the offices, idly fingering things people had left on their desks. Lots of drawers were open, left that way in people's frantic efforts to grab whatever they felt was important enough to save from the "bomb." Thinking about all the bomb threats we made caused me to smile for a second, but the thought of having to wait about ten hours until being able to rummage around in the contents of certain trash containers was too depressing. I left the Transamerica Building and walked through the chaos of downtown. In a daze, I made it all the way to the Cannery. Shit, the tourist shops are still going strong, like the robbery's not even happening. I walked past Ghirardelli Square, then up the street to a revival movie theater. There, too, it was business as usual. They had *The Big Sleep* and *The Maltese Falcon*. Perfect. That was just the kind of distraction I needed for the next few hours. I paid my way and entered the black-and-white world where happy endings were always in plentiful supply.

Six

"Mr. Falkes? I have a videotape that you'll find very interesting. You're the star."

"Who is this?"

"Nat Fisher of Milo Security."

"Oh. How did you get this number?"

"The phone company."

"This is an unlisted number."

"Not if another member of the phone company calls and gives the right verbal cues."

"I don't understand," he said.

"Look," I said, "we're getting off the topic. Obviously I did get your number, so let's leave it at that. Do you want to see the tape or not?"

"What tape?"

"The tape I made of the activities inside your warehouse yesterday." Silence. All I heard was heavy breathing on his end of the line. "You making an obscene call or what?" I asked him.

"So this is blackmail," he said at last.

"Call it whatever you like," I purred at him. *"Do you want to see the tape? It's not very good. Black-and-white. Kind of dark. And you are seen from a bad angle, but—"*

"How much do you want?"

"Let's not discuss it over the phone. Can you get to the office by eleven?"

"The office?"

"Yes. You remember, the rectangular room in which business was discussed?"

"You mean at Milo Security?"

"Bingo. So, can you make it by eleven?"

"Well . . ." he said, and hesitated.

"I'd really like it if we could be out of here by one o'clock. That's when the cleaning people show up, and I think we should be alone for our little transaction, don't you?"

Silence. Then: "Uh, yes. Yes, of course. I'll be there in twenty minutes."

I hung up and frowned at the phone. Either he's coming to kill me or he's taking off for parts unknown. Either way I was about to lose a client.

"Did he take the bait?" It was F. J., coming in from his office.

"Maybe. He's on his way over. I think. Or he's off to the Malay Archipelago."

"How do you want to handle it?"

"Oh, I don't know. How about we just knock him unconscious the second he walks in the door?"

"Sorry, Nat. I'll just listen in from the next room, all right?"

"Fine." I smiled at him.

F. J. was a good guy. He was worried about the setup. But then, so was I. If this was going to be the scene of Falkes's attempt on my life, it could get very messy. Oh, sure, I could take care of myself, and I could yell for F.

J. anytime I wanted. But that wouldn't do much good if Falkes pulled a gun and started blasting away. That wouldn't be the work of a pro, but Falkes didn't strike me as a pro. And amateurs with firearms were always dangerous.

F. J. had reports to write, so he hightailed it back to his desk. He was—is—a fine investigator, but since he opened this establishment he's become one of the fullest of full-time paper pushers. Budget reports. Trial reports. Case reports. And the most delicate of all, the reports to clients who were not going to be pleased with what we'd found out for them. Spouses cheating on them. Offspring getting involved with all kinds of chicanery. Business partners skimming off profits. Security systems that were neither secure nor systematic. Employees involved in thievery, large and small.

True, it was always better to know the truth so you could do something about it. But still, the truth often brought about a profound sadness and sense of loss, and the way F. J. worded things could mean the difference between heartache and heart attack. We favored the former.

I was tempted to put on a cassette—I had Kitaro's Silk Road in my hand—but I switched on the radio instead. I like feeling plugged in to the city every now and then. Listening to the various stations always gave me a sense of the great, coarse cross section of humanity that was lurking out there. I tuned in Helpline, a phone-in talk show.

". . . filling out the forms. It can be a little bit frustrating, but if you take it slow and easy, you'll find that you make it through them all right. And your insurance company representative can usually tell you over the phone whether or not you're covered for a mattress burning on your lawn. Okay?"

"Yeah, thanks."

"*You're welcome.*" *There was an electronic click, and then the announcer continued, "This is* Helpline. *You're on the air.*"

"*Hello, I was kind of wondering what's going to happen at all the banks on Monday morning. I mean, if all the money was stolen, what if we go down and can't get our own money out?*"

"*Oh, I don't think there's any danger of that. The thieves didn't take all the money in the world. They didn't take all the money in San Francisco. Your money is insured at your bank, and it'll be there when you want it.*"

"*Well, isn't the bank out all that cash?*"

"*I don't think so, no. The bank is also insured, I believe. They'll get their money back from their insurance company. So don't you worry about—*"

"*Where does the insurance company get the money?*"

"*Well, the insurance companies charge premiums to all their customers, and they use some of that money to pay out whenever there are claims.*"

"*It's kind of like robbing Peter to pay Paul, if you ask me . . .*"

I didn't pay any attention to the rest. I began thinking about the money. Over eighty bank branches had been hit. Over thirty jewelry stores. Over two hundred markets and liquor stores. And that didn't begin to count the stores that were looted.

Robbing Peter to pay Paul. The people who organized this mass holdup would want a share of all the swag. How would they get it? Where did all those garbage bags end up? Were they still in the city?

I switched off the radio. Nothing like a good talk show to get your mind off your current problems. I don't know why I liked teasing my mind by listening to stuff like that. Maybe I felt superior to the participants. I know I felt inferior to the guys who had pulled off this *series of heists. How did you coordinate something as big as that? You didn't just pick up the phone and tell your friends, "Say, I've an idea. Let's tie up all the emergency services of the whole city next Friday at, say, noon, so a bunch of the fellows can knock over a few banks."*

The front door to the office has a push button that sets off an annoying bonging sound in the hallway.

"God, I hate that gong," I said over my shoulder to F. J. as I flicked on the hidden tape player.

"All set?" he asked me.

"As set as I'll ever get. I don't think he'll shoot at the doorway. He'll want to come inside and talk about it, or at least get his hands on the tape."

"I think you're right," he said absently.

"Could you try to be a bit more convincing with your line readings?" I said, prompting him.

"Sorry."

The gong bong came again.

"He's anxious," F. J. remarked.

"Yup," I said.

Then we both stood there, letting Mr. Falkes think about things while out on the stoop. We like to throw off the expectations, the timing, or the momentum of anyone who is against us. We'll do almost anything, in fact, to get that little extra edge in the encounter. Letting Falkes stew in his own juice outside was as good a way as any to do it. The nice thing about working with F. J. was that we just did stuff like this naturally, without discussing it.

More bonging from the damn gong.

There was a smile at the corner of F. J.'s mouth. It became infectious, and suddenly we were both grinning about our little ploy.

"Well," I said, "that was fun. Battle stations?"

"Battle stations," he agreed, and headed off to the office next to mine.

I went down the hall to let in a very worried Walter Falkes.

"God," he said, "I thought something had happened to you."

"Nope. I'm fine. Come on in."

He stepped over the threshold nervously. I pointed him down the hall to my office. Every time we passed an empty office, he tried to peek into it, but he was trying not to show his interest.

When he got within a step of my place, I told him, "Hang a left."

He hesitated, and I wondered if we'd have to go through the rigamarole of him making some excuse to look through the place. Yup. We'd have to.

"Um, I, ah, have to use the rest room. What direction, um, is it?" He was hoping it was farther on down the hall.

I didn't disappoint him. "Farther on down the hall," I said. "Let me take your overcoat." I stepped forward to help him remove it.

"No, no, that's all right," he said too quickly. He was already moving away from me. "Maybe you could get me that coffee," he said as he headed back along the dimly lit corridor, the soft carpeting making his footsteps practically soundless.

"Will do," I said, loud enough for him to hear.

I thought about playing games with him, turning on the hall lights or even all the office lights, but I figured he was playing games enough for the two of us. At least I knew that the bulge in his overcoat pocket was more likely a gun than a present.

I went into my office to pour him a cup of coffee that I thought he'd never get to drink. The lighting seemed overly bright by comparison to the darkened offices we'd just passed. I went over to the VCR and hit the play button. The image of Walter Falkes, checking his big clipboard and passing out money rolled twice,

*settled in on the screen. I went over to the desk and
wondered how F. J. would play his part. Either he could
slip behind the last panel of the bookcase, in which
event only a full-on search-and-destroy mission would
find him, or he could be "discovered" by Falkes, forcing
Falkes to (probably) draw his gun right away. Nah, I
thought, we don't know enough yet for the latter
method. F. J. would remain hidden, and Falkes would
appear alone in my doorway.*

*Falkes appeared alone in my doorway. He spotted
himself on the screen and said, "Shit."*

"Yup," I agreed. "But then, I warned you the picture
wasn't too good. Dark, grainy, and a poor angle. And
that fish-eye lens doesn't do you justice."

"I want that tape," he said angrily, moving across
the room to the screen.

"Take it," I said. "The eject button is on the top row,
at the far left." It took him several tries to punch the
right button. The screen bounced with visual static as
he removed the cassette.

"Now I want the other copies." His voice was stronger than when he was at the front door. His confidence
was coming back. "Where are they?" he demanded. "I
want them."

"No can do, amigo," I told him. "From now on we
have to discuss fees. The copies are in a safe place,
away from here. But you can buy them. One at a time.
Mail order, you might say."

"How much?"

"I admire your directness. Let's say ten thousand
apiece."

"That's ridiculous."

"I don't think so."

"What if I don't pay?"

"Have you ever watched cable TV?"

"What?"

"Cable TV. There's something called the community

access channel. For a small fee they'll let you show just about anything on it. I was thinking that your little performance might make a terrific show for them. Oh, I know what you're thinking—that the ratings will be really low. But we're not talking blockbuster here. We'll just contact the appropriate people before the show and let them know you're going to be on. You know, people like the Chamber of Commerce . . ." I paused a second. "The local police." Pause. "Certain local, ah, business people. Like, for example, Martinelli." Pause. "Henderson."

"All right," he said softly.

"Foley," I added.

"*All right!*" He spat it out so hard, he wound up wiping his chin. "Jesus Christ, I'll pay you the fucking money."

"Goody," I said. "Okay, then, send us a check made out to Milo Security. Mark it 'For Security Consultation and Services' and we'll predate an invoice for the same thing. That'll get us going. Then we'll bill your office the same way until we run out of tape copies or you run out of money."

He gave me a look that would have melted metal.

"Hey," I told him, smiling, "don't look so spooked. I was only kidding. We've only got ten more tapes. A bargain. Cheap at the price and all that."

We stood there for a moment. He eyed me with as much hatred as I'd seen in a while, and then he slipped his hand into his overcoat pocket.

"Easy," I said. "Guns have a habit of going off, and then where would we be?"

"Just remove your hand from your coat," came a voice at my door. F. J. stood there with a very evil-looking sawed-off shotgun in his hands. Considering that it would have sprayed me with about one fifth of its pellets, I wasn't as relieved as I might have been to see him there. On the other hand, the ugliness of it was *calculated to have an affect on an amateur. It did. Falkes was frozen, mouth slightly open, staring at the big bore of the weapon. I moved back against the wall, and F. J. moved into the room toward Falkes, taking me out of the line of fire.*

"Wh-what is that thing?" Falkes said at last.

"Scattergun," F. J. told him. "Put about two hundred holes in you," he added authoritatively. "Now slide your hand out of your pocket slowly."

Falkes did as he was told. F. J. moved around behind him, putting the double barrels right up against the man's back. Then he reached inside the bulging coat pocket and removed a Smith and Wesson revolver.

"We'll just take this in trade for that first tape," F. J. told him. "Now, I'd appreciate it if you'd leave us. We have several others to contact. Your little caper will turn out to be quite profitable for us, I think."

F. J. prodded him forward. I quickly slipped out the office door and hit all the lights. Having a murky hallway was not conducive to the feeling we wanted to impart to Mr. Falkes. He was marched down the corridor, eyes blazing, his fingers white around his first copy of the incriminating tape.

After he left the building F. J. slid the bolt on the door and activated the alarm system. I knew we'd be on alert for the next few weeks at least.

"Did you see his reaction to those names?" F. J. asked me as we walked back to my office.

"Plain as day. Henderson and Foley got to him, although I think he's more afraid of Foley. I think Martinelli got to him, too, but he didn't really explode until Foley."

"Let's play it back."

I rewound the tape and we listened to the whole sordid interview. Several times. We still couldn't pinpoint Falkes's reaction to the mention of Martinelli's name, but we were positive about the others.

"I just don't know," he said.

"I don't know, either."

We kicked it around some more. No matter how we made the facts stack up, we had to have some of the big boys like Martinelli involved in the series of robberies. It was just too big for a small-time operator. And we couldn't conceive of Falkes having the muscle to pull it off himself.

"By the way," F. J. said after a pause, "do we have someone tailing our Mr. Falkes?"

"Wright.'

"Good. Who is it?"

"I just told you: Wright."

"Oh, I thought you were saying 'right,' not his name."

"I know. Sorry. Oh, I also have a tap being put on Falkes's phone and a bug in his car."

"Hmmm. This is getting expensive. After all, we're going to have to turn his money over to the police when we turn him in."

"Turn him in for what?" I asked.

F. J. knit his brow over that one, then said, "I see your point, I think. You're suggesting that there is no obvious connection between Friday's robberies and the actions of Mr. Falkes on that tape?"

"Right. As in 'affirmative.' "

"But we believe there is a connection."

"Right again. But let's wait until we can prove it. We'll be conducting a parallel investigation to that of the police."

"Hmm."

"You said that before."

"But eventually we'll have to turn him in," F. J. insisted.

"What?" I said in mock horror. "And lose our best client?"

He smiled. "Yes, a hundred thousand in security

consulting is quite a coup, especially for doing next to nothing."

"Why stop at a hundred thousand?" I said.

"We have only ten tapes."

"Sure, now. But those are copies. And we can just keep on making copies."

"Surely you're not suggesting that we actually black-mail him?" my very nice boss protested.

"Don't call me Shirley," I told him. He made a face. "Sorry. Old joke. No, really what I'm suggesting is that we play Mr. Falkes for all he's worth to see when and where he cracks. To see who he goes to for help. To see what happens when the screws are tightened."

"He's likely to come after us. Or, rather, send someone after us."

"Yup."

"That could be dangerous."

"Yup."

"And you're loving it, I suppose."

"Yup." I grinned at him. That's the kind of gal I am.

Seven

HERE IT WAS Saturday, and I was still in town. Why?
Well, greed for one thing. Before Tommy—Tommy
Weisberg, my partner until the fence blew him
away—I wasn't so much into grabbing all the mar-
bles. But Tommy sure had a way with spending. He
made it fun. Live for today, you know? Well, he taught
me how to enjoy spending. And that meant grabbing a
larger slice of whatever was up for the grabbing.

So we came up with this crazy idea to rob an entire
city. And we pitched it to the big boys and they bought
it. We never really knew why they went for it. Maybe it
was a desire to "get back into the action," like one of
'em said. Maybe it seemed like a good way to be able
to pull off some deals that would have attracted too
much attention under normal circumstances. Then,
too, I'll bet some of the guys had some scores to settle,
and they figured to do it in all the shooting that was
sure to happen.

Only there wasn't much shooting. Couple of shots
fired at a liquor store. Some turkeys shot up a bank

accidentally by tripping over something, I guess. But not much gunfire for so many holdups. That's what made some of the factional disputes stand out. I mean, here was half the county being robbed with a total of a half dozen gunshots, and then these four or five guys get wasted without even getting their wallets lifted. Pretty suspicious, if you ask me. Sure, whoever did it tried to make it look like some random weirdo killing, but weirdos—even weirdos who kill and forget to steal anything—wind up killing some innocent bystander, and every one of these dead guys had a record as long as both your legs put together. Plus, every one of the dead guys was connected with Foley somehow or other. The betting was that Martinelli had had it done, but I don't know. I think Henderson was just as good a bet. For that matter, I think Foley himself was just as good a bet—I wouldn't put it past him to have had several of his own men shot just to make some trouble for Henderson and Martinelli.

After Tommy and I had been working on the plan for about six months, and right after we had convinced Henderson, Foley, and Martinelli to throw their muscle behind the project, we were joking about all the things that could go wrong during the robberies. The humor got pretty black, but that just seemed to make us laugh harder. I had come up with a thought that was funnier than anything we'd said so far. "It'd be great," I hissed out, gasping for air, "if, after the deal goes down"—breath—"and the bags of cash are in the trash containers . . ."

"Yeah," Tommy said, still laughing.

"And then the City Sanitation Department"—breath—"sends their trucks around collecting trash on a *new* day . . ."

"Yeah."

"And they pick up all the stuff"—breath—"before

we can get any of it"—breath—"and they don't know
what's in there—"

"Yeah . . ."

"—and they dump it into the landfills."

"Arrghhhh!"

We both busted up at that. Imagine going to all this
work, pulling off the biggest mass robbery in the
history of crime, and then the trash dumpsters we use
for the drops are all cleaned out by real trash guys, and
the money and jewelry just disappears.

"Just buried under a ton of banana peels and shit!"

"Yeah, under the fucking garbage!"

We both thought of it at the same time, I think. We
were still laughing, but the breathing was coming
easier as we sobered up.

"Wait a minute . . ."

"It could happen—"

"The trash—"

"We could get it all, man."

"It could be picked up!"

"We could make the collection early . . ."

"Shit."

"Yeah. Shit."

We just stared at each other. No more laughter. Do
you think it would work?

Suddenly we were laughing again, big, rolling belly
laughs pouring out of us like ripped-open sacks of
grain, laughter so hard that it hurt on the underside of
the ribs and you make wheezing sounds in your throat
because you had to force air into your lungs in
between the whoops of joy. Jesus, we were going to
make the biggest killing in history. Not just the biggest
robbery. But also the biggest two-man payoff.

The key to it was Henderson's garbage trucks. They
were big enough to roll on through crowded streets,
tough enough to push past burning cars, and innocent-

looking enough to get by any cops. Besides, even if they were searched, all you'd see inside were plastic garbage sacks mixed in with real garbage. It just didn't seem likely that anybody would climb inside to rip open one of the sacks of money.

"If you take one truck and I take another," Tommy said, "we could hit all the drops between midnight and four A.M. That's about when they start their regular runs."

"Naw, they don't start at four. The drivers may get to the yard by four, but they don't head out for pickups until much later."

"Yeah, sure, much later . . . like about four-thirty. Believe me, I know, 'cause they wake me up about every other Saturday."

"Every other Saturday?"

"Sure, the Saturdays when I get to bed early—like around three."

"Yeah."

We had just about decided to do it when Tommy brought up a slight flaw: "Wait a sec. Oh, shit."

"What?"

"We don't know how to drive one of those big rigs."

"What do you mean, 'we,' paleface?"

"You know how?"

"Uh-huh."

"Bullshit."

"Bullshit, my ass."

"Where'd you learn?"

"Same place I learned to train all those bozos how to blow up power plants, cut phone lines, make homemade car bombs, roll eighteen wheelers . . ."

"All right, all right. Shit. What were you in the army, anyway—a terrorist attack drill sergeant?"

"Next best thing. I was in Supply. Anything that came through the whole camp came through us. If it looked interesting, I asked to inspect it. What I didn't know, I got somebody to tell me. It was great training for my chosen profession."

I thought about this conversation when it came time for me to take one of the big Sanitation Department refuse-collection vehicles, as they call them, out for my midnight run. Getting into the yard was a little trouble. I had to shoot the gate guard. Jesus, what the fuck did he want to stop me for? Who would steal a garbage truck, anyway?

The city was a freak show of clogged streets. I smashed the big rig through jumbles of smoking, smoldering cars, many of which were parked at crazy angles in the middle of the road. I rolled up on the sidewalk to get past one impossible pile of wreckage where someone had artfully added plywood and old mattresses to an already burning heap comprised of a Toyota pickup, a '73 Caddy, and a Ford wagon. Someone shouted at me from the shadows. It was an incomprehensible stream of high-pitched foreign noises.

After making the first three pickups I began to get into the rhythm of the city. Everything seemed normal, just at a different pace. I had to go slow with a heavy vehicle like the garbage truck, and I went even slower whenever the bonfires blocked too much of the roadways.

Along about pickup number fifteen I began to get tired, but there were still seven spots to go, and it became important, somehow, to get everything. Crucial, in fact. "Nothing left for the vomit-brained sons of bastards," I vowed.

The smoke was worse in this section, so I put on the mask usually worn by the trash handler as he wrestled with the cans outside the truck. Like some greasy bandit, I thought. The mask helped with breathing, but it didn't stop my eyes from stinging and crying.

The ache in my arms from manhandling the oversize steering wheel was getting sharper by the minute. I used to work out every morning, but this last month or so had been so exhausting, I had stopped. The muscles had gotten used to the inactivity, and now they were strained to the limit. I missed a shift, then another, grinding the gears badly. I began jerking the wheel to turn the truck, throwing my whole body into it. We lurched and jerked up to the last couple of drops.

But I did it. Collected it all. All except that one burned-out one. For you, Tommy. And now, all for me.

I drove to the Candlestick Park parking lot, rolled through the barricade, parked near the van I had left there the day before, and dumped the load of garbage and money right on the asphalt. Climbing through the rotten fruit, coffee grounds, wet newspapers, cat litter and crap, bones, half-empty cans, broken bottles, ripped panty hose, used paper towels and tissues, and all the other remains of everyone's life was not the most fun I've ever had in this world. But it was the only way of getting the money and jewelry out of the shit. I was almost three-quarters through when I saw that it was going to be a tight squeeze in the compartment Tommy and I had built into the back of the van. I ended up stomping on the sacks of money, finally jumping in at them at a crazy angle, throwing myself down on the pile over and over again, grunting and sweating with the effort. I just had to get them to fit in my hiding place.

Done. I lay there a minute or so, big droplets of sweat flowing off my nose. For a couple of weeks I had thought about this moment, when the first part was all over. I had planned the end scene over and over in my mind. I would get into the van with a swagger, savoring the moment of triumph. I'd fire up the mother and stick it to the floor and jam out of there fast.

Instead I dragged myself into the van's front seat, totally wasted with exhaustion. The engine died twice before it finally caught, and I revved it long and loud before putting it in gear and gingerly rolling out of the parking lot. I couldn't help thinking of Tommy and how he would have enjoyed this moment despite the exhaustion. We had worked so hard on all the plans together, taking the time to check and recheck the routes, planting the right evidence to be found after we'd gone, finding the right guys to kill . . . .

That was the best part of the Plan. We kept going over all the parts of the robbery, but we hardly gave a thought to what would happen afterward. Until one day Tommy said, "You know that the only way we can come out of this alive is to die."

"The fuck are you talking about?"

"Dig it: We pull off the biggest grab in history, and we take the goodies right out from under the noses of the biggest badass crime lords in the city, right?"

"And?"

"And so we've got everybody after us. The cops, the guys we hired to pull the jobs, and Henderson, Foley, and Martinelli. Hell, the feds'll be in on it, too, because of the military payroll. No way are we going to get out of it alive, unless . . ."

"Unless what?" I said impatiently. He was hitting a bad nerve with this talk.

"Unless we find a couple of guys about our size and arrange for them to die in some way that disfigures 'em. Like a fire or something. We leave behind some of the jewels and marked money and shit, and everybody'll think we bought it."

"You ever been to the dentist?"

"What?"

"The dentist? You ever go?"

"Oh, shit. The dental X rays."

"Bingo."

We were silent for a moment. "You know," he said at last, "it'll still work. We find a patsy who is about your size, okay? Then we get his dental records and exchange 'em for your dental records. Then everything'll match when they check. It'll work. It's just a little more complicated, is all."

"Oh, a little more complicated? I've got dental records from the army. How do you propose I change those?"

"Shit."

"Yeah."

Which was where I left it until it occurred to me that I had been to the dentist about four times more often out of the service than in it, and a lot had changed. I decided to risk it. Besides, what choice did I have? Tommy's plan had a better chance of working than just making a run for it.

So we looked for some guys to die for us. It's not easy. The guy had to be in pretty fair shape, yet he had to be a down-and-outer so that not too many people would come investigating his disappearance. Then, too, it had to be somebody we could get close to—close enough to find out the name of his dentist, anyway.

Tommy found his mark almost right away. I had to keep on searching until about two weeks before the big Friday. I was getting worried, but it all worked out just fine. Well, not for the guy I picked. On the way over to where my body double lived, I thought it was funny how Tommy's man would go on living because Tommy hadn't. Oh, well, that's death.

When it came time to kill the guy who was supposed to be me, I went into a sort of mental cruise control. It must have been the exhaustion of picking up the money. But the scenario of the murder had been rehearsed so many times in my mind that I didn't really have to think about it very much. It was as if I were a camera watching the whole thing.

. . . the van slows to a halt in a deserted, dirty street. The sky is still dark, but it is near dawn. A cat hisses and spits at me as I climb the wooden stairs of the old tenement house, carrying a small package of jewelry and currency. The door splinters easily from the crowbar wedged between it and the jamb. A voice, tired and husky, calls out from the darkness. The voice calls again, louder, and I silence it with a punch to the man's throat, then another to the side of his head. Got to make sure he's out cold for the next twenty minutes. The jewelry clatters as it's dumped on the floor. The stacks of bills crinkle as they slide from the plastic bag. The window frames squeak as I shut up the place and turn on the gas after blowing out the pilot light. The little windup alarm clock, carefully reworked to include a flint-and-striker mechanism that produces a large spark, makes a tocking sound as I tiptoe out of the room, sealing the broken door with industrial glue. The cat is hissing at me again on the way down the stairs.

The street gleams in a prelude to sunrise. I get in the van and drive slowly away. And suddenly the silence in my head is broken by more than those clattering sounds right up close. I hear the van's engine echoing off the buildings along the street. I hear other cars and trucks, early Saturday workers. I hear the roar of a plane arcing out over the ocean. And finally, mercifully, I hear my own heartbeat.

I drove carefully to a place near Mt. Davidson Park from where I could see the explosion with a telescope. Swinging it across the houses, the blur and swirl of color making my eye feel as disoriented as my brain, I thought about Tommy. Who am I kidding about this?

I didn't do this in his memory but for the money. I could have let it go by, just used the escape route with my share in hand, but no, here I was, trying to make off with the whole bundle.

I glanced at my watch. Close to zero hour. As I put my eye back to the lens, a gull flew past the line of sight between me and the tenement house. It was a blue-white splotch that filled the magnified view for an instant and then was gone.

Seconds dragged themselves out, time stretching as if to grant my man extra life. Come on! I wanted to see it—to feel it, if possible—and I dared not look at my watch for fear of missing the—

There. No sound, not this far away. Just a flash, followed instantly by a convulsive shimmy to the whole building. The windows shot out, up and away from the structure, which was a red-and-black roiling cloud of flame and debris. The fireball was impressive, even from here, then thick, ugly smoke alternately settled and swirled around the place.

Well, that was good. More exciting, somehow, than the whole heist scene. Relief took over and I found myself laughing out loud in the front seat of the van, shaking with hyena like howls that started hurting my sides after a while.

The euphoria of that moment may have been what made me delay my departure. I had made a tiny mistake—leaving a set of keys back in the crummy apartment I kept in the Potrero district. During the slow drive through rubble-strewn streets I bought a paper from an old guy on a corner. He was touting the *Examiner* coverage of "the crime of the century." Sounded okay to me. I didn't much care for the place, but I wanted a little downtime before getting out of there. It was another mistake. You shouldn't go around any of the old spots when you're trying to disappear. I started reading about my front-page exploits. The article went on and on about the mass hysteria and confusion. I skimmed along until I reached the really good part—about the money.

THE AMOUNT OF CASH REMOVED FROM THE COMMERCIAL BANKING ESTABLISHMENTS AND OTHER CASH BUSINESSES MAY BE, ACCORDING TO ONE POLICE DEPARTMENT OFFICIAL, "THE LARGEST SINGLE DOLLAR AMOUNT IN THE HISTORY OF CRIME," POSSIBLY REACHING THIRTY MILLION DOLLARS. "COULD EVEN BE MORE," ADDED THE POLICE OFFICIAL, WHO ASKED TO REMAIN UNNAMED.

I think my eyes glazed over at the mention of thirty million bucks. With visions of hundred- and thousand-dollar bills swishing through the air around my head, I fell asleep. It was my third mistake of that Saturday morning.

The dream was filled with flying. Swooping past the tops of tenement houses, being buffeted by the shock waves of the explosions inside the buildings. Over and over the houses blew up, sending shards of glass and bits of wood careening and tumbling through space, and right at my face. In the distance alarm bells clanged incessantly. The bells had a pulsing, echoing sound, gradually coming closer, closer, closer—

The phone woke me up. I fumbled for it, got it. Fourth mistake.

"Yeah?"

"Danny? It's me, Walter. Walter Falkes."

"What time is it?"

"It's about twelve-thirty. Listen, we've got trouble. That Fisher woman and her boss at Milo Security are blackmailing me."

"Uh-huh."

"They've got me on videotape at the warehouse."

"Good for them. Where are you?"

"At home, why?"

"Jesus," I said, and hung up on him. Great. First

they get him on video, now he lets them get him on reel to reel. Next time I only work with professionals. 'Course, with what I've got in the van, there doesn't have to be a next time.

I quickly gathered up the paint cans, brushes, stained tarpaulins, and sawhorses, and took them down to the van as the phone rang and rang just like in the dream. The bottom of the van had been lowered to make a nice little bed for the money, but there was so much of it, I had to go back to the original plan where the cash was stuck inside watertight bags and stuffed into the paint cans. That was a messy job and took forever (mistake number five) but the wet paint that got spattered over me and the van only added to the effectiveness of the ruse. By pushing and prodding, it was possible to get all the cash and jewels into the paint supplies and still make the van look like a journeyman painter's. After affixing two metallic signs (JOSEPH BENOV'S PAINTING & STUCCO REPAIR/ REASONABLE RATES), the van was ready. My paint-besmirched and dirty jumpsuit and a work order I had made up for a house-painting job out beyond Novato completed the picture. Tommy had arranged a similar deal but with a plumbing truck. I couldn't go for plumbing. The pipes reminded me of bars.

It took three hours to drive through the jammed-up traffic and the roadblocks. I had a sinking feeling in my stomach when a patrolman began poking around in the back of the van.

"What's in here?" he demanded.

"Well, I got my brushes and sprayers, plus the hoses and the compressor. Painting's more modern now, you know. And I got my paint and my ladders and my crosspieces for the scaffolding. Need the scaffolding 'cause it's a two-story job. One-story job and all's I need is my ladders."

"Kind of late for a painting job, isn't it?"

Here I got to play annoyed citizen. "Well, it wouldn't've been so late if you weren't tying up traffic like this. You know I spent three hours in this mess? Now all I'll be able to do is start on the inside of the place tonight instead of getting the first coat on the outside. Lucky the house is empty, so's I can sleep over. I don't want to have to go through here too many times. How long you gonna be doing this stuff, anyway?"

"We don't know that, sir. All right, you can go on through."

I breathed a lot easier as I headed up the coast. I even got some amusement out of the radio reports of my death: ". ... be some confusion about the identity of the man behind the series of crimes committed all across San Francisco yesterday. Police say that a large number of jewels and cash were found along with the remains of a man killed in a gas explosion early this morning in a rental building in the Potrero district. The man was an unemployed machinist known to residents in the neighborhood as John Schlott, but dental records indicate that he was Daniel G. Langer, thirty-two. Langer, formerly of San Diego, had served time in prison for running a bookmaking scheme. There is some speculation that the gas explosion that killed the suspect in Friday's series of bank robberies and sabotage might have been deliberately caused. Police officials say it is impossible to determine how much cash may have been destroyed in the explosion, which shook the neighborhood at five-thirty this morning, although they say the jewelry found in the rubble was about one fifth of the total amount stolen in yesterday's commandolike heists. Of the cash that was recovered, police would say only that it was 'under a quarter of a million dollars.' In a related story, the Bay Area Merchants League has entered a lawsuit against police and fire departments for what they term 'gross negligence in providing protection against organized crime and terrorism.'"

I had to smile. I didn't think they'd find the dental records that Tommy and I had switched so soon after the blast. The police, no matter what the Bay Area Merchants League might say, were busting their buns on this case.

It was a beautiful afternoon. Even the fog, which obscured the sunset, was gorgeous. All in all, I felt wonderful.

It's great what your own death can do for your outlook on life.

Eight

"Milo Security."

"Hi, Sadie. It's Nat. I just arrived at the station house. The guy on the case is Detective Dvorak. I'm going in to see him in a little bit. How's Wright doing?"

"Fine, Nat. He called in about ten minutes ago. That puts him only three calls behind."

I smiled. Wright didn't like our going on alert. He hated the routine of calling in every hour or so, or of calling before you left a place and then calling after you arrived at the next place.

"So, did he get anything?" I asked.

"He said that this Daniel Langer has at least a half dozen names. Want them?"

"Sure."

She told me and I made notes. They were just names.

"Okay, Sadie. Thanks. I'll call you when I leave here."

"Everything A-okay?"

"Absolutely. Bye."

"Bye."

Detective Dvorak was one of the new breed of police. College-educated. Community-minded. Politically aware. Not necessarily committed to spending twenty years on the force—if a private-sector job came along, he'd probably take it. No, I'm not psychic. Dvorak told me a lot of this himself. Not in so many words but by his manner, attitude, and the fact that he asked me at least as many questions about my job as he asked about my connection with Falkes.

"Very interesting tape, Miss Fisher."

"Fascinating."

"Don't know what we can do about it."

"You don't have to do anything about it. We'll keep tabs on Falkes. And if the money from the big Friday heists did all burn up in the explosion that killed Langer, then Falkes isn't going to have the bucks to buy the copies."

"Well, you don't know that, Miss Fisher. He could still want to protect his good name, and he is a wealthy property owner."

"That's just it. He isn't wealthy. He owns that run-down warehouse, which is empty and has been that way for over a year. He has three mortgages on his house. He's down to one car from a total of six he had just a few years ago. He had money, but he doesn't have any now."

"You've been working hard, haven't you?"

"Thank you."

"How does that go? I mean, do you have field investigators running around for you, or what?"

"We have a couple of field people besides me. We also have lots of other cases. Now, what I'd like to know is how I can get a look at some of the videotapes of the bank holdups."

"That's part of our investigation."

"True, but we've brought you in on Falkes, so we'd like to be brought in on some of your data."

"Miss Fisher, the police cannot let outsiders view pieces of evidence. You know that."

"Sure. I also know that it's possible to work together on an investigation. Milo Security has done it many times in the recent past."

"Look, the department is very grateful you brought us the Falkes thing. But we can take it from here if it seems like a worthwhile way to go."

"Come off it."

"I beg your pardon?"

"I said, come off it. You can't cover all the leads you've got on this thing. We've got Falkes right where you want him. Let us play him until we see if he's worth reeling in. If he is, you make the bust and Milo Security gets the reward money that the local businesses have posted. You do it any other way and Falkes will slip through the cracks. Come on, Detective, loosen up a little. You know that we can obtain evidence in ways that you often can't."

"I didn't hear that."

"Okay. I didn't say it."

"Ah, what ways are those, exactly?"

"Well," I said, lowering my voice, "since we're not having this conversation, I certainly won't tell you about using computers to break into other computer files to trace people."

"Uh-huh, uh-huh," he said. "Break into computers."

"Not into computers. Into the records. The stuff won't stand up in court, but it's nice to know what's what. In our business, it's often enough. In yours, well, you can usually find the evidence you need a lot faster if you know where it is you're supposed to be looking."

"Computer records, huh? How's that work, exactly?"

"Just like in the movies, only a lot slower and a lot more boring. You get your computer talking with somebody else's computer and you try to crack their security."

"And you've got computer people to do that for you?"

"Sure." He looked relieved, so I added, *"And I do quite a bit of it too."*

"Oh," he said, looking worried. Then he brightened and announced, *"That's illegal."*

"You bet. But since we're not talking about this, I didn't admit to it."

"Yeah. Right."

"Now, Detective, how about letting me see the videotapes from the bank jobs?"

He still hesitated. *"Well, let me get this straight. You stay on Falkes, feeding us any and all information you dig up. If we decide it's time to move in on him, we make the bust and you put in for the reward, right?"*

"That's it," I said.

"Okay. It's showtime. Come with me."

On the way to a small viewing room he asked me more questions about the security business, including why we weren't going after the insurance companies to let us try to recover some of the stolen merchandise.

"You don't have to have their permission," I said. *"If you recover something, you can turn it in for the percentage they offer."*

"Or you can keep it, right?"

"Depends what it is."

"How's that?"

"If it's intrinsically worthless but was heavily insured for other reasons, it may be better to contact the owner, who can then cancel the insurance claim and deal directly with you."

"Oh, yeah," he said. *"Well, here we are. Officer Chambers, this is Miss Fisher. She's helping us with the bank robberies, so would you roll the videotapes for her?"*

"Well, we're about to view them with some of the bank people. Would it be all right to have Miss Fisher there? We've got enough chairs."

"That's fine. Miss Fisher, it's been a pleasure. Please check in with us every couple of days, or if you find out anything. Just ask for me or Officer Chambers, here."

"Got it."

The tapes were boring. Most of them were alike in nearly every detail. Only the interior layouts of the banks seemed to vary. First, three or four figures clad in dark jumpsuits and striped ski masks ran into the bank. They carried long-barreled weapons—rifles, mostly—although there were a few with shotguns and a couple with automatic weapons that were not legally available to the public.

One or two of the figures would climb up on a table or counter near a corner and wave his weapon around at the occupants of the room. All of the masked figures appeared to be shouting orders, really barking them out—you could see the jerking motions of their heads as they yelled. One team avoided yelling by lugging an amplified bullhorn along.

While the people in the bank were herded into the center of the lobby and made to lie down on the floor, one, two, or three of the robbers swung their weapons over their shoulders and began stuffing cash into plastic garbage bags. Sometimes they would take a bank employee into the safe; sometimes they could get into it on their own. Either way, all they wanted was the cash. No violence (with two notable exceptions), no hysterics, no hostages.

The first incident involving violence was actually pretty funny. The guy who leapt up to watch over the crowd misjudged the angle, catching his foot on the edge of the table on his way up. On his way down, his gun became caught between him and a stand-up poster proclaiming this Car Loan Month! His body doubled over on the gun, sending him and the poster rolling off the table. The force of his landing jarred his trigger finger, and the gun went off. His fellow scofflaws, *thinking he was engaged in a life-and-death tussle with the poster, raced over to his rescue. Unfortunately the floor had just been mopped by the maintenance crew, and two more masked marvels hit the tiles.*

By this time, the bank security man, a retired shoe salesman, had managed to load his gun and fire at point-blank range into the pile of thieves.

Two men were hospitalized, one in intensive care, the other with multiple flesh wounds, and one to the chest. It is with these two that the police feel they can begin getting enough information to drag people like Martinelli into it. I doubt it, but you never know. Don't get me wrong—I feel that I can get some names at the top too. I just don't think we'll ever get anything that will stand up in court. Which is why Milo Security concentrates on returning people for the reward money (paltry) and for the publicity (sometimes quite substantial). And, of course, returning stolen property for the insurance fee.

The other incident of violence involved a team of bandits who were out of uniform, so to speak. Two members of a four-man team did not wear ski masks. Instead they wore leather bondage hoods. One had metal studs crisscrossing the back of the head. The other had large red stitching around the eyeholes and the mouth opening, giving it a hideous, voodoo-doll appearance. The man with the metal-studded hood also wore thick leather wristbands. That stirred something in my memory—didn't one of the guys paid by Falkes have big wristbands? Yes, that's right. And he was wearing pants that could have been leather.

Just as this group invaded the bank, the security guard was passing near the door. Two of the armed men used the butt ends of their weapons to beat the guard in the head and face. They hit him several more times than necessary, battering him into unconsciousness even before he crumpled to the floor. The two scum—one in a ski mask, the other in the metal-studded hood—squared their shoulders together and slapped hands. It was as gruesome a bit of strutting gleefulness as I've ever seen.

The room in which we were sitting had been mostly silent up until this point, but now the two women were exhaling and inhaling at top volume, saying non-sentences, such as "Oh, I never," and the three men were sputtering with rage.

"The son of a bitch," one said.

"Both of them," I said.

The rest of the robbery went according to plan. The men were unusually aggressive in the way they went about their actions, but no one was seriously hurt, not even at the end when all four raced across the lobby in a tight cluster of men, bags, and guns—and all four were firing just above the heads of the prone employees and bank customers. That doesn't sound like a big deal, but to maintain covering fire in four directions while moving at a good clip in lockstep formation takes practice—the kind you might get in the military. Add in the fact that they had semiautomatic and some fully automatic weapons and you've got a strong link to the armed services.

We saw a few more tapes, and everything became dull again. When the screening was over, Officer Chambers had to bear the full brunt of their questions.

"What are you doing to find those men?"

"Who was behind it?"

"When will something happen in this case?"

"Where did all the money go?"

"Was the man who died in the explosion the leader?"

"Have you made some arrests?"

Chambers finally was able to quiet them down and get a word in edgewise.

"Ladies and gentlemen, please, we're doing everything that can be done on this case. Every able-bodied
member of the force is at work. All leaves have been
canceled. We are working with the FBI, and that means
we'll have access to all sorts of federal help that
ordinarily we wouldn't have. We have made several
arrests and are getting a lot of valuable information
from these suspects. The police commissioner himself
will be making the announcements of all the latest
developments in the case tomorrow morning at eight.
I'm sorry I can't comment, but I must observe the
proper protocol and go through the right channels like
everybody else. But be assured that with the commissioner taking an active part in this investigation, and
with the FBI working side by side with us, we will have
a satisfying conclusion to the case very, very soon."

*Well. I was impressed. Rarely is the gift of lively
extemporaneous speech found in one who truly believes
the complete bullshit contained in his flowery sentences. But his manner was so convincing that it
worked. Sure, they had more questions, but they were
calm, not frenzied. And they were easily put off with
non-answers and platitudes.*

*I called the office, told Sadie my next move, made
some requests for the initial work on the military and
leather-boy connections, and then asked to speak to
F. J.*

"Nat?"

"Hi, F. J. How are you—knee-deep in paperwork?"

"Hey, fornicate yourself, my darling Dauntless one."

"It's something I've been meaning to try. Listen, I'm
about to leave the police station with a bunch of bank
bigwigs. Well, at least one of 'em is big—his suit is one
of those sixteen-hundred-dollar handmade rigs."

"Yes. And?"

"And we've all been handed a load of crap by some
public-relations smoothie who is really good. So, do I

keep quiet or make a grandstand play for Mr. Big, plugging the wonders of Milo Security?"

"I suppose you're itching to show up the P.R. smoothie?"

"Not exactly. I'd like to maintain a truce at the moment. I was thinking of going out with them and catching them on the steps—oop, they're leaving. I vote for the big play."

"Go for it, then, and good luck."

"Thanks. Bye."

I caught up to the crowd of bank folks without seeming to. They were making reassuring noises at one another. Gosh, I really hated to break the mood, but that's how we sometimes get clients.

"Excuse me," I said. "I'm sorry to break in, but I'd like your opinion of what happened back there."

"Who are you?" This was from Expensive Suit.

"Natalie Fisher. From Milo Security? We're working with the police on this case."

They introduced themselves.

"What are you doing to help the police?" Suit again.

"It's a big case, as you know. We're running down quite a lot of paper trails—checking computer records, pursuing the less obvious leads, and generally shaking down some of the guilty parties."

"I beg your pardon?"

"We've got a line on one of the middle-level crooks, and we're applying a bit of pressure."

It might sound like I was giving away too many secrets at this point, but it seemed like a safe bet. If they kept the information to themselves, then everything was as it had been. If they talked and word got to Falkes, it might provoke him into something rash. And that could get interesting.

"Are the police aware of this?" Fancy Pants was a bit incredulous.

"Of course. I'm interested in knowing how you feel

about what Officer Chambers said," I said, coming to the point. My point.

"Well, and I think I speak for all of us, it is, ah, reassuring to know that so many people and organizations are working on the case."

"Oh."

Silence.

"How, ah, do you feel about it?"

"Glad you asked," I said. "I think it's bunk."

"What do you mean?"

"A load of hooey, a line of bull, a crock of—"

"I think we get the point. I thought you said you were working with the police."

"We are. But not with the slick P.R. types like that. Did his kind of dada really pull the wool over your eyes?"

"Young lady"—Expensive Suit sniffed—"if you have something to say besides these aspersions against police personnel, then I strongly suggest that you—"

"I think I get the point," I said. "Okay, how about this: There has never been an instance of the local police working with the FBI. They barely tolerate each other. It's not so much a case of working side by side as of working at cross-purposes."

"Well," he said, frowning, "don't you think that federal assistance—"

"—will muddy the waters? Yes, I do."

"Still," one of the others spoke up, "the police commissioner is—"

"—just an administrator. The man's a paper pusher. Always has been. He's had twenty-five years of desk jobs that were no more on-the-street than Officer Chambers's. You'd better hope the commissioner is just a figurehead on this case, or it'll be messed up royally."

"Are you suggesting the case wouldn't get solved?" Expensive Suit again.

"Worse," I said.

"What's worse than not being solved?"

"Being incorrectly solved. We'd get a solution, all right; it just wouldn't be accurate. The media would be satisfied, you might be satisfied, but the real perpetrators would go unpunished. And, of course, the money might never be found."

"Didn't the money burn up in that gas explosion?"

"Maybe some of it did. But since not all of the gems were found, it's reasonable to assume not all the money was in that room."

"Wait just a moment," another of them said. *"The officer mentioned some arrests, that they'll have an announcement in the morning. What about that?"*

"No biggie," I said. *"If any of the suspects was high up in the scheme, the commissioner would have mentioned it on TV already. No, they've caught a bunch of small fry, and they hope that lumping them together will make it look like more has been accomplished. If these small-timers can't directly implicate the big boys, basically the crime will be a success. And besides, the police are only making their announcement so they can show the media they're not just sitting around waiting for the FBI to do something. Just watch what happens —the FBI will call its own press conference a little later. In it they will trot out the usual platitudes about modern criminology and computerization of criminal records, and that magical fingerprint file. And I'll bet they give a detailed rundown on Daniel Langer's past. They're very good at instant biographies of dead suspects."*

I stopped. Out of breath more than anything. They looked thoughtful or skeptical, or both at once. I nudged them with the finale of the grandstand play.

"Watch and see if what I just predicted does, indeed, happen. If so—and you'd like that kind of analysis to

be applied to other parts of this case, or on any other security problem—give us a call." I handed Expensive Suit two cards, my own and F. J.'s. "You'll find F. J. much less outspoken than me. He's more refined, more corporate. Just as truthful, mind you, but a lot more politic. Call him if that's more your style. Otherwise call me. I'll be seeing you one way or the other. Oh, and thanks for being a wonderful audience."

I left them muttering to themselves and went and grabbed a cab. I felt odd, but then I always felt funny after a performance like that. It's fun while I'm doing it—hey, I'm as much a ham as the next failed actress —but it's a draining experience, and not a little demeaning. That sort of thing is really a bit of a hustle. Still, it had to be done every now and again— opportunities to drum up business don't often present themselves. F. J. has done wonders with his corporate seminars on the uses of security analysts, and the interest in computer security has given rise to a whole new branch of the private-investigation trade. This biz is getting fragmented, specialized, and downright trendy. Boy, I sure hope that Wright will always be a shamus and I'll always be a sleuth. No matter that we might take on the odd corporate assignment now and then. And no matter that we rely on computers and tape machines and hidden microphones and cameras and high-power lenses and electronic gear. All that stuff goes right out the window when you're out on your own tailing some joker at four in the morning and he does something unexpected.

When it comes down to it, what Wright and I do for a living involves tenacity, psychology, street smarts, and that word I can never say without getting my tongue all tangled up in my throat: chutzpah. Or what my mom used to call "damn high gall."

You know, I'm really going to have to learn to get control of myself. Getting this worked up about a simple, fun, showy, salesy display like I put on for the bank people isn't healthy. It takes up even more energy, so you're left feeling even more drained. And it's very distracting. For example, I didn't notice the guy standing in the shadows near my apartment until after I paid off the cab and sent it down the now darkened street.

Nine

I NEVER LIKED the ocean, so the idea of traveling to South America by boat wasn't exactly my favorite part of Tommy's and my escape plan. Still, he had managed to convince me at the time, now that all the papers were arranged and the special double-hollow centerboard was welded into place, so it was really the only way to go.

The centerboard was something we thought of while watching reruns of *Hawaii Five-O.* I don't remember if the story was about somebody smuggling stuff in a hollowed-out centerboard or if a character on the show just mentioned something about a centerboard, but all those scenes in the harbor got us to thinking about how you hid something in a boat.

"Easy," Tommy said. "In the water."

"Sure," I said.

"No, really. If you make your bundle watertight, you could just tow it underneath the boat."

"Get tangled in the prop."

"Naw. Keep the line short."

"Put a lot of drag on the boat. Better just to get a monster powerboat and outrun everybody."

"C'mon. You can't use a fast boat for every situation. They attract too much attention. We got to look normal. No, what we need is some way of getting the bundle up on board, or back in the water real fast."

"And not be seen doing it," I added.

"Yeah, right. Like the centerboard on one of them big pleasure boats. It goes up and down underneath the boat."

"Only on sailboats, though, right?"

"Christ, I don't know. What's the difference?"

"I don't know if you can add a centerboard to a boat that's not designed for one. And besides, if you put one on the wrong type of boat, you'd still get caught if divers go looking under you."

"C'mon, cops don't have divers."

"They do if they're serious. Besides, the Coast Guard has divers."

"Shit."

We stared at the pretty moving pictures on TV.

"We could—" he started.

"What if—" I began.

"Sorry."

"No, go ahead."

"Okay. We could put the money inside the centerboard on a motorized sailboat."

"Right."

"Has it been done?" he suddenly asked.

"Probably," I said.

"Oh. Too bad. They'll look there. What were you going to say?"

"I was going to say pretty much the same thing, except that I don't mind if they look there."

"What do you mean?"

"We'll put something else in there for them to find. Right on top. Something we'd like to have hidden.

You know, a lot of duty-free liquor, cigars from Havana, whatever."

"Something just illegal enough to seem okay, but not bad enough to get us arrested."

"Exactly," I said.

"But the real stuff is inside another compartment that's inside the first compartment?"

"Something like that."

"I like it." He smiled at me.

"So do I."

So we did it. And so here I am, bobbing up and down in a big tub I hate, with thirty million bucks in the centerboard and a seventeen-year-old runaway I picked up along the way. She's really built and that's fine, but what actually attracted me to her was her snappy dialogue. Not the part about "seeing life all over the world" but the part where she said, "I know how to navigate a boat." I didn't like the way she said it—sort of in a half whine, with the accent on every other word. But I liked the content of that sentence just fine.

Truth is, I didn't think I could make the trip on my own. People have always called me a loner, but they didn't get that right. I'm not attached to anyone or anything (except that thirty mil down below), but I'm not alone very often, either. Sure, I'm not exactly with friends, but at least I'm not alone. There's always somebody to do a deal with, or looking for action, or needing help with a plan for a job, or trying to put money down on something. Always. In every town and every city. You just have to put yourself in the right place.

Anyway, I wanted somebody to make the trip with me. It's a big boat. When the kid popped up at my elbow, I wasn't too inclined to shoo her away because of her curves. We joked around a bit, and I was making with the rich-guy routine, saying this scow

was just my small boat for knocking around in . . .
and then it hit me: I *was* a rich guy. A *very* rich guy. A
very rich guy who had to get out of the country and
who didn't know what he was doing with a big boat
that had sails and a motor and a very special centerboard.

And then the curvy kid claims to know how to
navigate.

"Really?" I said.

"Uh-huh," she said.

"Come on. You don't know how to navigate in open
sea or anything like that, do you?"

"Sure," she said. "I grew up around boats."

"Nearby?"

"Nope. Michigan."

"They don't have an ocean. Just a lake."

"You haven't been in the middle of Lake Michigan
in a squall," she said petulantly. "It blows hard out
there, and the swells get as big as you ever sailed in."

"Okay," I admitted. "You can ride it out. But could
you pilot something like this"—I jerked my thumb at
the boat—"to another country?"

"What're you tryin' to do, talk me onto your boat to
prove it to ya?"

Actually it seemed like she was the one doing the
best to talk her way onto the boat. "I don't think your
parents would think much of that, kid," I told her.

Big mistake. She flared up like one of her Michigan
squalls. She said she was no kid, and she swore like an
army grunt to prove it. I had obviously struck a nerve.
The words kept spouting out of her.

"And if you're not man enough to do something
about what you've started, then you're worthless, no
matter how big your boat is. Big boat but little
dick—is that it?"

"Whoa," I said. "Time out. Very impressive. Great
vocabulary. Nice touch at the end there, impugning

my manhood. I'd like to, ah, discuss that with you privately sometime. Thing is, you're not legal yet, know what I mean?"

We argued about that for a while, she insisting she was eighteen, me saying sixteen, until we split the difference and agreed she was seventeen. Still jailbait, but close enough to legal for being out on the ocean together. Then we got a little serious about her parents and her past—enough to hear the same stories that half the runaways in California have to tell. And enough to establish that no one in the immediate vicinity was about to come looking for her right away.

"All right, Miss Spunky," I told her. "Let's you and me go for a boat ride so you can prove some of those tall tales of yours. Navigate us the hell out of here and head south down the coast. First calm and private place you find below San Francisco, put down the anchor and we'll see how much of a woman you really are."

"Hah," she said, smiling. "How much man you are, you mean."

She liked having a strong effect on men. She told me so as she was having a strong effect on me. She teased, stroked, posed, touched, and moved just right. She was intoxicated with her own sexuality and wanted everyone around her to share the feelings of ecstasy. It may have been just sexual games for her, but it felt good to me all the same.

We weighed anchor and headed south again. She came up into the wheelhouse wearing a University of Michigan Wolverines T-shirt that was at least one size too small. She brushed up against me to show she was still firm—as if I couldn't see that through the thin material. She was very proud of her breasts. As she told me earlier, "They stay up high whether I wear a bra or not." Now she sauntered away from me across the cabin and gazed out at the sea. It was at that point that I noticed she was wearing only the T-shirt and nothing else.

"Forget something?" I said.

"Nope. I didn't." It came out "dint."

"Nice tan line," I said.

"I don't have a tan line."

"That's what's nice about it."

She slowly turned her head back toward me, then slowly—very slowly—she also turned her body toward me. Nothing new in what she had. It was just put together better than most. Well, okay, a lot better than most.

"Think you can keep your mind on where we're heading?" she asked.

I glanced forward. We were heading straight in toward the shoreline.

"Shit," I said, and spun the wheel over to get us back on course.

"Try to be more careful, huh?" she told me reproachfully. But I noticed she was smiling with satisfaction.

"I'm going to my cabin," she said. "If you start feeling down about anything, let me know and I'll"— pause—"get you up again."

All in all, a not unpleasant way to travel, I thought.

Ten

The guy was big. How could I have missed him? I wondered. It couldn't have been easy hiding a body as big as a horse out in front of my building. All I could think of was the shrubbery.

"You were hiding in the bushes, weren't you?" I said to him as he came at me.

"I got a message for you," he growled. Jesus, he doesn't even sound like a human being.

"Gosh," I said, "I hope you aren't hurting your voice. Maybe you should come back later."

"Shut up," he said raspily, and used his body to push me up against the side of the apartment wall.

"Fresh," I said, and tried to get my hands or elbows in a position to do something violent when the right time came.

"Stay off the Falkes case," he sort of said.

"Oh, is this a message from dear Mr. Falkes? Because he could just as easily have called the office and—"

"You're not listening," he croaked out at me. He punctuated his next sentence by bashing my shoulders back with the palms of his big hands. "Stay"—shove — "off"—shove— "the" — shove — "Falkes"—shove — "case"—shove.

The right time had come. I lifted my right foot and placed it against the front of one of his massive legs, right on the shinbone. Pushing the side of my shoe into his leg as hard as I could, I jammed my foot downward, scraping him a bit.

"Hey," he said. It was the most articulate I'd ever heard him.

The scraping of my foot came to an abrupt halt about one second after it started—right when my heel landed on his instep. That brought about a loss of concentration on his part. We had been playing patty cake up to then, with my efforts to get my arms and hands free going for naught. He forgot about my hands for a second, just enough for me to send my own palms straight out and up at his fat head. Bull's-eye. Or rather, bull's-nose. The idea with this movement is to jam your attacker's septum right up through his frontal sinus, so I put my whole body into the quick arm thrust. His head snapped backward. I quickly pulled my arms back, then shot them out again, this time with fingers held rigid and extended with just a slight curve. I aimed a little lower than last time: right at his trachea. Bull's-eye. Or rather, bull's-neck.

He grunted and gurgled, and I wriggled past him with a shove from my elbow. I thought he was making animal noises before, but that was nothing compared to his guttural, rolling, low-pitched scream of rage. The screaming noise came up behind me as I tried to get into the apartment's front door. He closed in from the side and clamped his paws on arm and waist. We spun around, and he picked me up and tried his very best to throw me right through the sidewalk. I was lucky we were in a spin because he put me into too much of an arc to accomplish his purpose if I could go into a roll. I went into a roll. I got bumped and bruised, but there were no sounds of bones breaking.

Now that I was down on the ground, I decided it was my best bet to stay there. Back in my first self-defense class, I was always best in the ground-level stunts. I became queen of what they called "the chicken position."

I got my legs between me and the human mountain and tried to look helpless. It wasn't hard to do. He came lumbering over, still in his screaming fit, only now punctuating his squeals with gasping breaths. I hoped he made another mistake and planted his feet too close to mine. He did the next best thing: He hopped onto one foot and swung his other leg back, preparing to placekick me out into the bay. I slid on my rump toward his planted foot, stuck one of my feet around the back of his ankle, and sent the other foot lashing out at his knee. I'm not going to say bull's-knee, because that would be tiresome. Let's just say that I heard a very satisfying crunch.

He went down in a heap, positively shaking with pain, bellowing like the wounded animal he was. Windows opened across the street. Someone I recognized but didn't know came out the door of my building. I asked them to phone the police, ask for Detective Dvorak, and get them to send a patrol car and an ambulance. Then I tried to get something useful out of the bawling blimp. He didn't want to talk at first.

"Get the fuck outa here," was how he put it. "Fucking Christ, my knee. Jesus."

"Listen, butterball," I said straight into his ear, but I didn't get any further because he swatted at my head with one of his shovel-sized hands.

I chopped him one in the gut. That brought his head up off the pavement slightly. I punched down at his *forehead, sending the back of his cranium into the unyielding concrete.*

"Lie still," I told him.

He tried coming up again. I bounced his dome off the sidewalk. We did this routine a couple of times. I tried using words he was probably used to: "Stay, boy, stay. Down, big fella." It didn't work. "Okay, ace," I said. "You asked for it." I hit him in the knee.

If the human voice was like fireworks, he would have lit up the sky. I waited until the first rush of pain subsided, then I hit him again. I think I finally had his attention.

"We can keep playing this fun little game, but I suggest you listen to my questions without moving, then try to answer them. Truthfully and quickly."

Sweat was forming all over his face.

"What'd ya wanna know?"

"Who sent you?"

"Some guy. Never seen 'em afore."

"What did he say?"

"To scare the dame off."

"Scare me off what?"

"I dunno. The Falkes case."

"What's that?"

"I don't know! Fuck, get some help. I need a doctor."

"One's on the way. What did the guy look like?"

"Little guy, 'bout five ten or eleven. Bald with long black hair on the sides. Weird for a young guy. Aw, Jesus."

"White guy?"

"Yeah."

"Thin? Fat?"

"Thin. Jesus Christ, get somebody!"

"Coming. Where did you meet this guy?"

"Warehouse."

"On Pier Sixty?"

"Yeah. Think so. By docks."

"How did he talk?"

"Fuckin' A, he just talked."

"High voice or deep voice?"

"Ah, shit. In between."

"Did he kinda talk like dis? Or did he pronounce every word exactly?"

"In between."

"If you had to give me one fact about him that would help anybody identify him, what would it be?"

"Shit, I dunno. Fuck."

"I think I'll practice my bongos on your knee," I said, moving toward his leg.

"No! Wait! Shit, let me think. Uh, he, ah, he had real funny skin."

"Go on."

"It was like . . . oily, you know?"

"But he was a white guy, right?"

"Yeah."

"But his skin was smooth and looked like it was covered with oil?" I guessed "smooth," but I wanted to hear him.

"Not dark oil. Light oil or something."

The cops arrived just about the same time as the paramedics, so we had to end our delightful little chat. I began telling everything to the police. Well, almost everything. I didn't feel like prolonging things with a discussion of some unknown male caucasian, youngish, balding, with long black hair and oily skin.

The cops finally had enough of my side of it and left to charge Blimpy with assault. They reminded me to show up to press charges tomorrow. I went to the kitchen and made myself a Texas bloody Mary—beer and tomato juice. I put on a tape: Yearning & Harmony by Tri Atma with Klaus Netzle, and their synthesizer and Indian rhythms worked their calming influence.

I hit the playback button on my answering machine and heard Wright's usual charming message: "Give me a call, bitch. Some of us work for a living."

For some reason, abuse from Wright always made me smile. Shit, I forgot to call in. I didn't think Sadie would still be on the board—we get a second- and third-shift person in whenever we go on alert—but she was the one who answered.

"What are you doing still at work?" I said.

"New girl's just about to take over. I'm showing her where everything is. Oh, that means we're on the backup code."

That meant the same as asking "A-okay?"

"Everything's hunky-dory. I'm home now, and I plan to stay until, well, who knows. Any messages?"

"Yes. Wright wants you to call him at home."

"Wright called to tell you that?" I asked incredulously. A message on my machine once in a while, sure. But a call to the office? Unprecedented.

"I know it's odd, but he said it's very important. He also said that from now on we're to assume our phones are tapped and to conduct business accordingly. F. J.'s going to check out the office phones tomorrow."

I thanked Sadie and hung up. I had to talk to Wright, tap or no tap, although I wondered how he'd get anything of importance over to me if we behaved as if the line were dirty. Wright answered in yet another way calculated to discourage the casual caller: "This better not be a wrong number."

"Heaven forbid," I said.

"Hiya, legs. Listen, you're not going to believe what I got. Remember that we have in common a certain blue book that must needs remain nameless right now?"

I had to think a second. Oh, the Bartlett's. We had the same edition. "Right," I told him.

"Get it."

I got it.

"Now," he said, "read stanza forty-one on page 572. Silently, of course."

"Of course."

I found it: a quote from Shelley's Adonais that went, 'He lives, he wakes—'tis Death is dead, not he."

"Okay," I told Wright. "Now what?"

"Take the Sam on page 210, then take the D-O out of the Savage on page 536 and put in a G-E."

"What is this?"

"Just do it and shut up."

I sighed and flipped pages. On page 210 I found Samuel Daniel, a sixteenth-century poet who had penned Sonnets to Delia. On page 536 was Walter Savage Landor. If the two offending letters in his last name were dropped and—

"Jesus," I said into the phone, "are you sure?"

"Yup. Let's meet and talk. We'll need a noisy place."

"There's a free concert at SFAI."

"Perfect. Look for me at three o'clock."

We hung up and I went to change clothes. Three o'clock meant he'd be as close as possible to the far right side of the audience as viewed from the area of the main entrance. I think the thing that made Wright so good at this business was his love for these sorts of code phrases, methodologies, and rituals. Why the hell he refused to check in with the office to let them know his whereabouts is something I've never been able to fathom. He enjoys the other rigamarole. Where else could you have the delicious, adolescent delight of sending secret messages to another person who—I confess—shared your delight? Using Bartlett's Familiar Quotations to tell me that he discovered that Daniel Langer did not die in that gas explosion was the kind of good fun one did not have in the more normal lines of work.

If Daniel Langer was indeed alive, then we were on to something interesting. Something the bank boys *would pay for. Something that might show up both the police and the feds. It also meant that something was funny with that gas explosion, and that meant there was the possibility that there were still jewels and paper money to be tracked down—we could then deal with the insurance people, or with the owners, on a direct basis. I couldn't wait to talk with Wright. I got dressed —more for fighting or running, just in case my large attacker wasn't acting alone—and called the office with my upcoming movements. The last thing I did was something that seemed to be happening on more and more cases: I went to the front closet, spread apart the coats, removed the false drywall, unlocked the cabinet that was built into the back of the little room, opened it, and selected a gun to tote along on my travels.*

I used to think packing a rod was exciting. Then I got to the point where I avoided it because guns have a habit of getting used, and when guns get used, people get shot. Now I'm sad every time I feel the need for the iron in my purse or in my holster. But the need is there, I keep telling myself. I'm not creating the need, am I? No, there are people like the blob who started bouncing me off the side of my own building. And there are the people who hire the people like that. I took a .38 and a shoulder holster (nice thing about San Francisco is that it's almost always chilly enough to wear a jacket to cover up the weapon), sighed, slipped it on, and left to hear the details of what might make an interesting case also a profitable one.

At the Art Institute a free-jazz student group was honking its way through what sounded like Ellington's "C-Jam Blues." Wonder how the Duke would feel about that treatment. Wright was right where I expected, snapping his fingers.

"You dig that?" I asked.

"Good tune. Fractured tempo, but they're going to be okay. Let's move around."

We moved among the crowd, mostly students. Alternative modes of dress were, shall we say, in evidence.

"Tell me," I said.

"I was playing the tapes of the tap we've got on Falkes. We have one where he calls someone named Danny right after you put the screws on him. We know that the call was made at 12:26 on the afternoon of the day of the gas explosion."

"Could be a different Danny."

"Could be, but it's not. We took the tones of Falkes's dialing and came up with a number. I checked it out. It's to an apartment in Potrero. Guy used his real name. Daniel Langer. We got a picture, and—"

"You did? Where?"

"It's in the Examiner, *dummy. Where've you been?"*

I told him about the battering blimp.

"Jesus," Wright said. "Remind me never to try to kick you when you're down. Anyway, I took Langer's picture over to the apartment and showed it around. They made him."

I smiled.

"Looks like we've got profit potential."

"Looks like."

"How do you suppose the dental records of the guy in the gas explosion got switched?" I asked.

Wright said, "You answered it yourself. Langer went in and made a switch."

"Of course, but how? Inside job or break-in?"

"What's the difference?"

"If it's inside, we might be able to put pressure on somebody there. And if it was a straight break-in, then maybe we can learn something from the police report."

"Long shot. Better to concentrate on Falkes, that oily-faced geek, and Langer. I'll take Langer, since you're already started on Falkes and Oily."

"But Langer's the man with the money. I want him. You take Falkes and Oily."

"No way."

"Come on, Wright, let me have Langer. I'll owe you one."

"Forget it."

"I've got a better idea," I said. "We'll both work on Langer and let F. J. send somebody after Falkes and Oily. He's going to have to put a lot of work into this thing, anyway. Besides, half of the work will be with the phones and the computers."

"Maybe."

That was close enough for me.

"Okay, so that's settled. Now what do you know about military training that would lead to four men running in precision formation while facing all points of the compass?"

"Where'd you get that?"

I told him about the image on the bank's videos.

"Sounds like some sort of commando thing," he said. "Might make it easier to check their records."

"Think we can crack 'em again?"

"Why not?"

We have a computer whiz who maintains there isn't a computing installation in the world he can't crash. We get some of our contract work that way. We bet he can break into their system; they say we can't; we do; they put us on retainer. Fender is the guy's name. "Fender the computer nerd," as he calls himself. We always say, "Oh, Fend, you're not a nerd." He likes to hear us say it. Fend has a friend who crashed the Pentagon computers (you may have read about that). Fend says it doesn't count if someone else can tell you crashed it. Makes you wonder about your computerized bank statement, doesn't it? Anyway, we would have to unleash Fend on the computer storage vaults of the armed forces. It would be no contest.

"Let's call Fend," Wright said.

"Now?"

·"*Might as well get him started. He likes working at night, anyway. Phone lines are freer.*"

We made the call from a pay phone right off the courtyard from where the jazz was blasting. Wright had to shout a bit to be heard. That was okay. Wright's good at shouting when he has to.

"*So how's about we check out this group?*" *he said after hanging up the phone.*

"*Nope,*" *I told him. "I'm out of here. It's been much too long a day as it is.*"

"*Want me to drive home with you?*"

"*No, you stay and listen to the music. I'll be fine.*"

"*You check out those shadows this time.*"

"*I'll do that.*"

I did more than that. Not only did I ask the cabbie to stay until I was inside the front door, I kept my hand inside my coat, resting lightly on the butt of the gun. Something about being attacked makes you overly cautious.

Nothing happened outside my building. Nothing happened inside except sleep.

Eleven

WE ALMOST DIDN'T make it as far south as Monterey. The Coast Guard cutter that sliced across our bow was filled with stern-faced men looking for a chance to use some of the military hardware they had at their command.

"Heave to and prepare for boarding," came the voice over a bullhorn.

I found myself shouting back at them even though there was no way my words could have reached them across the patch of choppy water between us. The wind probably carried my protests all the way back to Alcatraz.

"Heave to and drop anchor," came the solid, electronically powered voice.

"Jesus," I muttered. Now, the key to getting out of this would be a good acting job. What would an ordinary tax-paying citizen do in a situation like this? Especially a tax-paying citizen with enough money to buy a boat this size. Why, he'd be fucking indignant, that's what. So I was.

"What the hell do you mean 'drop anchor'?" I shouted. "Get the hell out of my way. I pay your fucking salaries!"

I told the girl to go around the cutter.

"Are you sure?"

"Yeah."

"They look like they mean it," she said.

"Hey, so do I, goddamit." I gestured violently at her to steer our boat around theirs. The gyrations were primarily for their benefit. I wanted them to think I was hopping mad. I went to the wheel and picked up the radio and started making calls over a frequency I was pretty certain they would be monitoring. I invented a pal on shore named George and began laying it on thick: "George! George! Come in, George. If you can hear me—and I know you can—you get on the phone to the senator and you tell him some jackshit two-bit toy sailors are trying to stop us from sailing our own boat along the coast. Then you get Maury to bring the videotape crew from the Pacifica construction site and get all this down on tape. We're just off San Pedro Point, and they can be here in ten minutes if they hustle it. I'm going to sue these bastards for every cent in their military retirement fund. You do it, George, or it's your ass." I tossed the radio handset down and hoped my performance hadn't been wasted.

"Heave to, or we will be forced to shoot." Bullhorn again.

I went out where they could see me. It was a surprise to see how big the cutter looked up close. They were within a few yards of us, again blocking our path. I began a tirade that was very strong on taxes, political contributions, connections with Senate investigating committees, and the lack of any intelligence among the military. The girl finally broke in at one point.

"Will you shut up a minute, for chrissake!"

"The fuck do you want?" I shouted at her.

"Look, mister, they're going to board your boat whether you like it or not. Let's let her drift alongside and throw them a line." She indicated the small boat that was being lowered into the water next to the cutter.

I threw up my hands in disgust and walked away to the far end of the boat. She did what she said, and in a few minutes she was staring face-to-face with an ensign, who climbed nimbly aboard. I had been smiling a little at my act, but now I got myself into another rage and stamped over to the two of them.

"You ask permission to come aboard?" I said.

"Yes, he did. Jesus, cool out, why don'tcha?"

"What's the meaning of harassing American citizens in American waters?"

"Sir, thank you for your cooperation. We have been ordered to stop all commercial and pleasure craft en route from the San Francisco area unless subjected to a search conducted with or without a warrant at the owner's or captain's request. Do you so request?"

"What the hell—?"

"I can repeat our orders for you, sir. Is that what you wish?"

"Naw, I heard you. Jesus. You're stopping every ship unless you search it? Without a warrant? Jesus."

"We will be happy to obtain a warrant, sir. If you will allow us to tow you to harbor and wait while we obtain it, the Coast Guard will be thankful for your cooperation."

"Yeah, yeah, I heard that too. What happens if I don't cooperate?"

"We are free to use whatever force is necessary to maintain order along the coast." He paused and looked hard at me for the first time. "In this case I don't think we would have to do any shooting. You look like a man who knows the military, sir, and you know that we can follow orders the hard way or the easy way. Let's make this an easy one."

I just stared at him for a few seconds. I couldn't help wondering if he could tell I was ex-army, or if he was just making a guess.

"Aw, shit. Search away, then," I told him. "Jesus Christ, what do you think I've got on here, marijuana?"

"No, sir. We don't think that." Not a trace of a smile.

He signaled for the rest of the men in the small boat to come aboard, and they made a very efficient search. I followed along with the ensign, saying things like, "Hey, careful with that" or "You break it, you buy it." It seemed in character.

When we got below decks, they stood right next to the centerboard. The ensign came over to me and said, "You have a nice ship, sir. Very impressive. You sail it by yourselves, just the two of you?"

"Thanks. Yeah. Well, actually, she does most of the work. This'll be her toy one day."

I tried not to pay too close attention to what the men were doing around the centerboard. They seemed to be looking at the bolts that held the cover in place. Once again Tommy had known just what he was doing. "We paint the bolts every time we open and shut the stash. If it looks like paint is chipped off the bolts, then it looks like we've been in there recently." Good old Tommy. He even put some gray paint into the can of white we used on the bolts so it looked like the white paint had been on there a while, fading a little with age. It worked. The men left the centerboard and filed past me to go back up on deck.

"Thank you for your . . . patience," the ensign said.

"Yeah. My patience. Sure."

The men were already getting back in the boat when

I got back up on deck. No more words were exchanged as the ensign joined his men and they made their way back to the cutter.

"Do you always get so upset?" she asked me.

"No."

"I thought you were going to bust a blood vessel."

"Good. Just the effect I wanted."

We headed the boat down the coast. After we got past the cutter the day turned out to be great. The girl was pouting at first but then began getting flirty. She kept coming up to me with one less article of clothing each time we passed on the way to the galley or up to the wheel. The effect was like a prolonged strip routine. Only this act was better, because she would get real close, brushing up against me every so often. Near dusk she was down to bra and panties as she steered us into a little cove, and we let down both anchors. She took off her bra and headed below decks.

"You're a real tease, you know that?" I said to her back.

She stopped and turned slightly, letting me see just enough of her. "If you get to do what you want afterward, it's not a tease."

She had a point.

Twelve

"Hello?"

"Nat? It's F. J. Turn on your TV. The police commissioner is holding his press conference, and that FBI guy, Rutterman, is up on the dias with them. It could be good. I'll call you back when it's over. Bye."

"Bye."

I flicked on the set.

". . . bringing the total to twenty-seven suspects now placed under arrest by your city police department. These suspects are all undergoing extensive questioning, and several patterns are beginning to present themselves, patterns that are rich with avenues for our continuing investigation and the ultimate solution of this well-planned series of commandolike robberies."

There followed a general mass confusion as the media horde jockeyed for position to see who could ask the next question.

"Yes?" the commissioner said, pointing to one reporter.

"What about the dead bodies found on the outskirts

of the city? Were they gangland people? Were they victims of execution-style killings?"

"Well, we are also continuing our investigation into those crimes, but there is no reason to suppose that they're connected with the robberies."

Again the babble.

"Commissioner, isn't it true that none of your twenty-seven suspects are ringleaders?"

"We don't know that."

"But aren't they alleged to be just drivers and a couple of burglars?"

"Well, in a commando raid everyone is important. All twenty-seven arrests are crucial to the police department's ultimate solving of the case."

"Does the lab say that most of the thirty million dollars was destroyed in the explosion that killed Daniel Langer?"

"Treasury agents have conducted tests on the remains—uh, that is, not the human remains—and it is not possible to state the amount of money destroyed in the explosion and fire."

"Are local labor leaders involved?"

"We don't know that at this time."

"What is the FBI doing?"

"Well, perhaps Special Agent Rutterman will care to comment on that."

"Yes, I would. We have obtained the criminal records of all twenty-seven of the people arrested by the police, and we will be making this material available in due course. We have some information on Daniel G. Langer, alias Daniel Joseph, Joe Lansky, Dan Landerman, and so on. Mr. Langer was thirty-eight years old, had served four years in the U.S. Army, serving in America and in Mexico, and had a criminal record. He had been arrested six times for grand theft, three times for illegal gambling, and convicted once for *grand theft and the fraudulent sale of government property. He does not have any surviving relatives . . ."*

There were further details, none of them significant in the least, and many additional questions to Rutterman and the commissioner, most of them calculated to make it easy to get the two men to agree to a shocking revelation—something that would look good in a headline.

The whole affair had gone pretty much as I had predicted to the banking men and women. F. J. told me later that before Rutterman could even finish his spiel about Daniel Langer's background, one of the banking bigwigs called to put us on retainer. F. J. later signed up two other banks and three savings and loans, some for consultation, some for security seminars, some for both. That's how money is made in the modern detective firm. At this point, anything we came up with on the actual case would be gravy. Now Wright and I could get on with the real stuff. After F. J. called me back, we agreed on how many of the in-house agency people could be put on the case, and I handed out the assignments: trace Langer (sure, the FBI has big computer files; they also have unmotivated, bureaucratic nonentities poring over their work, and they could easily miss something); look into Langer's friends and associates; check out Falkes and any of his associates (got to get a line on Oily Face); and see about Fender and his work on the military records of the hooded creeps. All this would be electronic, using normal data processing/modem/Fax transmission of information. By having Wright and me out in the field, we'd be doing as much as we could. We would, of course, monitor the police as much as possible via the radio.

The job itself is frequently a question of tenacity. You knock on doors, buttonhole people, find out something else to run through the computers of America (whether

*America knows it or not), hang out with court reporters
and crime reporters (boy, oh boy, do they ever think
there's a difference, so don't ever get 'em mixed up), try
to find somebody who'll become a paid informant, and
just generally run down every straight or silly idea that
pops into your head. The trick is to run it all down
before moving on to the next idea. Or you try to palm
off the really boring stuff to your partner. (Of course,
he's busy trying to palm stuff off on you.) No matter
what happens, you always keep coming back to what
you already know and try to add facts to it and follow
the trail from there.*

*The doors I knocked on and the people I buttonholed
were all in the area of Daniel Langer's apartment.
Sure, Wright had hit it right on the money—no sweat.
But we had nowhere to go with the story. So he had an
apartment in the neighborhood. (So he faked his own
death and is gallivanting around with thirty million!)
So, what were his habits? Did he have a car? Who were
his friends? His business associates? Could we prove
that the body in the exploded room wasn't his? In which
direction did he run? Who the hell was it who got blown
to smithereens?*

Other than that, we were really cooking.

*Armed with a couple of reproductions of Langer's
tight-lipped countenance, I went through the standard
litany of questions and explanations: "Have you ever
seen this man before? No, I'm not a cop. This is to help
get some of the money back for the insurance companies. Would you take another look at the photographs?
Yes, they aren't very good photos. They never are. Yes,
they're probably giving a reward for the return of some
of the jewelry. Are you sure you haven't seen this guy?
Thank you for your time." And so on. And on.*

*Gradually I worked my way into the life of Daniel
Langer. It took several days, and lots of frustrating
talks with Dvorak at the police department (he always*

had to have the facts dragged out of him, and he never seemed to listen to the little tidbits of information I gave to him, which was okay with me, because the longer we had exclusivity on the possibility of Langer still being alive, the better our chances of cracking the case ourselves). By cross-checking everything with what we could get via computer, then going back to more face-to-face work, Wright and I began to get a picture of Langer's life.

Small-timer. Gambling. Numbers. Insurance scam or two. Pretty smart as petty crooks go—always figuring the angles so that he came out on top. Well, almost always. He did do one stretch in prison, and one stretch in the service of our nation. His most recent partner was the late Tommy Weisberg, the guy who was fished out of a sewage tank just before the big robberies. Weisberg had been involved with the fence who was killed in Falkes's warehouse. We couldn't account for Langer's time on the night of the fence's death. Might be a connection. Langer was point man for many of the groups of people involved in the robberies. He gave them their instructions, helped get them the proper equipment, coordinated the schedules, and even had the muscle to keep some of them in line.

It looked like Langer was the only connection between the robbers themselves, the truckers who blocked off the traffic lanes, the guys who cut the phone lines, the messenger boys on their motorcycles, and the trash-truck boys. Now, the interesting thing is, Langer himself didn't have the clout to make all these groups of people do what was necessary to pull off the robberies. He could handle a couple of guys at a time, but no way could he get the truckers to roll their rigs at precise locations all over the city at exactly the right time, for example. But Martinelli could get his truckers to do it—and he could get it done without having it traced back to him, leaving Langer or some other poor *schnook out to dry. Langer couldn't get all the numbers runners in the city to turn in false alarms, cut phone lines, knock off liquor stores, etc. But Foley could control them. And Foley could control his dope runners so that all the deals would go down at about the same time—Jesus, it must have been snow city out there. The same thing applied to Henderson's trashmen, construction/strong-arm boys, and maintenance crews. And the newspapers were hinting fairly strongly that some cops had to have been involved in the deal.*

We found out more about Langer. He owned a van. He hung around an unemployed machinist named John Schlott for a while, even helped him get into an apartment, then didn't show up in the neighborhood again. His friend Tommy also owned a van—a van filled with plumbing equipment, or so it appeared. If you pulled a certain way on the pipes, a hidden compartment was revealed. He had a magnetized sign that read STAR PLUMBING. *He had papers that said he was going to Mexico and Peru.*

As things sort themselves out, you just keep plugging away at it. You walk through the city, noting how the crews are cleaning up the burned vehicles, boarding up the broken windows, repairing the phone and alarm systems. Sometimes you confirm things with Fender. Sometimes you talk with the cops. Sometimes you get to meet Wright for lunch.

"So?" he said.

"What do you mean, 'So?' Don't you call in to Sadie?"

"Naw. I knew you'd fill me in."

"Damn it, Wright, you might have something we needed."

"If I had, I would have called. Let's order."

"But we've got to trade information more often than this." I glared at him. "Jesus, Wright."

"Hush, woman. Order your eats. Then let's talk
about a certain individual with a viscous visage."

"You found the oily-faced man?"

He wouldn't talk about it until we ordered.

"Come on, Wright. Give."

"Okay. I started with a little visit to your assailant's
hospital bed. He still hasn't forgiven you for making
him a cripple."

"That's not a nice word," I told him.

"Uh-huh. How 'bout gimp?"

"Not funny."

"Hopalong?"

"Stop it."

"You're being a bit sensitive over this one, Natalie
Dauntless."

"Yeah, I know."

"Do you know why?"

"Well . . ." I hesitated, then went on. "I think it's
because I don't really feel much. I mean, when I kicked
him and I heard the snap of his leg, I knew it was all
over. And there was a certain relief. And some satisfaction, because I had done just exactly what I aimed to do
right then. But I didn't feel like 'Hah, he got what was
coming to him' or 'That'll teach you to come after me'
or anything like that. Now, when I should either be
feeling a little sad for him or looking to joke with you
about it to show how 'professional' I am, well, I just
don't feel like it. I don't feel anything other than 'It's
over,' and I lived through it, and, well, that's all. Finis."
I paused. "You think something's wrong?"

"No," he said. "I think you have finally gotten over
thinking of this business as a game. It's now that you're
closer to being 'professional,' as you call it."

"Hope you're right."

"It's just . . ." he began.

"What?"

"Well, dammit, Nat, I still think it's a game. And that fat hobbler got precisely what he deserved. Finis for me."

"Oh."

The food came and we began eating slowly.

"So tell me about the oily-faced man," I said.

"Not until you joke about the gimp."

"Knock it off."

"Well, you almost did. Okay, I'll accept that as a joke. But I'm warning you: You've got to be wilder than that in the future."

"Very funny."

"I'll loosen you up again, Natalie Dauntless. Swear to God."

"Fine."

"So, anyway, I tried getting a little more out of Fatty. Said it'd go better for him to talk. Didn't much convince him, but he did describe the guy who hired him. He could see the value in bringing somebody else down with him."

"Does this mean I don't have to go to the station and press charges?"

"Up to you. We tie him to Falkes, and Falkes to Langer, and the cops will be very interested in Fat Boy. And it's not as if he can run very far right now."

He put the accent on the word run, just to see me react. I made a face but no comment.

"Next I went to see your Mr. Falkes. Had to get very insistent with his hired help. Started talking very loudly about videotapes. Finally got to see him. Did you know he was into amateur theatricals?"

"You mean, like little theater groups, that sort of thing?"

"Yeah. Very little groups, from what I can make out. He fancies himself a great makeup artist. Almost a master of disguises, you might say."

"The oily guy is Falkes?" I said.

"You got it."

"How corny."

"It worked. Fat Boy didn't know Falkes when I showed him a photo."

"Well, still," I said, "people only do that shit in the movies."

"Yeah, well, maybe that's why it worked."

"How'd your talk with Falkes go?"

"Fine. We're great pals. He 'n' me are like that."

He held his hand up, thumb and little fingers straining to stay as far away from each other as possible.

I smiled. Weakly.

"Nice try," I said, "but you'll have to do better than that to loosen me up."

"These are just the preliminaries, woman. God, you're a bitch."

"Thank you."

"Welcome. Anyway, I had a nice chat with Falkes. He was pissed about my coming there when he thought he had a deal with you and F. J. I said we were pissed at him for sending Fat Boy. He denied it. I demonstrated how I could break every finger on his hands. He panicked and drew a gun."

"He does that."

"Yeah, well, he won't be doing it again anytime soon."

"What did you do?"

"I went for him."

"And?"

"And he shot me."

"Yeah?" I said, half joking.

"Yeah. Right in my bulletproof vest."

I didn't know if I should believe him, but he sat back from the table and showed me a hole in his shirtfront.

"See?" he said matter-of-factly.

"*You take too many chances, Wright.*"

"*Anyway,*" he said, "*I think I broke his hand when I took away his gun. I tried to get from him who he was tied in with—Foley, Henderson, Martinelli. I don't think he dealt at that level. He may have only been contacted by phone. You know, it occurs to me that our Mr. Langer may have it made if Falkes is the quality of person who's after him.*"

"*Oh, thanks a bunch.*"

"*Besides us, of course.*"

"*I should say so.*"

"*We'll have more out of him by the end of the day. I put Freddie on him. Freddie could get a mute to talk.*"

"*You put Freddie on him? Where?*"

"*Out in his own warehouse. Seems like a nice quiet spot.*"

"*Shouldn't you have turned him in to the police? We sort of promised we would if we got anything else on him.*"

"*They didn't want him,*" he said.

"*What?*"

"*You know your Detective Dvorak, the guy you've been checking in with for the past few days? I got him on the phone, explained the situation, and asked if they wanted me to hold Falkes or bring him in. He said neither, that their case was about wrapped up and they didn't need any loose ends.*"

"*Wrapped up? Jesus, they've arrested fifty people who made phony calls, cut telephone wires, and set fire to parked cars. They've got nobody of importance in the whole case.*"

"*I know. Interesting, ain't it?*"

"*Jesus, Wright. Something's fucked.*"

"*Such language from such a pretty girl.*"

"*Does F. J. know about Dvorak's statement?*"

"*Yeah, I called him before meeting you. Seems that*

*there's to be another press conference at two o'clock.
That's why I've been dawdling over luncheon with you,
darling. There's a TV in the bar of this place, and we
can go watch it in there."*

"It's almost two. Come on."

*It was a travesty. The multisyllabic words flowed like
compliments at a wedding reception, but not a whole
hell of a lot was said. It boiled down to: The job was the
work of outsiders, masterminded by person or persons
unknown—possibly a foreign government as part of a
terrorist act—and most of the money was probably
destroyed in the fire that killed someone whose dental
records said he was Daniel Langer. The fifty-nine
people who had been arrested were misguided souls
who acted on impulse or who were swayed by the
anarchistic talk of the commando leaders.*

"This is total bullshit," I said to Wright.

*"Yup. Might just work, though. It's just crazy enough
to sound like a real, honest-to-badness conspiracy."*

"People are going to be asking lot of questions—"

"And there will be lots of answers, Nat."

*"But the answers aren't going to make sense,
dammit."*

*"Yeah. Just like life. Look, kiddo, somebody put the
fix in, or our own government is running a scam for
some reason."*

"Why?"

*"Don't know. Either way it puts Langer out there
somewhere with a pile of money."*

*"Could it be some elaborate sting operation?" I
wondered.*

*"Who they trying to sting—depositors of the First
National Bank?"*

*"This is actually one crime where the little guys were
pretty well protected. Deposits up to a hundred grand
are insured."*

"Yeah, well, somebody's insurance rates are going to go up. And I'll bet that means somebody else's mortgage rate is going up too."

"I've got to talk to Dvorak," I said.

"Good luck. I don't expect him to be overly talkative," Wright said sardonically.

He was right. Detective Dvorak was elusive, evasive, and grumpy when not being noncommittal. Hell, it was hard to find him in the first place, and he started putting on his coat when I did finally locate him. All I got from him were grunts and excuses about being busy on other cases.

"What the hell happened to this case?" I asked, following him down the hall.

"It's over."

"Bullshit."

"Get a copy of the commissioner's report, will ya?" he said. He increased his pace.

"I'll read it," I said, "because of my love of fiction. Jesus, what's the matter with you? What are you scared of?"

He stopped and whirled to face me. "Hey, I'm not scared of anything, sister. I got pretty damn far on this investigation, and I'm stopping because the case is closed, okay? Now get the fuck away from me." He headed down another corridor.

I stayed right with him. "I read you, Dvorak, but please tell me who to watch out for. At least give me that much, because I'm going further with it."

"That's what you think."

"It's what I know. We've got too much to stop now. Shit, I'll go public with it if I have to."

He stopped again. "Look," he said, "you've got a boss over there. B. J., C. J., something like that?"

"F. J."

"Right. When he tells you to knock off, that'll end it. And he will *tell you."*

"No way."

"You watch, girl. And as for your going public, what will that do except cause a lot of confusion and cause everybody to go into deep hibernation on this thing? Then where will you be, besides being dead?"

"You really think this is closed for right now, don't you?"

"It is closed," he said.

We stood there a moment.

"You, uh . . ." he began. "You could get a shitload of garbage dropped on you if you're not careful."

I waited for him to elaborate, but he just stood there, staring at me, almost daring me to . . . to what? Continue the case? The conversation? Both?

"That's it?" I said.

"That's it."

"Okay. Thanks."

"Sure."

"Catch you later," I told him, and walked away. Garbage, he had said. Henderson was the man with the trash contracts in this town. I had to get to a phone and let Wright know to tell Freddie that Henderson was more likely to have something on Falkes.

I got Wright at his place.

"Talk," he said. He always had a great way to answer a phone.

"It's Natalie. Listen, Dvorak let me know he knows this whole thing is screwed. He also said that garbage could fall on us if we're not careful. Henderson's the garbageman, right? So tell Freddie. Maybe it'll help with Falkes."

"Can't do it."

"Why? Don't you have the number out there? The warehouse has a phone. I've seen it."

"Nobody but cops to answer it out there."

"What?"

"Just heard a couple minutes ago. Falkes and

Freddie, both shot. Killed. Pro job, like the ones on the hill.''

"Wright? Are you staying at your place?"

"Not too much longer."

"Where can we meet?"

"Canada's nice."

"Be serious. We've got to talk."

We arranged it so that I'd be on a certain street at a certain time. I figured I was safe out here, so I made another call. A private number that rang wherever F. J. happened to be.

"Yes?"

Nobody in the whole organization could answer a phone like a normal person.

"F. J.? It's Nat."

"Natalie, we have to talk."

Uh-oh, I thought.

"We **are** *talking, F. J."*

"Where are you?"

"In a phone booth. What's wrong?"

"I'll meet you at the office. Come on in."

"Where are you?" I asked. The phone could be set to ring in his office, his car, his house, his boat.

"I'm in the office."

"Good. Pretend I'm there and let's talk now."

I filled him in on the situation as I saw it. He didn't argue. But he did as Dvorak predicted. He said he had to stop the investigation.

"Why?" I said warily.

"It will be better in the long run, Natalie, believe me. I'm sorry, but we must officially put an end to this case."

"And unofficially?"

There was a pause.

"I see," I said. "What if I solve it? Then what? Do we hold on to it just for ourselves? Or do we let the banks

and other clients in on it? And what about the insurance companies—do we tell them or just keep whatever money we find?"

"Natalie, you might get killed."

"Yeah, and I might, anyway. Freddie did. How do you know they aren't after all of us, whoever 'they' are?"

I paused a second at that thought.

"Come to think of it," I continued, "who are you dealing with on this, F. J.?"

"Not on the phone, Natalie."

"Oh, so what do we do—meet in the shower? You tested your end, didn't you?"

"Yes, but—"

"Fine. I'm at a public phone booth. You think it's tapped?"

"I, ah, actually don't know about that, Natalie."

"You don't know about that? What the fuck is going on here, anyway?"

"Natalie, officially Milo Security is no longer involved in this affair. Come to the office tomorrow and take a look at some new assignments. You'll find we have several very lucrative new retainers, many thanks to you personally."

I didn't say anything.

"Natalie?"

"I'm going to get the money back from Langer," I told him quietly.

"Natalie, you can't. I'd have to let you go."

"You mean, fire me, F. J. The term is fire."

"Yes, well, I'd have to do that."

"I've got some vacation time coming up."

"I'll pay you for that."

"Fine. I'll come get the check tomorrow."

"Natalie, please don't go."

"Then tell me what this is all about. Now."

"Natalie, I could lose my business!"

I had not heard him so excited. But then, Milo Security was pretty much his whole life.

"Keep your business, F. J. I'm going to do mine."

"Natalie—"

"Look, we've seen this coming. I don't mind the fact that this business is changing into computerization, seminars, and all that shit. But this case is one big field job, and it looks like we've got a clear track right now. Besides, I am getting really pissed about people not telling me the truth. If Dvorak came out and admitted that he was being told to drop the investigation because Langer's involved with some foreign government we don't want to embarrass, okay, I could weigh that information and make a choice about continuing. Or if you told me that the Treasury Department told you to drop it because the money Langer got is counterfeit or something like that, again I could decide what to do. But no—everybody starts lying to me, saying I can't go on with the case. Like hell I can't. I'm going to find Langer. I'm going to get the money. I'm going to bring back the money. And if I'm employed for myself, then it's my company that's going to get the publicity, not yours."

He was silent for a moment. Then: "Natalie, I can't tell you what this is all about, but I will not risk my business over Daniel Langer, and that's what it would mean to continue. As for you continuing on your own, well, I just don't think you can do it without the resources of the team behind you. Natalie, I just can't tell you—"

He was right. I hung up on him. I went to meet Wright and see what we could make of this thing. The severing of the five-year relationship with Milo Security was frightening, and more upsetting than I thought it could have been. That's probably the case when something unthinkable happens. You feel punched in the gut, disoriented, lost. You don't notice what's around you. You don't even feel the wind because of a wild rushing sound in your ears, a sound that seems to come from inside your soul. You don't notice lots of things, like where you're going. Christ, I was on the wrong side of a long block of big, old apartment buildings, each with those jutting bay windows that look like they're about to fall off. I saw a cruising cab and almost flagged it down. Then I pulled back. Frugality, I said to myself. I must learn to practice frugality. After all, here I was about to go chasing after some guy, supposedly dead, who just maybe had some stolen money, who was off God knows where, and just as soon as they figure out what happened, four or five very high-powered organizations were about to join the search for the guy, only they also wanted him dead . . . and I was doing it on my own savings. No more income for a while. No more frivolous cab rides for this Natalie Fisher.

Jesus, it's bad enough when people start babbling; now I was babbling inside *my head. Stop feeling sorry for yourself. Move it, girl. Get on over to meet Wright. Got to talk about your plans, discuss your options.*

It was getting dark and cold. Good thing Wright was on time. I thought he'd be in a cab, but he drove up in a Saab Turbo.

"Where'd you steal this?" I said, sliding into the passenger seat.

"Bought it from my courtroom work."

"Oh."

"Where to?"

"Just drive? No, I need to pack some things. Think we can hit my place?"

He moved us.

"You talk to F. J.?" he asked.

"Yeah, I talked to F. J."

"So you know he called it off?"

"Boy, do I ever."

"So?"

"So I'm going after the money and I'm fired."

"Shit."

"Yeah," I agreed. "Shit."

"Want me to come along?"

That took me by surprise. I glanced over at him. He was staring out at the road, keeping a cool head and driving us expertly through the city traffic. Every now and then we'd pass a liquor store with the boards still up in place of window glass. Once we passed the remains of a burnt-out car.

"City tow trucks must've missed that one."

"Yeah," I agreed.

I still didn't know what to say. He didn't press. He was good about that.

"Wright, I need a think session. Let's get my stuff, find a place to hole up, and go over what we know on this thing. Then I can tell you what I want."

"You bet. Although with F. J. pulling back, it's probably safe to stay at your own place."

"But I haven't pulled back. And besides, communication among bozos who kill people for a living isn't exactly state-of-the-art. They don't usually carry beepers."

"Okay," he said. "We'll get you packed and head for a hotel. I've always wanted to shack up with you, anyway."

"Oh, and I with you, big boy."

"Seriously, Nat."

"This has got to be a working session, Wright. You know that."

"I know, I know."

I had never heard him repeat himself before, at least not with a sigh built into one of the refrains. Wright's a good-looking guy. I had checked him off in my mind as a fair-to-middling prospect for a girl, but that was before I heard about his habit of stepping in front of

llets as a test of his nerve. It never occurred to me
at he would show any interest in me other than the
ual boy-girl partner flirtation. But that sigh seemed
al enough. Still, we had work to do, and I put it out of
y mind. We got my things packed without incident; I
lled a friend to come take care of my plants and the
t (her mrreough seemed inordinately friendly, with
: undercurrent of concern; Wright said I was project-
g my feelings onto the cat); and we checked into the
otel Essex, one of my favorite landmarks because of
eir habit of disconnecting the el Es from their giant
on sign so that the night sky is filled with red letters
oclaiming Hot Sex.

"Okay," I said, settling onto the bed, "let's recap."

"Okay," Wright agreed. "We got a two-bit hood—"

"Two two-bit hoods. Daniel Langer and Tommy
eisberg."

"Right. They plan a preposterous raid on the whole
ty."

"Right. But they need too many people—"

"So they go to the big guys: Foley, Henderson,
artinelli."

"Who get their people to do all the dirty work."

"Which consists of blowing the city's communica-
on—"

"Transportation—"

"Emergency services—"

"Et cetera, and knocking off banks, savings and
ans, the racetrack—"

"Right after the military begins using local banks for
eir payroll."

"That's right. Good timing."

"Now, were the little robberies part of the plan? You
iow, the liquor stores, jewelry stores, groceries?"

"Some were, some weren't. I'll bet a lot of the
ink-job guys went right from their big heists into a
uple of quick little ones."

"So what was Falkes doing paying off these guys i
the warehouse? They could've kept the money from th
heists."

"Not if Martinelli and Henderson told 'em not to
They might have skimmed some of it, but with th
motorcycles right outside the bank doors, they wouldn
have had much chance."

"And when they were inside the banks, they wer
being taped on video."

"Right. So Falkes was just a payoff for the boys wh
did the work."

"But why right then? Why not later?"

"Maybe that was the only way to get full coopera
tion."

"Okay, then why use Falkes?"

"Why not? He's not connected to anybody big. He'
in debt and needs a quick cash score."

"Then there's the police investigating a murder, and
he's fucked."

"Until Milo Security saves the day."

"Sort of. Then the tables get turned on him."

"Right. Leading to Oily Face's makeup job and th
hiring of Fat Boy."

"And your taking him down for the count," Wrigh
said. Was that a trace of admiration in his voice? H
was impressed when he first heard about it, but he wa
never emotional this late after the fact.

"I still don't see why they had to dump the money
into trash cans," Wright said.

"Because nobody would think to look there?"
suggested.

"Yeah, but then Henderson would have it, and I can'
see Martinelli and the others going for that."

"Maybe not all the money was put in trash cans
Maybe Langer only got away with part of it."

"Or maybe he's just a decoy."

"Then the police and FBI would also be after him,"

said, "and they act like they don't even care about Langer faking his own death. Also, from what we've seen, somebody doesn't want us to follow through on this case."

"So what's he doing down there? Financing a revolution?"

"No, he took off on his own. He screwed Henderson and the rest. That's why they're shooting each other. Each one thinks the other has all the money."

"Or at least is responsible for Langer."

"Right."

"What did they want the money for, anyway?"

"What does anybody want money for?"

"I know, but these guys have their money-making schemes pretty much under control right here in town. They look legit to the cops and the IRS, but they've got it wired some way. Why run this risky a deal?"

"To finance a bigger deal?"

"Possible. Okay, what kind of deal? Drugs?"

"Maybe. Could be anything. Arms shipments, counterfeit goods, restricted goods, counterfeit money—"

"Or even insurance?"

"Insurance?"

"Yeah. They knock over all these places, which jacks up the insurance rates, then they go legit and sell insurance."

"Hmm. Are these guys into insurance?"

"Maybe. Who knows? I'm just trying to account for their having done this kind of strong-arm stuff. They don't mind using tactics like that to prove a point, but they don't like one-time payoffs as much as the long-term, steady paying deals."

"What if this thing was just a way of making a point to the city?"

"What do you mean?"

"As if to say, 'We're in control.' To show who's boss."

"Farfetched," he said.

"So's the whole setup," I pointed out. "Robbing San Francisco is definitely farfetched."

"Right."

"Then again, maybe we're dumb to be looking for a conspiracy beyond the fact that some big, fancy crooks got together with lots of little, average crooks and pulled a heist. A modern, all-stops-out, ballsy heist."

"Just to have some action, you mean?"

"Yeah. Like the good old days, something like that."

"Shit," he said.

We sat and looked at each other.

"This thing with F. J.," he said at last. "Why's he pulling out?"

"He's scared of something. He said he could lose the business."

"And the cops have pulled back. As well as the FBI?"

"Guess so."

"Why?"

"Some other organization is stepping in?"

"Like who?"

"I don't know. Interpol?"

"CIA?"

"God, none of this makes any sense. What about a foreign government?"

"Why?"

"Beats me," I said. "Okay, maybe the FBI isn't pulling out. They just want Langer to think they are."

"Or they want the people here in town to think they are."

"Or both."

"Then why threaten F. J.?"

"So they don't have any interference."

"Farfetched. Again."

We sat and looked at each other some more. Then we went over everything again, trying to put the pieces together in some way that made sense. We got no further than before.

"Look," I said at last, "no matter how we figure it, Langer's out there with as much money as he could steal from all the other crooks. Sooner or later everybody's going to be after him. I might as well go after him first. Seems as good a way as any to launch my new detective agency."

"What are you going to call it?" he said.

"Something very corporate. I've seen that the real money is in computers, seminars, consulting, and stuff like that. So having the word security in the name doesn't make much sense. However," I said pointedly, "there will always be room for a good field operative."

"I'll think about it."

"Meanwhile let's call Fend and see what he's come up with."

We called and got the latest poop on the leather-hooded guys—unsavory characters, to say the least—and arranged for him to work with Wright on my behalf from now on. He seemed to like the possibility of working for my new company as long as he could still work out of his home, something that F. J. wouldn't permit, insisting that Fender be free-lance. We were about to hang up when I had a thought.

"Hey, Fend—how hard would it be for someone like you to make it look like the FBI was issuing a directive, and maybe have that directive backed up by some governmental source?"

"Well, I don't mind breaking into their systems, but I don't want to futz around with any hard-copy rat-fucking like that."

"No, I don't want you to," I said. "What I'm asking is, could someone with a bunch of equipment like yours do it and pull it off?"

His answer was a bit disconcerting.

"Easy as pie," he said.

We ended the conversation. Wright and I considered this new possibility.

"*Maybe you've got something,*" Wright said. "*Langer could have done it himself.*"

"*Or any of the big guys here in town.*"

"*Or some private party who wants Langer all for himself.*"

"*It all comes down to my going after him,*" I said. "*From what we know, he's made some contact with people in a town in Peru. I think I've got to chance it and get down there.*"

"*I'll keep on it up here,*" he said.

"*How? F. J. said—*"

"*Fuck F. J. I'm working on this at this end, and the minute you need anything, you call me. In fact, you call me collect every day. If you don't, I'm coming down after you. I mean it, Miss Fisher. You read me?*"

I smiled and said, "*I read you. Thanks, Wright.*"

"*So you'd better get some sleep.*"

"*I'm not tired yet.*"

"*You want to talk about your first move down there?*"

"*Sure.*"

"*You're going to need a cover story.*"

"*Photographer working on a travel story. Give me an excuse to prowl around.*"

"*What if it's some godforsaken place?*" he asked.

"*Then: photographer working on a nature book.*"

"*Okay. And what's your interest in Langer?*"

"*Well, he's not bad-looking, and he's American. It'd be natural enough to be interested in talking with him.*"

"*I don't like it personally, but it'll do for you to start. What if he doesn't want to talk with you?*"

"*By that time I'll be able to watch him. And I can always play the woman scorned.*"

"*Weak, but it'll do. What are you watching for?*"

"*The money,*" I said. "*The money's the key. What do you suppose he's going to do with all that money?*"

Thirteen

COCAINE IS SUPPOSED to be the best high in the world, but sex and cocaine together is even better.

It's amazing, but the stuff is hard to come by down here; at least it's hard to find in the form I'm used to. Once it has been processed, it's shipped out. You can get coca leaves to chew, but that's a hard switch from the powder form. The first night we were in the hotel, the kid was taking off her dress to change into her swimsuit when she said, "Do I have to chew more of these fucking leaves? They're rotting my teeth." I told her we wouldn't have too long to wait.

Making coke deals in South America isn't the safest thing to do, especially for a gringo who doesn't speak Spanish. So I went looking for outside distribution. First, I sent a cashier's check for fifty thousand dollars to the Soviet embassy in Lima. No note accompanied the check, just a scrawled line on hotel stationery: "With the compliments of Daniel Langer." It got me the meeting I wanted.

The embassy official was courteous but noncommittal as he listened to my proposal. He said it was "interesting," but he would have to think about it. In other words, he wasn't the decision maker. I asked to speak to whoever was in charge. That ended the interview. Jesus, people are so uptight about their own importance. It took them a whole three weeks to agree to test my plan.

In the meantime I needed protection and information. I found both in the form of Luis and Humberto. Luis was strictly small-time in the coke trade, but he knew absolutely everybody at every level of the lucrative, illegal business. He made his living by knowing what was what and moving fast enough to profit by his knowledge. His friend Humberto was a professional giant. Literally. Physically huge and very powerful from several years of cheap labor, Humberto found there was a good living to be made from throwing small people up against walls until their wallets fell to the ground. He was currently employed by the number-three coke distributor in the region.

"How'd he like to be working for the number-one C-man?"

"I do not unnerstan'. He is to change jobs?"

"Nope. Number one and number two are going to go into another line of work. Number three will be number one."

"Oh, that will be very hard to do. They have many guards, many guns."

"You haven't seen guns until you see the people I work for," I told him. What I was doing was a variation of a scam Tommy and I had pulled when I'd gotten out of the service. We set things up to look like we were just the little guys who were doing the bidding of some very nasty and very powerful people who chose to remain behind the scenes.

I explained to Luis that I represented an organization that was interested in establishing some nontaxa-

le economic relations with some of the local inde-
endent growers and refiners. I told Luiz that the
cally big money in this game came to the guys who
ook the stuff into the United States. That's where a
narkup of several thousand percent was not uncom-
mon. But the people who were growing the stuff and
urning it from coca leaves into snow and crack were
nly making a fraction of the money that was in-
olved. Now, I said, was the time to change things.
veryone who switched to the number-three distribu-
or would be paid double. There would be rewards for
ecruiting people from the other coke dealers. There
vould be instant retaliation if the number-one or
umber-two dealers tried coercion.

What I was proposing was an economic revolution.
s such, it was guaranteed a lot of attention and some
nstant loyalty—as long as the money lasted. Luis
cted as representative of the number-three distribu-
or. I asked Luis if it would be possible to arrange for a
mall shipment as a test. It might be, for the right
rice. Would a fifty-percent cash advance payment be
cceptable? It would. And would Luis make it clear to
veryone that the people involved would be watching
very move that was made and that they were of a
articularly ruthless and unforgiving nature? Oh, yes,
eñor, Luis assured me, it would be made very clear. I
ave him a piece of paper with an address on it.

"What is this?"

"The address where I want the merchandise sent."

He looked at it again and was puzzled. I nodded and
miled. He looked at me skeptically and rose slowly.
Ie left without saying anything.

"What was that all about?" the kid asked me.

"Poor Luis doesn't know what to think."

"About what?"

"About the address I gave him."

"You going to tell me?"

"Later. Let's go out to the boat."

We got in the launch and had the boatman take us out into the bay, out past the smaller fishing boats, out to our glorious motor-and-mast beauty with the centerboard that was going to make everything possible. A mansion, servants, some more bodyguards to go with Humberto.

In the launch, she put my hand under her skirt and said, "While you think about doing whatever you want, tell me what made Luis act so funny back at the hotel. What was the address you gave him?"

"The Russian embassy."

"What for?"

"That's where we're sending the cocaine."

"I don't get it."

"Diplomatic immunity."

"So? I still don't get it."

"Look," I said, "they want to make trouble for the U.S., right? So smuggling crack to America makes trouble—trouble that doesn't get traced to them. They even make a profit on the deal."

"But how—?"

"We send the coke to their embassy. They take it into the U.S. in their diplomatic pouches, and it gets distributed from there by our people."

"Why don't they do it without you?"

"They probably do, but this way they run almost no risk because we take care of the planting, growing, harvesting, refining, and distribution. They're just shipping."

"Why don't—ooh."

"You ask a lot of questions, honey."

"Wait," she whispered. "Not here. You can do that when you've got my legs tied apart. Besides—"

I wasn't listening anymore. Every time she said something about her body being tied up, a thick, delicious sickness would close in over me. It was sensual but upsetting, like being hungry and too full at the same time. The coke seemed to intensify it, string it out, make it last, let it spread through my whole being.

"Are you there?" she said.

"What? Yeah."

"I said, what's stopping Luis and his friends from getting rid of us? Couldn't they just go to the Russians on their own?"

"Yeah, well, we pay better. What are these panties made out of?"

"Stop. Just play with the legs."

"You're not getting prudish?"

"Ha. Wait'll you see what I'm wearing on top."

"Let's see now."

"Keep your hand down here. Just play with the knees and thighs. You'll get everything else in a little while."

We reached the boat and sent the crew back to the dock. She went below. When I went down after her, I found her on a chair, her dress pulled up around her hips. She had put two long lines of coke on her thighs. I grinned at her, took the silver straw she handed me, and made the lines disappear.

She took off her dress.

"Like it?" she asked. "I think this outfit is naughty. I should be punished for wearing it, don't you think?"

She was always saying things like that. I told her I liked that in a woman. I think she liked being called a woman instead of a girl.

"You know," I said, "this setup is just about perfect. The Russians are afraid of me and Luis because they think Luis is part of some private army of cokehead drug runners. And Luis and his friends are afraid of the Russians because, well, because they're Russians."

"But Luis and friends aren't afraid of you."

"They soon will be."

"Oh, yeah? Why?"

"Because Luis is going to disappear."

"Oh?"

"Yeah. Now, you take the coke Luis has brought us. It's very pure stuff."

"It's good, yeah."

"But one of these times they'll try lowering the quality just a bit. Just to see if they can get away with it. I won't say anything. You won't say anything. The Russians won't say anything. But Luis will disappear. He'll just . . . vanish. And that will scare the shit out of everybody. That's just what I need to make everything work out just right. Then everyone will believe that there are some powerful people behind me."

"How will Luis disappear?"

"Easy. We're going to kill him and dump the body at sea."

"Oh."

No shock, no indignation, no disbelief. Just "Oh." She thought about it for a while, looking out at the water. Then she turned and came over to me, looking very earnest.

"Can I kill him?" she said.

Fourteen

The flight down to Lima was uneventful. Which is to say, the flight was a good one. "May you have an eventful flight" strikes me as a curse the likes of which you wouldn't wish on an ax murderer.

The bus trip to Callao and Chimbote, two port cities up the coast of Peru, was equally mundane. This is where you expect to find peasants carrying pigs and chickens. Instead I had people in clean casual wear and a few folks in business suits. The bus was air-conditioned, clean, and perfectly boring. It gave me time to think about Wright.

The scene at the San Francisco airport had been strained. Wright was mostly silent. I didn't have much of anything to add to his lack of conversation. Our silence was doing the talking between us. Then, just as they announced the boarding of my flight, we both snapped out of it at the same time.

"So, I—" I started.

"Well, it—" Wright began.

"I guess this is—"

"—it," he finished. "Still think it's best that I stay up here?" he said, trying to remain businesslike.

"Yes. Yeah. Yes. I'm going to miss you, Wright." We paused a second. "Oh," I said too quickly, "I forgot to get my check from F. J. Can you go and—"

"Already taken care of," he said.

"Thanks, Wright."

"No problem. And you have a present from F. J., unless you figured that out already."

"A present?"

"Yup. A kind of bonus."

"What is it?"

"You're holding it."

"What? My ticket?"

"He called the airline this morning and put it on his card," Wright explained. "Now, Natalie, you didn't think they upgraded you to first class out of the goodness of their hearts?"

"Is that what the woman meant? I thought she was hyping the airline, saying they ran a first-class operation or something."

"What a detective," Wright said.

"Come on, Wright."

"Such powers of observation."

"All right," I said.

"—comprehension—"

"Enough, Wright!"

"Okay. So I'll work with Fend and keep asking questions, and maybe I'll get something you can use. You keep checking with me, you hear?"

"I hear." I smiled at him. "And see if you can find out what the hell is with F. J."

"I have a feeling that finding out will help tell us where to look on this whole case. Whoever's pressuring him has clout."

The second boarding call was announced over the airport intercom system.

"*Either they've improved those things or they're hiring people who can enunciate. I actually understood every word that time.*"

We grinned at each other. I extended my right hand for a friendly, businesslike shake. He raised his eyebrows in a mock grimace, brushed my hand aside, and stepped forward. I had arms full of man, pressing, holding, nearly shaking as we swung slightly back and forth together.

I whispered to him, "Good-bye, Wright."

"You take care, because I want you in one piece when this is over."

"Right." I laughed. "Right, Wright. And thanks."

"Bye, Natalie."

"Bye."

Before I knew it, we were zooming down the runway with that lurch and runaway-elevator-stomach-to-the-floor sensation you always get at takeoff. For some reason I looked for Wright in the airport parking lot as we floated past. Dumb. The big plane climbed, banked, straightened, and shot through the cloud cover to emerge into blinding, blue-white, sunshiny skies.

They had a movie, Blame It On Rio, *with most of the breasts edited out. I put on my Walkman and fell asleep listening to the finely played dobro of Jerry Douglas's* Under the Wire *album. When the tape ended and the machine shut off with a little click, I barely noticed.*

Fifteen

LUIS WAS BEING very uncooperative. He was taking a long time to die.

Some people are like that. Tough, resilient, a real fighter. Killing someone quickly and silently can be a struggle if the person is young and strong. Besides, silent killing isn't something most of us practice. Guns with silencers weren't available in the shops, so we had to make do with other tools.

There is a sequence in Alfred Hitchcock's *Torn Curtain* in which Paul Newman and some character actress really work up a sweat trying to kill a foreign agent. The scene drags on and on because the guy keeps fighting back. I believe they had the same problem the girl and I were having with Luis. Using a gun would call attention to what was happening.

So she and I wrestled with Luis in the murky moonlight, our perspiration-soaked bodies chilled by the night breezes or suddenly sticky-hot in the stillness. The grunting and groaning went on and on, me with my arm around Luis's throat, she reaching in and hitting him again and again with the club. We thrashed around on the ship's stairs and then tumbled down into the main cabin. Every time I thought I had the death grip on his windpipe, he'd twist and flail about, hitting the boat and deck as often as he hit me but slipping the hold just enough to go on living. He'd have to pause then to gulp more air, and the girl would tentatively move in to bring the stubby wooden club down on his torso. She went for his head once and got part of my arm. I yelled at her to go for the ribs instead, figuring that would slow him down enough for me to get a proper choke hold applied. If I had been able to get my arms positioned properly in the first place, it'd all be over by now.

We didn't have much time, either. The way we'd worked it out was to call Luis from the boat, saying that we couldn't get the launch started, and would he row out in the skiff. Once he arrived, we figured we'd have about two hours to kill him, weight him down with anchor chain, row the skiff out to a point beyond the breakwater, dump his body, row back to drop me at the boat, let the girl row the skiff to the end of the pier, tie it to a piling, and swim back to the ship. Two hours, more or less, because the tourist ferry came through around ten P.M., and the harbor patrol made a final sweep around midnight.

We wanted the patrol boat to notice the skiff tied up at the end of the pier, but we didn't want to take the chance of being seen by the ferry. Seeing the skiff probably wouldn't cause the patrol to do anything right then, but they would tell the harbormaster the next day. The harbormaster, an uppity, dim-witted, fat slob, would investigate this outrage to his position. He would find that Luis had borrowed it to go out to the Americans' ship. We were going to leave a couple empty bottles of cheap local beer and a half-empty bottle of expensive Scotch whiskey mixed with salt water in the skiff. This would make it seem like Luis had been boozing it up. I would complain about missing a new bottle of Scotch when the harbormaster came to talk to us about Luis. The girl and I had all the details worked out. We even had a few parts where we didn't quite agree with each other but were close enough not to make much difference. It would be perfect. No hard evidence to connect us to Luis's disappearance, yet the signal to his partners would be clear: impurities in our substances would not be tolerated. On top of everything, it would look like we had help from some unknown party on shore.

As for the killing job itself, she had been quite serious about wanting to do it herself. I couldn't understand it. Murder was something you sometimes had to do, but you didn't go looking for it.

"I wanna," she said.

"Why?" I asked.

"'Cause I've never done it," she replied. "Have you?" I didn't answer. "C'mon," she pressed. "Didja ever kill anyone?"

"Yeah," I said, looking out at the water.

"Bullshit."

I turned, looked her straight in the eye, and said, "Bullshit." I held her eyes.

"Okay, okay," she said. "Sorry." I looked away again. She said, "No fair counting it if it was in the army."

I had to laugh. Then the faces of the guys I'd seen die right in front of me came back into view. Nothing seemed so funny all of a sudden.

"It wasn't in the army," I said quietly. Then I added, "Hell, the most peaceful time of my life was in the army. The fucking war ended right after I went in."

"Well, you've done it and I haven't. I want to do it once."

"Jesus."

"At least let me see how it's done."

We went back and forth on it. Finally I convinced her she'd be doing a hell of a lot just helping me kill him without making much noise.

Trouble was, we didn't seem to be doing it too well. After getting through to Luis on the ship-to-shore, we made all friendly and eager to party so he'd think we just wanted to get to the hotel quickly. We watched with a pair of field glasses as he got the skiff from back behind the dilapidated boat houses at the shore side of the pier. He started to row out to us just as the ferry slogged through the harbor, its overly bright lights sparkling against dark water and sky. I busied myself with a drink before glancing out to check on his progress. He was still only halfway to us. He had waited for the wake of the ferry to completely subside.

After what seemed to be an hour and a half of slow rowing, Luis brought the skiff alongside the ship and tied up. His head appeared up the ladder, then his whole body. Jesus, he was still moving in slow motion.

"The launch, señor?" he said.

"Yeah," I said. "I don't know what's wrong. Can't get the fucking thing started."

"We see," he said, and went to haul on the line that secured the launch to the ship. He slowly pulled it along, then deftly leapt into the cockpit. He tried the starter, found that I'd shut off the fuel line, opened it, fed it some gas, punched the starter, and the engine gunned to life. I did one of those "I coulda hadda V-8" hand slaps on the forehead and grinned stupidly down at him. He just shook his head, as if to marvel at the Americans. He shut off the engine and climbed back aboard the ship.

"Hey, sorry, pal," I said. "Listen, have a drink on me." I went to the bar, muttered about the "goddamn ice maker," and took a tray into another part of the ship.

That was her cue. She quietly entered the cabin where Luis stood waiting. Her skin glistened in the cabin light. The tiny swimsuit gleamed darkly in the small areas where it hugged her body. She walked past Luis to the other side of the cabin. He did what anybody with male hormones would have done. He turned to watch her curves as they sailed lightly past.

"You think this is good stuff?" she asked him.

Luis replied in Spanish. It's probably just as well she didn't understand him. I only said things like that to her when she was tied up. Anyway, that was my cue. I stepped out from behind the bulkhead. A three-foot length of oak was in my hand. I raised it over my head to bring it down at the back of Luis's head, but the low cabin ceiling screwed things up. The club hit it, causing Luis to turn suddenly as I brought the club smashing down on him. Still, I got a fairly solid hit on the side of his noggin and he went down. I thumped him again and he stopped moving.

"Jesus," I said.

"Did you want him to turn?" she asked.

"Fuck, no."

"Oh."

"Oh nothing. Get his feet, and hurry."

I took his arms and began pulling him toward the cabin door. He slipped down in a heap.

"Shit. Wait a sec and I'll get him."

I got my arms around his torso and shuffled backward while bent over him. At that point he regained consciousness and I nearly got my teeth handed to me as a present.

"Fuckin' A," I said, and punched him as hard as I could. "Get the club!" I yelled at her as he came up off the deck at me, fingers clawing for my throat. I twisted around him and got his head between my arm and my ribs. That wouldn't last long.

"What do you want me to do with this?" she said, none too hurriedly.

"Hit him with it!"

"In the head?" she asked calmly. Too damn calmly, if you ask me.

"Fuck, no," I snapped at her. Too late. She swung at him, clipping my elbow in the process. Jesus.

I worked my way toward his windpipe with the crook of my arm as she thwacked him once, then twice more. We writhed and rolled and rocked and bounced around some until I felt my grip being loosened.

"Hit him some more, dammit," I snapped at her. "Get the ribs."

I tried to roll him so that she'd have a clear shot at his torso. I shouldn't have worried. He had one arm down to protect his rib cage. She smacked it a good one, and he shot it out of the way. Then she broke at least one rib with a wicked shot that I felt go all the way through his body. He tried to double up on himself, probably an involuntary move. I took advantage of that to really get ahold of his neck. He knew it would only be a matter of a few more seconds.

"That's got it," I said as he flailed away at my arms with progressively weaker fingers. She stepped in and swung one last time, the club practically whistling through the air. I thought she was going for the ribs again, but she brought the wood down on his groin. His whole body jerked sideways, then lay still. He went limp in more ways than one.

The force of that last swing toppled her over on the two of us. We all lay sprawled in our own sweat, two of us pumping hard for air.

"He's dead now, isn't he?" she said. More of a statement than a question.

"Yeah," I said. "He's dead. Congratulations. You've just been to your first murder."

"It was kind of exciting," she said matter-of-factly. "We'll have to do it again sometime."

I just looked at her like she was a bug crawling across my dinner. Jesus H. Christ, what a weirdo.

"Shouldn't we get a move on?" she asked.

"Yeah. Let's get him into the skiff."

We dragged him up and wrestled his deadweight over the side and somehow got him into the small, low-slung old boat. Then we clambered down after him and I rowed out toward the point. We took a good long length of rusted anchor chain and wrapped it around his body, fastening it with silver wire, then pushed him up over the gunwales. The sound of the splash was quiet, mocking.

"That's that," she said.

"Not until we get the skiff back," I said, and began rowing to our ship.

"Why don't we just turn the skiff loose when we get back to the boat?"

"Because I want the bottle to be found in it. That's the fucking point of this whole thing. Jesus."

"God, you don't have to get so mad about everything. You better have some lines when you get back. Just cool out."

Yeah, that would be good. Things were sure fucked up in the world, but cocaine had the power to smooth everything out. You can put a real freeze on, and then everything gets clear. Life's better when you relax in your head and just sort of flex your muscles. Coke taught me that. Coke taught me so much.

I got the skiff next to the ship, grabbed the ladder, and pulled myself up. I paused after a couple of rungs, turned, and looked back down at her.

"You'll be all right?" I said.

"You know it."

She was already in position to row.

"You don't want a float?"

"No, I don't want a fucking float. Or a life vest, either. Landlubbers," she said derisively.

I shrugged and climbed up and on board. We were just going to make it for time. I got a glass of ice and some bottled water, then found the field glasses so I could watch her progress. She had a good rhythm going and was much closer to the pier than I expected. She looped around underneath it, brought in the oars, and leaned out over the side to tie the short rope to the pier. She timed the little current perfectly. It pushed her out from under the pier just fast enough to make the move worthwhile, but just slow enough to allow her to tie up. Then she steadied herself, crouched, and neatly dived over the side. She surfaced, shook her hair, the stream of water flying up and outward like in a beach-party movie, and began swimming out toward me. After *Jaws,* I just couldn't see anyone doing that, but she had suggested it, and it did seem like the best way.

I went and got some coke, took a couple lines into my nostrils, and then used a finger to put some on my gums. I liked putting a freeze on my whole mouth. The thick, sticky feeling would soon creep down the back of my throat, anyway, so might as well get the taste buds numbed and the roof of my mouth wiped out.

I brought the glasses back up and saw that she was still pumping away. Putting the glasses down, I could see she was about halfway to the ship. That's when I heard the harbor patrol boat.

Shit, they were early. I moved forward to get a better angle on the patrol and the girl. She had increased the speed of her strokes and was almost three-quarters back, but the boat was coming into

view and would go right over her if they didn't see her
in time. And they wouldn't see her. Why should
they—there was nothing in that part of the harbor;
they were supposed to look at the ships at anchor, and
at the boat houses and buildings around the piers.
That was their job.

They were bearing down on her. I saw her pause
slightly in mid-stroke to shoot a glance at the bow of
the boat as it cut through the water, nearer, nearer.
Jesus, right on top of her.

She raised herself up in the water, drew in air, and
dived under the waves just as the patrol boat churned
past. It seemed to take forever for the boat to go by.
The engine noise was deafening at first, then the
hissing of the water took over my senses and it was as
if a million gas-station air hoses were going off all at
once inside an echo chamber. The water behind the
patrol boat was foam-flecked, black-and-green, and
choppy. I searched the surface in horror, expecting to
see blood. Nothing. I glanced left, right, far, near. Still
nothing. What the hell? The seconds stretched out to
become heartbeats, vibrating inside my skull.

She came up much nearer our ship than I thought
possible. Once again her hair sent water arcing out
into the night sky. I heard her gasp for breath, big
coughing whoops, trying to fill her lungs in as short a
space of time as she could. I found myself grinning
and running to the ladder, slipping up and over,
grabbing her hands, half hauling her up, half guiding
her.

"Aaugh."

"Jesus."

"I didn't," she said, gasping, "think I could"—gasp
—"stay down"—gasp—"that long."

"I didn't think anyone could."

When she caught her breath, she wanted to take a
shower. Seemed like she had had enough water to me,

but then I remembered the look of the harbor, with all the oil from the powerboats, trash from the peasants, litter from the tourists, and I realized she was right.

"Music," she said, bouncing into the room after her shower. She opened the cabinet, fiddled with the cassettes, inserted one, and began moving to the sounds the second they boomed out of the big built-in speakers. She tried to tell me who was who among the black blues singers she loved, but I kept getting B. B. King mixed up with Albert Waters, or was it Muddy King with—no, it was Muddy Waters and Howlin' Wolf, and Albert, uh, well, he's also King. I think. Anyway, they played electric, powerful, undulating, and downright evil blues music. And what it did to turn her on was nothing short of fanfuckingtastic.

"Get the bindings," she said.

I smiled, got up, and went to grab the leather wrist and ankle bindings out of a drawer. We had had them made in Trujillo by an old craftsman who acted like we were crazy for ordering them. We also got several lengths of very finely constructed chain; so well put together with its small, interlocked links that it clicked when slid upon itself rather than clanking. Just thinking about fastening them to her body made me nearly queasy with pleasure. Sometimes she pretended to struggle while I held her down and fastened her arms and legs into the leather and chains, but the most exciting time was when she was quiet and just stood there, offering her body to the sacrifice.

That's how she was this time. She had another one of her costumes. Every time it was something new. This one was a one-piece job of sheer nylon, covering her breasts and reaching down almost to her hips.

"I have my tits covered," she said. "Do you mind? I thought this looked sexy, anyway. You can see me through it, and I think you'll like touching me through it. If not, you can just sort of pull it off me."

As she spoke, she pulled my hands to her body, placing them on her side and sliding them up.

"Put your hands behind your back," I said. She obeyed. I played with her body for a while, then ran my hands up to her face, ending on her lips. She licked them, touching my fingertips with her tongue.

"Come over here," I said, leading her to the room's one chair with extended arms. I sat down, and she stood very close, practically asking me to play with her some more. The coke was in easy reach, so we both got a good freeze on and then went back to the body work.

"Kneel down," I told her.

She did, placing her hands on the arms of the chair. I took a length of chain, fastened one of her hands to one side of the chair, passed the chain up to be looped around her neck, and fastened her other hand to the chair's other arm. I put my hands on her head, weaving my fingers through her hair, and pulled her down to me. Her mouth was already forming an "oh," as soon as my hands applied pressure on her head.

"I love this," she whispered, then took me with slow, expert movements.

At the climax I pushed up and into her, trying to get right down her throat. I grabbed her breasts and squeezed tightly, holding them for the longest time. The main time . . . the jolting, shuddering time. The time of total release, when all the shaking and queasiness gets transformed into violent spasms that mix with the coke sensations . . . all of it producing a form of pleasure that I never felt before and never wanted to give up. Not ever.

I sat there a while, running my hands through her hair. Afterward was sometimes awkward. Do I release her right away, or do I leave her tied up, maybe to come back and whip her a bit, just to see if I get excited right away and want to take her again? Usually the second time was with her mouth, and we'd just done that. So I unfastened her and watched as she slowly stretched out on the carpet. An attack of drowsiness hit me, and I barely made it to the bunk before giving in to it. I didn't budge much until I woke up very early in the morning as she tried to put one of the bindings on my wrist.

"What the fuck?" I mumbled, rolling over.

She laughed as she snatched the leather piece away.

"What's going on?" I said.

"I was going to surprise you," she said.

"I'll bet."

"No, really. I was going to, you know, tease you a little, like you do to me, and then you'd have me."

I just looked at her. Thinking about it, it seemed we had reached some sort of breaking point. The rest of the morning was spent in silence until about nine, when she stuck her head into the cabin where I was fooling with some of the coke baggies. "Are you going to do something about the radio, or what?"

"What about the radio? Play your tapes, for chrissake."

"Not that radio," she said.

"The ship-to-shore?" I asked.

"Duh, yeah."

Someone was trying to contact us. I punched the right buttons and got a flood of Spanish out of the speaker.

"Anybody there speak English?" I said.

After a pause another voice came over the airwaves: "I am Carlos, señor. You are the man who call Luis last night?"

"What's it to you?" I asked.

"The harbormaster, he must talk with you."

"So let him," I said.

"You come to his office? Soon?"

"Naw, I couldn't make too soon. Matter of fact, we're kinda stuck out here until Luis comes out to start the damn launch again."

After another pause the voice tried again: "The harbormaster, he talk to you on your boat?"

"No, the harbormaster's never been out here. Why do you ask?"

After another pause the Spanish started up again, this time excited and fast.

"Whoa there, partner. Sounds like the amigo's gettin' a mite testy." I covered the microphone, turned to the girl, and said, "I love doing this phony Texas accent." Then, back to the mike, "You all gonna explain what this all's in reference to, or am I gonna have to start guessin'?"

The one who spoke English came back on: "Señor, the harbormaster is going to your boat."

"He is? Well, I'll be hornswoggled." To the girl I said, "What the hell is hornswoggled, anyway?" To the mike, I said: "Say, does this harbor fella know anything about startin' up launches? After he gets my launch fixed, maybe he'll explain what he's doin' about gettin' some of the garbage out of his harbor. Ten-four, boys."

The harbormaster waddled on board like he was ready to sink the vessel with his own hands. Several men with uniforms and side arms came with him. One of the men tried to stop him from speaking, but he brushed the man aside and unleashed a sputtering flow of angry Spanish.

"I don't rightly know what tubby's sayin', but I don't care much for his tone. Somebody tell him he's going to be shark bait if he keeps it up."

I imagine what he said next was something very similar to what I just said. The uniformed man got him calmed down.

"Señor," the man said to me, "I am Carlos. I am chief of police here. Let us sit down and talk like gentlemen before we have international incidents."

"Sounds good to me."

The girl and I played out our parts, giving them exactly the impression we wanted. Carlos saw through my shit-kicker routine, so I dropped it after a couple of sentences. He looked at me with a kind of half smile and said something about being glad my health was improved.

"My health?"

"Si, señor. I notice your voice is now better than before."

The guy was sharp in other ways. He asked several questions we hadn't thought of, and he managed to find out that she was an excellent swimmer, knew her way around boats, and that there was some difficulty with her passport. We had bought a forged set of papers for her, but she was a bit hazy on some of the invented biography she had put in them.

"We will not bother you more," the policeman was saying, "after your embassy confirms you."

"Our embassy does what?"

"That maybe is not right, not the right word. We send papers about you to them, and they send some different papers back. This confirms you, no?"

"Oh." We hadn't thought of that, either. "I see," I said. "I guess that *confirms* is as good a word as any."

We all stood up. The harbormaster was still angry, but he didn't worry me anymore. We were about to have much too much official attention. After they left, I started checking our provisions.

"Whatcha doing?" she asked.

"Seeing what we need to get the hell out of here."

"Not by boat."

"What?" I said.

"Take a look."

I glanced in the direction she indicated, toward the mouth of the harbor. The patrol boat was slowly making its way across the opening. Then it turned and made its way back. Like a guard at the stockade, I thought.

Okay, that presented some problems. If we left with the money, we'd be carrying too much not to be conspicuous. If we left the money and just took off, we'd have to come back to get it, or trust someone to move the boat for us. Besides, they might rip up the boat while we were gone. Damn, I had to wire those explosives in there. I had some good plastique that I'd been meaning to install in the centerboard, but somehow something always seemed to come up. Shit. It began to look like our friend Carlos was going to have to be bribed. Maybe even brought into the operation. Which wasn't such a bad idea, come to think of it. He's the local law, and he has connections to all the other official parties down here.

After approaching Carlos with the proposition it struck me that this may have been his game all along. He didn't care one way or the other about Luis or the harbormaster or even the coke shipments themselves. He just was looking for a quick and easy score. Luis was just a good excuse to push into my scene and nose around for his share.

Taking care of the police with Carlos in on things turned out to be no problem. And Carlos took care of the harbormaster just fine. But we miscalculated when it came to the harbor patrol. They were officially part of the country's navy, and they weren't having anything to do with our efforts to work out a deal. Carlos began taking heat officially, and we began to have trouble getting anything on and off the boat. Carlos suggested we take a hike for a while, unless I felt like putting the entire Department of the Navy on the payroll. He said we should move on by car to another town, another harbor. Like Chiclayo, which had an airport, or even Guayaquil, which was even larger. Both had good harbors, and Carlos said he'd get the boat up to us. In the meantime the coke shipments would continue inland. I'd still get my supply, and things would go on as before. I didn't trust him as far as I could drop-kick him, but I figured I could always hire some real rough talent to come in and clean up the whole fucking town if I had to, so I was leaning toward taking him up on his offer. Then the navy boys tried to have us arrested, and when Carlos took us under "his jurisdiction," the girl and I got a car and made ready to hightail it the hell out of Chimbote.

I didn't sleep much that night. What a choice. Do I leave the money in the centerboard or try to take it with us up into the hills? The girl said we should split it, leaving half on the boat and taking the other half. I guess that's about the time I started hiring lots and lots of bodyguards for us.

Little did I know I could've bought the whole fucking police force, Carlos and all, for less than I was paying the private scum (plus Carlos on the side). But then, that probably wouldn't have prevented all the shooting. I don't think anything would have.

Sixteen

"Miss Fisher?"

"Yes?"

"My name is Daniels. H. R. Daniels."

"Congratulations."

"Special Agent H. R. Daniels. I'm with the CIA."

"What do the initials stand for?"

"Central Intelligence Agency, Miss Fisher."

"And the other ones?"

"Pardon?"

"The other initials. What do they stand for? I've heard of the CIA."

"Do you mean my initials, Miss Fisher?"

"Those be the ones."

"I use my initials instead of my given names. Now, I have a few questions that I'd—"

"Is this official?"

"Pardon?"

"Do you have trouble hearing, or are you just excessively polite?"

"Miss Fisher, as a citizen of the United States, don't

you wish to cooperate with a branch of your government?"

"Sure, but since when did the CIA become a branch of my government?"

He sighed. "Look, I think we can talk better if I could sit down."

"I thought you were sitting down. You're not really that short, are you?"

"I can make things very difficult for you, Miss Fisher. If you want to make this personal, I—"

"Okay, okay. Sit down, Henry."

"Henry?"

"I'm working on the H first. I thought I'd take them in alphabetical order."

He stood there, head cocked to one side, sighed again, and sat down at the café table opposite me. He slowly took off his coat and loosened his tie. As he worked his shirt's top button loose he said, "You're working on a case down here. On Daniel Langer. The San Francisco robberies. You quit your job to do it. You beat us to him, but now he's skipped out again. We want to know what you know. Then we want you off the case and out of the way."

"Well," I said, "that's up front. I think I prefer the straight poop laced with a bit of humor, but I can understand how out of practice you must be, working for an organization that issues winter suits to its Latin American operatives."

"The point is, Miss Fisher, we can make things very difficult—"

"Yeah, yeah. Difficult. You said that before. You want to get specific, or am I supposed to quake in my sandals just imagining you and the IRS cooking up something together?"

"We don't need the IRS. How would you like your passport revoked? Or your application for a private-

investigation firm denied?" He fell silent. When I
didn't answer, he said, *"Do you think I'm bluffing?"*

*"Frankly, yes. Enough people know who I am and
what I'm doing down here to make it hot for you to try
chickenshit stuff like that. Besides, anything that forces
me to go public with my story would show that you guys
either covered up the investigation in San Francisco or
you were too stupid to realize that Langer was alive."* It
was my turn to pause. When he didn't say anything, I
got up to leave.

"Where are you going?" he said.

"Oh, come on," I said in mock exasperation, *"don't
they teach you about tailing people? Planting bugs on
them? Checking hotel registers?"* I emphasized the last
one.

"You'll be at your hotel this evening?"

"Say, Hubert, you're quick."

"Hubert?"

"Humbert Humbert?"

"What?"

*"Oh, that's right. You said the second one was an R,
didn't you?"* I left him there. Since they usually work in
pairs, I glanced around as I entered the street, but I
kept moving because I had left Special Agent H. R.
Daniels with the check for my late lunch. I went to the
American Express office and bought myself an expensive phone call. As usual, it took a while to go through.
Also as usual, the wait was worth it.

"What now?"

*"God, it's great to hear you not answer the phone
very well, as usual,"* I said to him.

"Nat, why do you keep waking me up?"

"Because you choose to sleep when I have to call."

"Bitch," Wright said.

*"And besides, I have this fixation about you lying in
beds."*

"Oh, great. Now I get teasingly obscene phone calls long-distance."

"Wright, how about affording another return call?"

"Sure. Same number?"

"No, I'm not at the hotel this time." I gave him the number. We hung up. For some reason, even after the breakup of the U.S. phone system, he was still almost always able to get me back within a minute. The phone rang. "Hi," I said.

"Hi, yourself. Okay, let's have another yell-fest."

We felt like we had to shout over the long-distance wires, even when the connections were good.

"Guess what turned up down here?" I said.

"What?"

"Okay, okay, don't guess; I'll tell you." That was code for "code phrase coming up." "Comedy. Intrigue. Adventure." He got the initials. He asked for names. "I've only got one so far. H. R. Daniels. Won't tell what the H. R. is for, so it's got to be some sort of milquetoast thing."

"Interesting."

"The initials?"

"No, the company. Fender came up with the same thing, but it didn't make much sense."

"Maybe it does. Guess what else turned up."

"Uhhh . . ."

"Okay, don't. I'll tell you. Unibody. Solitaire. Sophistication. Romance."

"Oh." He paused. "Ohhhh, the immunity."

"Right. They're bringing it in, and Langer's getting the money somehow. Well, sharing it with them, anyway."

"Seems a kind of backwater place to initiate that kind of activity, doesn't it? Wouldn't they use a bigger embassy?"

"Well, hell, Wright, picture yourself in an embassy out here. You're lonely. Forgotten. Just a diplomatic *nerd in a backwater country. Suddenly you're offerred the chance to make some money by sending some evil shit into an enemy country. And you get some thrills out of it for good measure."*

"Yeah . . ."

"So I think Langer or his cokehead pals went to the embassy, made his pitch, and got himself some cheap distribution. If so, and if our guys know about it, it explains why our side is interested."

"Hard to prove."

"It's the only thing that makes sense. Besides, I don't have to prove it to bust it up. Anyway, so far I've talked to Luis's family—the guy Langer killed—and they admit to his being in the coke business. I've talked to some local businessmen who hint about the coke running from here, and how it and the gangland killings have increased since Langer arrived. I've gotten a total runaround from the local police—"

"You didn't tell me about that," Wright said accusingly. "That means your cover is blown."

"Well, yes, but it would have been, anyway, with H. R. Daniels and his friend hanging around."

"You didn't know that at the time."

"Look, Wright, what difference does it make now? At the time I did it, it seemed like the only way to force something to happen, and it worked. The cards are starting to get turned faceup on the table—I think I can get Langer, shut him down, and get the goods."

He was silent at his end of the phone.

"Wright?" I said.

"I'm here."

"Are you upset?"

"No. You did what you thought you had to do. Listen, kiddo. Your Mr. H. R. Daniels and the police chief . . . what's his name?"

"Carlos."

"Right. They could be a pretty potent combination

*against you. Add in the harbor patrol and you've got
yourself surrounded."*

*"Maybe. But soon I'm going to get a line on where
Langer and the girl went. I think that will give me a
line on the money. And I think I'm going to have to
take Langer in, or take him out, if I'm going to bust
this one. So listen, let me know if you or Fend find out
anything on H. R. Daniels."*

"Will do. You take care, Nat. Bye."

"Bye."

*And people say women are moody. That was about
as abrupt an end to a conversation as I've ever heard.
Even so, it was still great to talk to Wright. Personal or
professional, his conversation was, well, good for me.*

*I walked out of the American Express office right into
H. R. Daniels's partner. There was no mistaking the
guy. He looked like a taller carbon copy of H. R.*

"Miss Fisher?"

"What now?"

"Would you come with me, please?"

*"Who are you, where to, why, and how are you going
to make me?"*

*He smiled and said, "H. R. was right about you." He
looked serious again. "Okay. I'm Gary Anderson. Back
to your hotel, which is also our hotel; we want to swap
information with you; and, uh, well, I guess I'm going
to try carrying you if you won't walk with me."*

*I just stared at him. I had to grin. He looked so damn
hopeful. Whether he was hoping to walk or lift me up, I
couldn't say, so I said to him, "Well, I'll be damned. A
human reaction. That's very crafty of you."*

*"Isn't it?" he said, smiling. "I specialized in that.
Nearly got me thrown out of the firm."*

*"I'll bet. Okay, Gary. You may accompany me back
to the hotel. We'll first stop at a shop or two where I've
been dropping heavy coin, to establish our involve-*

ment, and then, when we reach the hotel, we'll have a debate about whose room will get visited."

"Careful, aren't you?"

"Absofuckinlutely," I said, starting back toward the hotel. "You guys have been known to make bone-headed, violent plays."

He looked hurt. "How can you say that, Miss Fisher? We've just met."

"Call me Natalie, and I can say that about your organization because it's true. How about that clown you let deal with the Libyans all those years while building up a personal fortune? How about those botched assassination attempts? How about—"

"All right, all right," he said, still smiling. "Some of my colleagues have not been the, uh, smoothest operators in the world—no puns intended. But I can assure you, Natalie, that I have never let any clowns deal with Libyans, nor have I botched any assassination attempts."

"Straight shooter, huh?" I asked.

"Absofuckinlutely," he answered.

Well, so far it sounded like the start of a beautiful friendship.

Back at the hotel, we compromised on the seating arrangements by grabbing the table in the farthest back corner of the bar. H. R. didn't like it, for "security reasons." Gary told him to lighten up. Oh, yes, we became Nat and H. R. and Gary for this conversation.

"So, I think it's up to you guys to start," I said.

"You realize," H. R. said, "we don't have to tell you anything?"

"Right," I agreed, "just as I don't have to tell you anything."

"You have a duty to assist the investigation of two government officers," he said pedantically.

"What investigation?"

"Our investigation of Daniel Langer."

"Langer? Never heard of him. Tell me more."

"Now look—" H. R. began.

Gary broke in. *"H. R., let's be fair about this. She did have us beat on Langer. We've been playing catch-up. Let's at least tell her what we know."*

"But that's not proper procedure," he said. He sounded genuinely offended at the very idea.

"You guys have got an interesting variation of 'good cop/bad cop' going here," I told them. *"It's sort of 'smart cop/dumb cop.' Nice. Next thing that's supposed to happen is that you"*—I indicated H. R.—*"act hurt and petulant, and you stalk off somewhere, leaving us two simpatico types alone."* I watched to see if they exchanged looks. Nothing. Gary looked hurt, which was a switch. H. R. looked puzzled. But then, that's how he'd always looked. Well, if this was a setup, these guys were damn good actors.

"Okay," I went on, *"speak to me about Mr. Langer. He's into coke. Take it from there."*

"First we want to know how you tailed Langer down here so fast."

"Easy. His dead partner had papers indicating he intended to come to Chimbote. With a little poking around we found out that Langer did too. Stupid of them to head for the same place. How about you guys—how did you wind up here?"

"We were already here. Or rather, in Lima. When some marked bills from the San Francisco robberies began showing up along the coast, everyone along the way was notified to watch for anyone with a lot of cash who showed up suddenly. We were just lucky Langer decided to stay in our jurisdiction."

"Yeah, lucky. So what have you got on Langer so far?"

They looked at each other, then H. R. shrugged.

"Well," Gary said, *"he's definitely into coke—*

growing it, refining it, and selling it. He's got a live-in girlfriend, a teenage runaway named Doris Yablonski. She's—"

"Doris Yablonski?" I said. "Not really."

"That's her name. Although she's got a dummied-up passport that says she's Diana Pamela Grier. Doris/Diana is seventeen going on forty and has a record of prostitution, narcotics, and accessory to armed robbery."

"The all-American girl," I said. Then I dropped a bomb. "So how's the Soviet embassy fit into all this?"

They exchanged glances. Another shrug from H. R.

Gary said, "Langer's boys take packages of cocaine to the Soviets in Lima. They use a fairly standard drop point. The diplomatic pouch is used to take the stuff into Canada, and from there a couple of guys in Seattle or Portland go up to get it and bring it into the States."

"Portland? That's a bit of a trip as compared to Seattle."

"Yeah," Gary said, "but Langer likes using two different sets of distributors."

"How's the money come back?" I said. They exchanged glances again.

"Bingo," Gary said.

They were silent again. I said, "What?" And then, "What's with the money?"

"Well," H. R. admitted, "we don't know how the money gets back. As near as we can tell, nothing ever comes back."

"You mean, the people at this end aren't getting paid for their shipments?" I said incredulously.

"No, no, they're getting paid. Langer's paying them. It's just that, well, we don't see any money coming back to Langer."

"Numbered Swiss bank account?" I said.

"Possible."

"Especially if the Russians are ferrying it for him."

"But then, how's he paying everyone?" H. R. said.

"Hey," I pointed out, *"he only stole thirty million."*

"But he doesn't have it with him," Gary said.

"How do you know?"

"We searched his boat."

"Oh, come on. He could have it in the bulkheads, under a phony piece of decking, dangling in the water on a string—"

"We checked."

"You checked every square inch on that boat?"

"Essentially, yes."

"You want to elaborate on that?" I said.

"Well," Gary said, *"it involves a piece of equipment that's a kind of density analyzer. You point it at something and it tells you the composition of it up to six inches thick. So we scanned the deck, the bulkheads, the furniture, the mast, the rails, the engine, the works. Wherever the readouts didn't match up with whatever other sections of the same target we'd already measured, we used another piece of equipment that's sort of like an X ray. Everything's as it should be on that ship."*

"I'm sorry, but it doesn't sound very precise to me. How many hours did you spend on this little venture, anyway?"

"We did it over the course of two days. Since he's gone and the boat is still there, we had plenty of time. We know something's going on with the boat, because the cocaine crew still goes out to it, so we figure Langer's still calling the shots from up in the mountains."

So they knew something about Langer's current location. I couldn't just come right out and ask about it. Keep 'em talking. I said, *"What about below the waterline?"*

"We had divers go over it. Nothing unusual."

"Did you use your gizmos underwater?"

"Well, they don't work in the water. Not yet. We're waiting to get some sort of watertight holder, then we'll have the boys go down again."

"So what are you doing here? Just watching the boat?"

"What are you doing here?"

"Me? Oh, just on a holiday."

"Now, look, if you think—"

"And while I'm here I figured I'd just recover the money and turn it in for the insurance reward. They pay ten percent, you know."

"Oh, sure. Just turn it in."

"Sure. It'd be illegal to keep it."

"Whatever you say, Miss Fisher."

"Ah, we're back to formality are we, Hilary?" H. R.'s eyes flashed. "You mean, that's correct?" I said.

"You told her," he said to Gary.

"Not me."

"No, I guessed. Now I've got to work on the R—"

"Look," Gary said, breaking in, "let's get back to basics. What are you doing down here if you're after the money? Why don't you drive up there and ask him for it?"

"Why don't you?" I shot back at him.

"We're not exactly sure if the money's the issue at hand. We're supposed to stop the flow of drugs into the States, and stop the flow of money out to the Soviets."

"And he's got a small army of people up there with him."

"Any women?"

"The women of the village."

I thought about it for a bit. If people were still going to the boat, that may have meant they were doing business there. But then again, I couldn't see Langer letting anyone dip into his stack of millions. Unless it was somebody he trusted. I said, "Does his girl go to the boat?"

"Haven't you been watching it?" H. R. asked me.

"I've seen people go out there, but I haven't been glued to it. For example, you may have noticed I'm not watching it right now."

"Well, we've seen her once, and we've heard her there a couple of times. We planted a few surveillance devices."

"Oh, call 'em bugs. Everybody else does."

"So what have you been doing this past week?"

"Well, finding out that Langer had Luis killed—or maybe did it himself. That he sent a message to the drug suppliers that he didn't appreciate his coke being cut too much. That the police are on Langer's payroll. That the Russian who's involved is named Svetlov. That Langer and Doris are using their own coke pretty heavily. That they're into kinky sex. That a girl could get herself killed for sticking her nose into the coke biz. And that Langer hasn't carried a gun, so far as anyone can tell."

"Shit. Who's working with you?"

"Nobody. I just lucked into a cop who felt he was getting a raw deal, and I put on a little pressure."

"How did you do that?"

"With my hands, silly. Here, give me your neck for a second." I reached out to grasp one of his pressure points.

"Hey!"

"See?"

"Fuck."

"Such language," I said in mock horror. *"That doesn't sound like basic government training to me."*

"You found out all that from one bent cop?" Gary spoke this time, sending sidelong glances at his partner, who was rubbing his sore neck muscles.

"No, I talked with a fair number of people. I'm afraid I blew my cover rather early in the game. Probably

when I broke the fingers of some clown who guards the coke run over the hill to the reds."

"You broke Humberto's fingers?"

"Is that his name? Yeah, he got a little fresh. I don't know why I bothered with him. He doesn't speak English."

"That guy's going to come after you."

"He already did."

"How do you know?"

"Look," I said, "when a guy that big shows up in your room in the middle of the night, you know he's there, okay?"

"I don't believe any of this. If that monster went after you, you'd be mincemeat."

"Bullshit," I said to him. "Check out your partner's neck."

"Yeah," H. R. said.

"No way did you take Humberto out unless you held a gun on him. And even there, I'm not so sure you'd win."

"Tell you what, next time you see Humberto, you ask him about it."

"I'll do that."

We gabbed like that for a while. They asked me for the names of the bozos I'd encountered during my week-long tour of this sweaty little place. I told them. I asked about Langer's habits up the hill. They told me. They asked me to forget the case and go back home. I told them to dream on. I asked to hear the tapes of their "surveillance devices." They told me to dream on. And so it went. After a while I figured that I'd have to offer them a deal. I didn't have much hope, but it was worth a shot.

"I think we should team up and get this whole thing solved."

"How do you mean?" Gary said.

"Let's go up there, get Langer, the girl, the dopers, and the money. You can return Langer and the girl to the States, turn in the coke runners and the crooked cops, and I'll make an anonymous donation to the bank account of your choice with the insurance money."

"Sure."

"No way."

"Are you afraid of Langer and his 'private army'?" I asked.

"The smallest weapon they've got is the Uzi. Hell, they've even got antitank guns up there."

"So you are afraid."

"Lady, you don't go up against that kind of firepower armed with a 9-mm Smith and Wesson."

"Is that the fifteen-shot automatic?" I said. "How do you like it?" We segued into a ballistics discussion. Here, they were pretty hip. We had the usual disagreements over weight of hit against number of bullets, and those quirks of gun owners everywhere about the "feel" of certain weapons. But all in all, these two knew their stuff.

"Naw," H. R. was saying, "the handle's too damn thick. You feel like you're holding a handrail on the stairs, not pointing a weapon."

"Well, it is a bit hefty, but it helps to hold it steady. That sucker kicks like a mule," Gary replied.

"Oh? And how does a mule kick?"

"Hard."

"That's precise."

"Thank you."

"You're welcome."

"Hey, can we get back to the subject at hand, so to speak?" I said.

"What's that—you mean, storming the hill against a bunch of cokeheads armed with enough weaponry to repel the Normandy invasion?"

"*Come on,*" I replied. "*I don't plan on going at them that way. What if we posed as buyers?*"

"*Forget it,*" H. R. said. "*They know we're on to them, and they know who we are. Shit, they made us as soon as we got off the plane.*"

"*Okay, then, how about we hire somebody to go in as a buyer?*"

"*I don't think so.*"

"*Why not?*"

"*Well, they're not in the habit of selling locally. They run a mail-order business.*"

"*Fine. So we have someone go in trying to set up a similar deal for some other part of the country. The East, the Midwest, somewhere.*"

"*I don't like it.*"

"*Gosh, and here I was running my whole life just to please you.*"

"*You think you can just hire some local greaser to slink up there and convince them he has enough bread to pull off a deal like that? You're full of shit.*" H. R. spat the words.

"*I think, with your obvious case of constipation of the brain, this discussion is going to have to be continued after you're deposited on the seat of your pants somewhere back in another corner.*" I spoke like my twelfth-grade math teacher.

"*Yeah?*" he half yelled, standing up. "*You don't get a lucky grab at my neck this time, sister. Come on and try it, you little bitch.*"

"*H. R., stop it!*" Gary said.

"*Why, Hilary,*" I said, smiling, "*you're quite a passionate and intense young man, aren't you?*" I stood up slowly. "*And so precocious too. Here he is, going out on his own and trying to start a bar fight just to impress his buddy in front of a girl.*"

"*Fuck you.*"

"*I don't think so,*" I said. I feinted at his head, then

counted on his confusion about his role in the rumble
he had started. I stepped slightly sideways, planted one
foot, and sent the other one straight out at his groin,
once, twice, thrice. Two of them landed right where I
wanted, and the third hit his hipbone because he was
twisting away from me. The force of foot on hip sent us
in opposite directions. I spun around and got ready for
the next phase of our little brouhaha.

"You slut!" he sort of screamed through clenched
teeth. "I'll kill you."

"Now that's hardly likely, Hilary. I can't imagine
they let you have bullets for your gun. You might do
yourself an injury."

Gary stepped between us just as H. R. threw himself
into a charge. They thumped together, briefly tangling
up arms and legs. H. R., in his rage, didn't focus on
Gary very well in the dim light. He tried to claw his way
past his partner but misjudged the angle and force of
Gary's efforts to stop him. H. R. was suddenly shoving
more air than partner, and he tumbled to the floor with
a yelp and a thunk and a grunt, as the breath was
forced out of him.

"Come on, now," Gary said to him, bending down to
help.

"I wouldn't—" I began, but it was too late. H. R.
rolled over, grabbed wildly at anything he could find to
help pull himself up. He got part chair, part partner,
and then Gary was down on top of H. R., this time with
two yelps and two thunks.

"This is great," I muttered. "All the agents in the
world, they have to send me the Keystone Kops."

I just stood there, watching two grown men flap their
arms while lying on the floor of a restaurant bar in
South America, their mouths gaping open as they
gasped for oxygen. Gary recovered first. Which was
only natural, since he had had the air knocked out of
him just once in the past two minutes, whereas H. R.

was laboring under the handicap of two lung poundings in the same space of time.

"Well," he said breathily, "this is another fine mess you've gotten me into."

"Fuck you," H. R. managed to say.

Gary got to his feet, looked over at me, and said, "Got the wind knocked out of me."

"No shit, Sherlock," I said to him. H. R. was rising too. He still seemed unsteady, so his quick two-step run at me was almost a complete surprise. I say almost, because I was watching him all the while and I noticed his eyes were on me even as his body was turned slightly away. He had been measuring the distance. He even got up in such a way that he ended up a step nearer. The quickness of his attack was unexpected, but the attack itself was signaled in advance. I sidestepped and prepared to hit him as he went by, but he pulled up short with a feint of his own, and so we ended up facing each other, knees slightly bent, hands out in front, muscles tensed and ready for action.

Gary made one more attempt to stop things. "H. R.! Knock it off!"

"That's what I intend to do," he said.

"Stop, H. R.," Gary said sharply.

"Stop, H. R.," I said lightly. "Heel, H. R. Sit, H. R. Down, boy."

He tried a kick of his own, trying for a direct payback of my earlier work. I saw it coming (he tipped his hand—or his foot—by leaning back on his other leg too soon) and stepped back, pulling one of the wooden chairs in front of me. I wasn't quick enough to have his foot hit the chair, but he banged his ankle knob on it as he retracted his leg from the thrust. You're supposed to get your leg back as quickly as possible after a move like that, and he seemed a little slow. Hmm, I wonder if I can make use of that fact. We circled each other a bit, and I noticed that some of the restaurant and bar *patrons, hotel guests, and various employees had gathered to watch the gringo man and woman go at each other in the semidarkness.*

"Gary," I said, "you want to collect an admission fee from the audience? Thank you very much."

H. R. became aware that we were giving a performance, and he figured I'd use this distraction to launch another kick, so I mimicked his sloppy technique and leaned back just slightly on one leg, as if preparing to kick with the other. He began his counterdirection movement too soon—before I had committed to the kick. I sidestepped toward him and jolted his head with a forearm smash, followed by a crossing blow to the face with my other hand. Not with the fist. The fist is for TV brawls. The fist is overrated. Unless you've got big hands—like a couple of frozen hams—you're much better off keeping your fingers tightly curled but away from your palm. You want to strike with the palm of your hand. It's a better weapon because it transmits the force from your shoulder through your upper and lower arm with more deadly delivery than does your fist. Take, for example, my blow, the one that caught H. R. on the cheekbone. It only traveled about ten inches, but I got everything behind it, and it bent him over and sent him down. It wasn't a knockout blow, but it had shaken up his cranium to the point where he was dazed. I stood there watching him squat on all fours, blinking his eyes. I turned to Gary and said, "You want to take him out of here, or would you prefer to have to order a new partner?"

"No, let me take care of him," he said, rushing in to lift H. R. to his feet and lead him out of the bar. About halfway to the door, H. R. angrily shook Gary off, staggered for a couple of steps, and continued on under his own power. Gary watched him go before returning to our table. The hotel management was very appreciative of our little dustup; they were putting another round of drinks on the table before we could sit back down. The waiter made a show of tearing up our check. I nodded to show my appreciation in return.

"You could have really damaged him at the end there," Gary commented.

"Yup."

"But you didn't."

"Nope."

"Why?"

"He's still one of the good guys. Not like Humberto."

"What did happen with Humberto, anyway?" he asked.

"Why don't you visit him in the hospital and ask him."

"You put him there?"

"I have that effect on some men."

"His pals might come after you, you know."

"That's why I want to get something going on this case. I found out a lot about who's doing what with whom, but I didn't know Langer was up the road a piece. So they've been letting me learn this stuff, thinking that they had the big picture covered. Meanwhile you've known about the private army up there, probably because of the bugs you planted, but you haven't done anything about it. So they're still winning. What gives?"

"Look," he said, "I shouldn't be saying this, and I'll deny it later if it comes to that, but Langer and the money and the private army aren't our concern. It's the Soviet connection we're interested in. We think they're becoming a big factor in the importation of drugs to the States. If we can involve them in it, expose just part of their operation, it would be a coup for us."

"Okay," I said. "So what do you have to lose by letting me hear your tapes, reading the reports of your

divers, and whatever the hell else you've got? And
what's wrong with trying to establish another drug
connection, like a sting operation?"

"Nothing, I guess. It's not SOP, but very little is at
the moment. All right. Come hear the tapes, read the
reports, ask your questions. We'll team up. Temporari-
ly. But as for the drug buy, I think H. R. was right. It's
not a good idea. Langer will never go for it."

"He might if the approach came from the Soviets
themselves." I let that sink in for a moment. I could
almost hear the little cogs and gears clicking inside
Gary's head.

Finally he spoke. "You just might have something
there."

"Thank you." Boy, this guy was slow. Nice, but slow.
Could he be putting me on, pretending the CIA hadn't
already considered this approach? We went upstairs to
give me a crack at their info. I had no idea that their
boring reports would turn out to save my life.

Seventeen

THERE WAS ALWAYS lots of shooting going on in our
camp. The ex-cops, ex-army, and ex-lowlife scum that
Carlos had recruited for me went totally batshit over
the automatic and semiautomatic weapons we passed
out to them. They were always going out for "target
practice," which for them meant marking off a group
of trees or bushes, then timing each other to see how
fast they could cut one down using Uzis from about
twenty feet out. I yelled about the waste of ammo, but
they rolled up an entire troop transport filled with
ammo clips, so there didn't seem much point. Not
that the weapons were going to last. No one ever
cleaned them, and they got tossed around with a
disregard that would have meant the stockade in any
civilized army. In the weather conditions down here, I
gave the whole arsenal about six months.

The camp itself was not too bad. The girl and I had
an entire bungalow to ourselves. It was supposed to
have been some sort of retreat for the country's

bigwigs, and there had been lots of money spent on creature comforts. The outlying bungalows were barely one step up from Spartan, but the men were always going down to Tingo Maria, or even Pucallpa, to buy or steal things that they wanted: mattresses, portable radios, liquor, clothing, even women. The place was beginning to resemble a summer camp for degenerates and hookers.

It was the women who caused the problem, although my own stupidity in not maintaining more control had a lot to do with the outbreak of violence. Shit, what I ended up with was a whole mountainside full of anger, greed, coke frenzy, and jungle madness.

The men were into coke every evening, as soon as the breezes broke through the lingering heat of the day. My little runaway would supply the camp with music, courtesy of her big stereo rig. She made sure it was cranked up, with the mechanism set to go for several hours of automatic cassette feed. It seemed to get louder every night, the whole hill and most of the valley bouncing to the beat.

"The guys have another girl," she shouted to me one night.

"Oh, shit. From the village?" We had nearly caused a revolution when a local teenage girl was taken up to the camp by one of the men.

"No," she said. "They got her from Ramon. He went to Mollendo to get them this time."

"Them?"

"He brought back a bunch of 'em."

"Christ. There's going to be trouble."

"Yeah," she said. "How 'bout some trouble between us right now?" She came over to me and led me to the bed. We went through what had become a ritual of teasing, binding, and feeling, and then suddenly we joined together, locked into the jam-socket tango.

When we finished, there was a fine aura of steam rising from our bodies.

I went to take a shower, and she went into the kitchen. The whoosh of the water melted into the drone of the stereo, and I spent too much time under the hot spray. It was a shock to hear voices talking too close outside when I finally turned off the water. It sounded like a shouting match right outside. But I couldn't figure out why all the voices were in Spanish. I quickly toweled off and got into some clean slacks. As I walked out of the hall I started to ask, "What's going on?" but stopped. There were about two dozen men in the room, and many more right outside the door. Toward the back of the crowd were several girls, probably the girls Ramon had gotten from Mollendo. Most of the men were peasants armed with machetes or knives, but Carlos's men had their guns out and were just itching to use them. I tried to quiet everybody down, but it had already gone too far. The assholes actually pulled their guns on me. Shit, I let 'em go on with their stupid shouting and went to get my Uzi from the bedroom. I got it out of the plastic wrapping, checked it over quickly, and headed back to the increasingly loud scene. A pushing match erupted right in front of me, and somebody bounced into my girl, who had been quietly standing there smirking at everybody. She nearly lost her balance but straightened herself and flailed at the man who had bumped into her, using the leather belt she had been holding coiled in her hands. She laid a long, vicious blow right across his face. He screamed and went for her with his fists. I didn't have a good line of fire but let loose a spurt, anyway, taking him out along with a couple of others who were right behind him. Then all hell broke loose.

Everybody started shooting at everybody else, both

inside and outside the bungalow. I hit the floor and
yelled for the girl to do the same. Somebody hit the
stereo, and the throbbing beat began all over again at
an ear-piercing level. All our shooting brought out the
whole camp, most of them firing wildly around the
bungalow. I scooted back against the wall, then skid-
ded on elbows and knees to get into the central
hallway. If we could get to the bedroom, it would be
all right. There was a trapdoor leading down to a
bomb shelter inside the bedroom closet.

The girl came skidding along after me, and I almost
shot her, thinking it was one of them still shooting up
the place in the other room. I don't know what the hell
they thought was happening, but nobody followed us.
They just kept on shooting each other, both inside and
outside the place. We got the trapdoor up, half fell
through it, and slammed it shut. I fumbled in the dark
trying to jam the lock until she found the lantern and
turned it up. We were safe for the time being.

Eventually the dull, popping sounds faded away
and all we heard besides the dripping water from a
pipe overhead was the huffing of our own breathing.

She whispered, "Do you think it's safe to go out?"

"Let's wait a bit longer." I used a whisper too.

"What's going to happen?" she said softly.

"Shh. Let's keep it down for a while. I think
whoever's left will probably go for the blow. And then
they'll try searching for the money. When they don't
find it, they'll start to tear things apart."

"They'll find us."

"Maybe."

"They'll kill us."

"Me, yes. You they'll rape."

"Oh, thanks."

"Shh. Jesus."

"What are we going to do, just wait for them to get
to us?"

"No, no. We'll go up soon. I just want to make sure they're over digging out the coke containers before sticking my head up there."

"Yeah," she said hesitantly.

We waited. And listened. The creaking of floorboards began in one corner of the ceiling and moved across the top of our heads, slowly, back and forth, then faster. Pause. Silence. Then running footsteps followed by the sound of gunfire.

"What are they doing?" she whispered intently.

"Killing each other over the baggies in the bungalow."

"Oh."

"Jesus," I said. "Wait'll they find the way to open the locks on the storage bin."

"Maybe they'll realize there's enough for everybody," she said.

"That bunch? They'll go crazy with greed."

"I hope so."

"In any case, it doesn't matter. I'm going to kill every one of them."

"You can't," she said. "There's too many of them."

I just smiled at her.

"You can't," she pleaded.

"One way or the other," I said evenly, "they're going to die. Violently."

We gave the silence five minutes, then doused the light, and I climbed up the stepladder to unlock the trapdoor. I slowly pushed it open, trying not to grip the Uzi too hard for fear of firing it accidentally. I got one eye above floor level, then the other. Nothing human in sight, so I went up and out onto the floor of the room. There was a bloody hand just beyond the doorway. No arm. Someone had aimed an automatic weapon right at the wrist. Lots of blood in the hallway. Many bodies in the main room, some with blood still oozing out of fresh wounds, but that was the only movement except for the front door swinging slightly in the breeze. I was tensed, half crouched, and ready to shoot any living being that came into view.

Gunfire out behind the house made me jump. I made my way toward the back door. There were seven of 'em left, all grouped around the iron door of the concrete structure. It may have been some sort of safe at one time. Its intricate series of bolts and locks made quick access impossible, but without the pattern for using the keys, it was a bitch to get open. They were lining up to shoot at it with the automatic and semiautomatic weapons. At the sound of the first blasting, I opened the door and stepped outside, raising my own weapon and bracing my legs for a good, solid firing position. One of the men went down just before I began shooting, so a ricochet off the iron must have struck him. With the rapid-fire delivery of the Uzi, I was able to hit all six remaining assholes before any of them could finish spinning to see what had happened. It seemed to take forever for the shots to stop pounding in the valley below us.

Very gradually I became aware of the breeze rustling the nearby trees. Another sound struck me too. A car was coming up the twisting roadway. About a mile away, it seemed. Time to move. Forget the coke. More of that available elsewhere. With Carlos's help the whole operation could be put back together in less than a week, and the Russians wouldn't even know the difference. No, they'd know—they were trying to expand the operation. Damn, they were sending their representative today. That was probably him in the car, undoubtedly with several jokers armed with Uzis, or something even bigger. I went and got the kid and said, "Let's roll out. Company coming."

As we passed through the living room she said, "What about her?"

I glanced at the body in chains. "Jesus," I said,

"how'd she live through it?" We took the gag and blindfold off and unfastened the chains. She'd have to do the rest herself. Other than a couple small burns and a few welts, she had gone through the shoot-out with everything intact. She collapsed to her knees and began working stiff fingers at the catches of the wrist and ankle bindings. "Come on," I said, heading for the front door. Too late. The car was just pulling in. "Shit. Head for the back door. Wait." That's strange. There was only the one Latino in the vehicle, the same one who had first contacted us. I glanced down the road and saw nothing. I stepped out the front door, saying back over my shoulder, "Stay inside."

"No need for weapons," the guy told me.

"I'll keep it, anyway, if you don't mind. Have you got the cash?"

"In the trunk."

"Open it."

"Don't I get to see the, ah, merchandise?"

"No. It gets shipped out later."

"Oh, no," he said. "I am to wait until the embassy cars arrive and watch it loaded."

"Suit yourself," I said, raised the Uzi, and blew him to oblivion. Yeah, I like the sound of that. Blew him to oblivion. Like crushing an insect. Shit, I should have found out when the embassy cars were coming. Then I had an idea. I got the antitank gun and drove it down the road to the first turn, pointed its evil-looking snout at the next turn after that, and locked it in position. That'll hold 'em for a little while. Next we opened up the coke bin and loaded the backseat with it. I took the fifteen million and jammed the boxes onto the floor, the remaining room in the trunk (the Russians' stack was barely a quarter of a million—just a satchel by comparison) and the floor of the front seat. We piled ourselves in and revved it up. I shouted to the girl inside to move her buns if she wanted out of there. We saw a sad face at the door, but she disappeared back into the dark. "Fuck her," I said.

"I'll bet you'd like to," the kid said from the passenger seat.

"Only you, honey. Boy, oh boy, am I gonna give it to you."

"Uh-huh," she said.

The sad girl appeared at the door holding one of the dead men's guns.

"Oh, shit."

"Move!"

We made it with only a couple of bullets in the rear deck. The damn car wouldn't accelerate very fast. Do you have any idea how much fifteen million dollars weighs? Or how much space it takes up inside a car? We could've built another bungalow with coke for mortar and twenty-dollar bills for shingles with what we packed into that stupid little car.

"Where are we going?" the runaway asked.

"Up."

"What do you mean?"

"I mean up," I said. "Up into the Andes."

"In this?" she said, indicating the car.

"You got any better ideas?"

"Yeah, a helicopter or a plane or something."

"Great," I told her. "Order one up for us, will you?" I looked at her for a second, hard. "We're leaving in the fucking car."

"But they say the road doesn't go anywhere."

"They didn't take the time to look. I did. We might not have any rubber left on the tires when we're through, but we'll make it."

"Make it where?"

"To whatever's on the other side."

Eighteen

The camp where Langer had been holed up with his private army was a mess. Mirandez, our front man for the Russian scam, was lying in the road in front of the main bungalow. Flies flitted and droned around his body. More bodies were scattered around the grounds and inside the main building.

"Natalie," Gary said, "you sure you want to see this?" He looked troubled beyond his years. "I mean, it's pretty gruesome stuff."

I wandered around the place once before heading up to the main house. The stench inside was ugly, snapping my head back and tightening my stomach. Bodies didn't keep well in tropical weather. Now I saw why Gary's men didn't stay inside very long. I pulled my blouse out of my jeans, ripped off the shirttail, and balled it up to hold over my mouth and nose.

Windows were open in the back rooms and the air was a bit better once you got past an insect-covered hand that was lying in the hallway. I poked around for

*a minute or two before seeing a rug that appeared to be
falling into a hole in the floor. Pulling it back gingerly,
I looked into a black hole. I went out to get a flashlight
or flare. The fresh air outside was a lovely surprise. I
had practically inhaled the tail of my blouse. The bile
rose up into my throat, and a brief dry retch sent a
convulsion through my whole body. Gruesome, Gary
had said. Yup, that was the word. Go ahead, be flip
about it. Might as well. Got to maintain some distance
from these dead souls.*

*H. R. came up from behind me and said, "Can't take
it? Too much for ya, tough girl?"*

*"Yeah. Too much for me. You can sure take it,
though. I've got to hand it to you. In fact, if you'll show
me where I can grab a flashlight, I'll take you somewhere where you can give yourself a hand."*

"What the hell's on your mind?" he said.

"Flashlight," I repeated.

"Yeah, well, there's one on the truck."

*"Thanks for all your help. Wait right here, H. R. I'll
lead you in."*

"In? In where?"

*"In the bungalow," I told him, already several steps
away. I wasn't going to waste any time with this bozo.*

"You've been inside the bungalow?" he called out.

*"Yup," I told him. I grabbed a torch and went back to
him. "Come on," I said. "You got a handkerchief?"*

"No, why?"

"You might want to rip off part of your shirt, then."

"The hell you saying?"

"Or you can just try breathing through your tie."

"You're crazy," he said.

*I had the piece of blouse up to my face as I stepped
over the threshold. I didn't stop to observe his reaction,
but when I got into the back room and glanced out at
him, he was attempting to eat his paisley tie.*

"Wheh thuh fuckh aryuh?" he said.

"In here," I told him. "Hang a left at the severed hand."

While I examined the mini bomb shelter, H. R. began some convulsions of his own and ran out of the place. Under other circumstances I would have smiled.

What's the matter with me? Has the trail of death, addiction, and perversion gotten to me somehow? Or is it the fucking failure of it all—the fact that I know what it is I'm here for but I can't seem to get off the dime and get it the hell done? I could have taken this clown Langer if only I'd gotten the phony Russian deal together sooner. And it would have been together sooner if I'd pushed Gary and H. R. to move on it. Jesus, those two could check and double-check any project to death. To death. Well, that's a fitting description of this caper, all right.

Stop this. Waste of time, girl. Focus, as your high-school math teacher used to say. "Focus, people." Okay. Langer has the coke, the runaway, the money, and a beat-to-shit mental attitude. He's in a small car, headed up a mountain that the locals say has no road. Either he knows something they don't, or he's going to have to come back down. Either way, if you just head on up the mountain, you'll find out more than if you stand here bemoaning the fact that you missed him again. What do you need to go after him? Food, water, weapons, a tent, and some transportation. Convincing Gary and H. R. to make the trip would require another couple of days. Planning, plotting, consulting maps. Maps—yeah, those would help. Seems to me that everything except the maps is sitting right there on the road in front of the bungalow. The truck had provisions, some rifles, ammo, and a couple of "shelter-pak" mini-tents. If I could get a map of the area here, on the mountain, and on the other side, I could just take off right now. I figured the direct route would be the easiest.

"H. R.," I said, "I'm interested in the subject of maps. I know you'll be able to help me. Give me a hand, you might say."

"Get outa here."

"There, there," I said. "You don't want to sever our relationship like that."

"I want you away from me."

"You know, H. R., you put your finger right on the crux of the matter. If I knew where the maps were located, I'd be over there reading them instead of here talking to you about my favorite movies."

"What?"

"The Hand, The Crawling Hand, Hands of a Stranger—"

"There're maps in the lead car!" he sputtered.

"Thanks, H. R. I knew I could count on you to hand me the right information."

"Fuck you."

"Only if you grow another six inches, pal," I told him, already walking toward the car that had led us up the road. Boy, H. R. really knew how to show a girl a good time: just be a straight man for my jokes. Lovely. And he had such a vile personality that it was fun to make him the butt of most of them.

I got into the car and popped open the glove compartment. Nothing but the warranty information and a schedule of maintenance that indicated this machine was about twenty-three thousand miles overdue on service. I shut the glove compartment, leaned forward, and felt under the seat. Couple of gum wrappers and some crushed, empty cigarette packs. On the backseat were two slim leather briefcases. One contained some blank Field Operations Reports and some other bureaucratic dada. The other held the maps. I got the ones I needed and was about to shut the case when something caught my eye. It was my name, neatly typed (although misspelled) on a white sticker affixed to a

*manila folder. Oh, what the hell. I took it. In for a
penny, in for a pound. Besides, I'd need something to
read by the campfire tonight.*

"H. R. says you want some maps or something like
that."

"Whoa, Gary, I didn't hear you come up on me.
Shit," I said, getting out of the car and using the maps
to cover the manila folder, "when we're around a bunch
of shot-up bodies, make sure you don't sneak up on
anybody." I looked him right in the eye and said,
"Otherwise I might overreact and turn you into another
H. R."

"What do you mean, 'another H. R.'?"

"A pile o' shit," I said. I started to walk away.

"Wait," he said, stepping in front of me. "Are you
saying you could take me like you took H. R. back at
the bar?"

"I sure am, toots."

"Hey, no way. Let's try it and see," he said with a
boyish smile.

Great. He wanted to play. I said, "Look, why don't
you boys get all the dead people arranged in neat little
stacks, and then we'll talk." He glanced around with a
worried expression, like he was afraid the boss might
catch him goofing off at the watercooler.

"Yeah, I'll bet." He turned and wandered off in
search of someone to supervise.

I got in the truck. Like so many government types
out on fieldwork, they had left the keys in the ignition.
Made things easier, although I was kind of hoping to
hot-wire the sucker. It was a Land Rover, and I'd never
lifted one. Wright and I have a contest going to see who
can lift the most, the biggest, the weirdest, and the
stupidest vehicles while on a case. We had to limit it to
while on a case. Otherwise we'd be snatching dump
trucks and cement mixers all over the city just to get
ahead of each other. So far he's got me on raw

numbers, but I've got the biggest (an entire diesel-powered train) and the weirdest (a so-called termite mobile, which was really an old Ford Fairlane with a fiberglass-molded body in the shape of a hideously oversize insect). Sometimes I tell Wright that it also counts as a runner-up in the stupidest, but he insists I only get one category per entry. Besides, he's got the leader in the stupidest (a Nash Metropolitan, a real tiny, tinny, putt-putt of a car that he used to chase somebody!).

I fired up the Rover, eased it into gear, and wheeled out of the short line of official vehicles to head up the road past the camp. I rolled almost to the edge of the clearing before anybody paid me any attention. A girl could get a complex with that kind of inactivity on the part of the nearby males.

"Hey!" Gary yelled. "Wait up."

That was more like it. I kept right on moving, exiting the camp at the rear. Gary was still mouthing off a ways behind me. I could see him halfheartedly running after the Rover as I glanced into the rearview. I stuck my left arm out the driver's-side window and gave him a friendly wave, as if to say, "Thanks for the loan of the utility van." I knew he'd try to follow in one of the cars, so I pushed pedal to metal and bounced up the trail as fast as the terrain would allow.

Coming up the hill to the camp, we had gone from asphalt to gravel to packed earth. Now, just a mile from the camp, the two ruts in the brush were all that indicated any hint of a trail. After four more twisting, vertigo-inducing miles, even those ruts seemed like an extravagance. I could barely tell that another vehicle had come this way recently. Then the going got really rough. Sharp rocks, slippery rocks, immovable rocks; sheer, soaring stone facings on one side; sheer, plummeting cliffs on the other. It was beautiful. Awe-inspiring. Breathtaking. Well, that's what I kept telling *myself, anyway: What a great view. Oughta get this on film, show it at the next party.*

Stop thinking things like that. Concentrate on the road. What there is of it. More like a path made out of debris, rock dust, and boulders. You'd think the four-wheel-drive would do more than this. The Rover feels top-heavy. If you feel it going over, throw yourself out and hope you land on land, not air. If it flips with you in it, you become one dead doll. Remember when you were young and riding in an elevator and someone said, "What would you do if the elevator cable broke and the elevator fell to the bottom of the shaft?" Remember how the smartass answer was, "I'd jump up in the air just before we hit the bottom," and it somehow seemed to make perfect sense? Then you learned about some natural laws, like that one about gravity pulling you down to earth at an increasing rate. Thirty-two feet per second per second. So if the Rover goes over the edge, you'd fall thirty-two feet in the first second, sixty-four feet in the second second, ninety-six feet in the third, and so on, until your crashdown. At which point you'd be traveling, let's see . . . damn fast.

I tried to work out the calculations in my head, but I'm too much a child of the ten-key pad. I could figure out how many seconds the Rover and I would be in free-fall, but converting feet per second into miles per hour was beyond me while wrestling with the steering wheel. It was tempting to stop, get out, and walk. But if I did, which way would I go? Forward, still after Langer and the money? Or back, away from the unknown cliffs around every hairpin turn? The maps were no help at all. They showed the road up about as far as the camp, and they showed a village about fifty miles inland. In between, all they showed was mountain. What if Langer was coked up and scared? What if there was no road through the mountain? Well, there is no road, exactly. My rump, ribs, and kidneys can attest to that.

Suddenly I saw the tracks. Some part of the cliff far above must have crumbled, sending pebbles, sand, and fine dust down on the odd trail I was violating with the Rover. In the dust there were some of the most gratifying tire marks I've ever encountered. Langer must have come this far, and he mustn't have turned back. Okay, so you'll keep going. Onward and upward. At least you hope it's upward, not downward.

A thought occurs. How much of a lead does he have? Wouldn't the wind have blown enough dust to cover the tire tracks? I stopped Rover (we were on a first-name basis after all the rump-bumping) and squeezed out, the door not opening fully because of the stone wall next to it. You know how, in the cowboy and Indian movies, some incredible scout or brave will be able to track anybody or anything through any kind of terrain? And how they'll come up to a marking on the earth, feel it, smell it, taste it—whatever—and announce how long it's been since the quarry has passed through this particular place? You remember that too? Well, I only believe it in the movies. I did everything but eat the sand, and I knew nothing more than when I was sitting in Rover. Well, there was one piece of information I got from rooting around in the dust: Langer's car was slowly leaking oil.

I got back in behind the wheel and started off, this time trying to figure out the flow rate for the oil loss he was going through. If he had loaded up the car with coke and bucks, then he was going to go stark raving apeshit if his only form of transportation went out on him in the middle of nowhere. The next two or three dozen turns were eventful only in my mind. I kept thinking I'd see Langer and his runaway—what's her name? Doris? Yeah, Doris Yablonski, but everyone knew her as Diana Pamela Grier—up ahead of me, leaning on a smoking, useless automobile, trunk open and clouds of greenbacks and cocaine swirling out of reach. No such luck. Not even a mirage.

Night came with the most singularly spectacular sunset I have ever witnessed. It nearly made up for everything wrong with this stupid trek across the mountain. I found the widest part of the trail that could still be seen in the dimming light, and pulled up to make camp. Or camp out, since the pup tent didn't come with any tent poles or stakes. Nice touch. Was this typical CIA-issue? The food was definitely the kind of thing you'd expect: freeze-dried, tough, and tasteless.

I had stuck my tape player in my purse. I popped in a tape of New Age piano solos by Jobson, Sakamoto, Kuhn, and Watson ("Piano One" on **Private Music**) and dreamed of the brilliant stars rotating, twisting, falling, and intermingling with white dust and paper money. The click of the player shutting off woke me for a moment. I got my bearings, shifted inside the sleeping bag, and went out like a power failure.

Nineteen

SOME ASSHOLE WEARING a leather hood was standing at the foot of the bed.

"Jesus," I said. "What now? Where did she get you?" He swung the leather truncheon at the shapes under the covers that were my feet. I barely pulled them out of the way in time. "Now knock it off," I said. "It's very realistic, but the act's not appreciated this early in the morning. Besides, whoever she ordered you from got it wrong." I swung out of bed and stretched. "It's girls in leather we want, not boys."

"What the fuck are you talking about?" Leather Head said.

"Isn't it hot in there?"

"Fuck this. Where's the money?"

"What?"

"You heard me," he said. He raised the club and started around the end of the bed.

"Hey," I said, suddenly waking up fully. Jesus, am I hallucinating this, or is it real? I hopped up on the bed, scrambled across it, and leapt off toward the bathroom.

"Son of a bitch," he said, coming over fast, truncheon arcing down at me.

"Look out," I yelled, and dropped down next to an armchair, pulling it over as hard as I could. The stunt worked—he smashed his hand into the chair, the end of the club missing my back by a couple of inches. I got my shoulder into the back of the chair and pushed as if I were in football training camp. I heard him *ooph* as the chair went into him, so I did it just like the coaches told me: Keep your legs pumping and your feet digging into the ground as hard and as fast as you can. The three of us—him, chair, and me—clomped across the room, banging into a closet door. I tried using the chair as a battering ram, bouncing it into his torso while he tried to twist away from it and land a good one with his short but deadly club. That was his mistake. If he had been able to ignore the pain of the chair crunching into his chest, he probably could have hit me. Or, if he had not been so intent on meting out some punishment, he probably could have gotten out from between the door and the piece of furniture I was using as a weapon. Finally he gave up on the club and used his hands on the armchair. When I saw he was going to get free, I hightailed it for the bathroom. My first thought was that this was a pretty chickenshit thing to do. Hiding in the bathroom was kid stuff, but I did it anyway, just barely getting the door shut before Leather Head crashed into it.

"Shit," he spat out. The sound of it was doubly muffled, once by the small mouth hole of the leather hood, and again by the closed door.

There was a second of silence before the door splintered right around the knob. He was bringing the truncheon down on the outside knob, and the cheap, hollow-body door was giving way under the pressure of the blows. It would only be a few more seconds until he was through, and then where would I go?

The shower had a flexible hose attachment to direct the spray any which way you pleased, so I grabbed it and spun the hot-water tap. Most hotels, even the ones down here in Greaserville, kept their water blazing hot because it caused the guests to use less of it. As Mr. Hood came crashing into the room, I let him have a good, solid squirt right in the eyes. He screamed and spun away from the spray, bouncing off the doorjamb as he did so. I kept the hose on him, burning his arms and, I'm sure, sending a nice stream of scalding hot water down inside his leather outfit. His body jerked away from the water in an amusing way. This was almost fun.

I held the hose steady but stepped back and as far to the side of the stream as possible, because it occurred to me that he would have to do one of three things: find the door, collapse, or rush me by coming straight into the spray. He chose the latter, swinging the club viciously ahead of him as he came blundering forward. He passed within an inch or two of me as he delivered a couple of blows to the shower stall. I let go of the hose and planted both hands into his back, right between the shoulder blades. He was catapulted into the tiled confines of the shower, where the hot water was now pouring out of the regular well-affixed nozzle. He was twitching under the water, slipping and sliding in wet leather, attempting to push himself out of the steaming hell. I was barefoot, but his head presented too tempting a target, so I waited for the proper angle and laid a solid kick into his cranium. It was like a perfect punt, his head taking the place of the football. His leather hood softened the blow on my instep, but the force of the kick sent him crashing back against the inside wall of the shower, where he slowly crumpled in a soggy, searing heap.

For a moment I considered letting the hot water finish him off, but the thought of having a human prune in my hotel-room shower was too much to take this early in the morning, and I reached in to shut off the tap.

"What happened?" came a female voice. I jumped about a foot. It was the kid.

"Jesus," I said. "Where the hell were you?"

"The gift shop," she said.

"Figures."

"What's going on?"

"This asshole came after the money."

"Who is he?"

"The fuck should I know?" I said.

"Let's at least take his mask off."

"Please do," I said, and went to get dressed. I heard her sliding a little on the shower tiles, then the sound of the shower again. "I think he's wet enough," I called out to her.

She appeared at the broken bathroom door and said, "I've got the cold water running on him."

"The cold?"

"Yeah. I wanna wake him up."

"Good God, what for?" I said.

"Find out who he is. Who sent him. How'd he know about the money. You know," she replied. "Don'tcha think that's a good idea? I can turn it off if you want me to. I just thought we should know if he's alone or if he's working for somebody. Maybe somebody back in San Francisco."

She had a point. "Yeah," I said. "Maybe so. Okay, let me know when he's awake again."

She looked back inside, and I leaned down to put on my shoes. When I stood up, she was standing by the splintered door, looking toward the shower stall, which was out of my line of sight around the corner.

She said in a monotone, "I think you can come see him now. He's awake."

"Right." I walked over to the door. "Let's see what the little punk has to say for his soggy self." I glanced at her, but she still had her eyes firmly fixed on the shower stall. I turned the corner and stopped dead. The stall was empty. "The hell?" I turned and caught fragments of the scene. The girl stepping out of the bathroom. The leather-clad lad looming up from behind the door. The layer of dust on the floor behind the toilet. The grain of the guy's leather pants as I threw my arms around his legs. The forced perspective as the truncheon came swinging down at my face. The girl at the doorway, holding the Uzi. The little flashes of light as the weapon burped out a dozen rounds. The blood on my hands from the guy's wounds. The girl turning the gun on me. The look of surprise on her face when it didn't fire. The red welt on her face after putting my fist into it. The way her hair got into her mouth as I slapped her head back and forth to get her to stop yelling.

"Shut up, you little bitch."

"You're going to kill me," she said, sobbing.

"And what would you call what you were trying to do to me back there?"

"I—I was shooting him."

"Oh, sure. If the damn thing hadn't gone empty, I'd be lying in there with him."

"No, no," she pleaded.

"Shut up. Just shut the fuck up."

"But I—"

"Shut it!"

She shut it. I told her to pack things up while I took care of anyone outside who had heard the gunfire. It's amazing what kind of privacy you can buy in some of these places. There was no one outside the door. If the gentleman and his young lady friend want to practice a little target shooting in their rooms, no problem. Even if they're firing automatic weapons. Shit, all I'd done was double what the desk clerk asked for the room and told him I didn't want to be disturbed. Makes you wonder what kind of hellfire and damnation I could unleash up here if I'd paid triple.

I went back inside. She was covering up her crying pretty well. Jesus, I had left her in the room with about four other guns. What was the matter with me? Some sort of death wish. I warily accounted for all the guns, putting one in my lightweight jacket, one in my waistband, and stuffing the others deep into the jumble of clothing inside our two brand-new suitcases.

"You're wrong," she said.

"Sure."

"Well, think about it. If I offed you, I wouldn't have the coke or the money, would I?"

It's true that I hadn't taken her with me when I hid the car, but it wouldn't have been that hard to dig it out. Hell, only about half a dozen people saw me drive out of town and walk back in a couple hours later. Yeah, there was a lot of room to lose something out there, but I figured the hidey-hole was probably only good for a couple of days. Which is all I really wanted in this backwater town.

"Let's go," I said.

"Where are we going?"

"We're going back to the boat, and then we're getting the hell out of this country."

I didn't count on there being more leather boys after us.

Twenty

After what seemed like an argument worthy of the General Assembly of the United Nations, my call went through from the only phone in the entire village.

"You better not be selling anything."

"Hello to you too."

"Natalie?"

"The same. How are you, Wright?"

"Fine. Where are you? Are you—is everything A-okay?"

I was touched. Wright rarely bothered to ask the code phrase, claiming that he's able to tell if something is wrong by the way the conversation goes.

"I'm fine. Tired. Worn-out. Pissed off. Stranded in the most godforsaken place you can imagine. Out of food. Out of patience. Out of water in the radiator of Rover. But other than that, I'm fine." I took one quick breath, then said, "Oh, and pissed off. Did I say that?"

"Rover?" he said.

"Rover," I said. "The Land Rover."

"Oh," he said. "Of course. How stupid of me."

"Goddamm it, Wright, I almost had them!"

"Fish story."

He always said that whenever someone starts to talk about their bad luck in trying to catch somebody.

"I saw their car at the bottom of the mountain. I was only about half a mile away, straight across a little valley. But it must have been five miles down the road, and by the time I got there, it was too dark to follow them."

"Big fish story."

"Stop saying that."

"Hey, so you came close," he said. "Big deal. Only counts in blackjack and horseshoes. Where are you? What mountain?"

I think that in addition to all my other problems, I was going trail-trippy—I forgot that he didn't know what was going on. I hadn't checked in with him for a couple days. I said I was sorry. I told him where I was. I told him I missed talking with him.

"About the case, right?" he asked.

"No," I said after a slight pause. "I miss talking to you, period."

"Thank you," he said after a slight pause of his own. "I feel the same, Natalie."

"Can you feel a smile through the phone?"

"Sure can."

"Great. That's the first decent emotion I've felt in forty-eight hours. Okay, what's happening out your way?"

"Big news is the crime war. Henderson vs. Foley vs. Martinelli vs. the world. Media's having a field day. Thirty-six people killed so far. Evidently Foley had laid off a huge amount of bets to Henderson, who had borrowed from Martinelli, who was involved with a big dope deal with Foley, and they all thought the score from the robberies would cover them with each other while the other action went down. And if you think that sounds complex, you should hear how they read it on the ten-o'clock news."

"So they were robbing Peter to pay Paul," I said.

"Sort of. Why?"

"Oh, nothing, really," I said. "It's just that I thought it was something like that back when I was still with F. J."

"Does it lead us anywhere?" he said quietly.

"No. At least, not that I can see."

"Then don't worry about it."

"I know. You're right. But what if we'd known it back then? Maybe we could have done something about it. Maybe things would have worked out differently."

"Yeah, and maybe then you'd still be here. Maybe we wouldn't have found out about Langer. Then you'd hardly be about to break the case wide open. Officially Langer's still dead, you know. Your bringing him in, or bringing in the money, will shock a few people."

"Yeah," I said. "I wonder about that. Our friends with the CIA aren't going to sit by and let that happen if they can keep from falling all over each other."

"Don't worry about them," Wright told me. "Watch out for those boys with the leather face masks. According to the word I get, they have some sort of fucking contest to see who can kill the most people while pulling a job. Or who can get paid for the most kills, or something like that."

"They didn't kill anyone in the bank," I said.

"They weren't paid to," he said. "I also found out one more thing from Fend."

"What?"

"Well," Wright said, "we can't get a precise fix on the names of these boys. Aliases like you won't believe. But when Fend did some cross-checking, he came up with a very interesting match."

"I'm listening," I said.

"Comedy. Intrigue. Adventure." He paused.

"You're kidding." It was all I could think to say.

"Nope," he said. *"I made him check it every which way we could. Still comes out that way."*

"But," I said, *"they wouldn't hire bank robbers."*

"Oh, come on, Natalie, they'd hire Khadaffi if they could get the money together for a large enough covert operation."

"Yeah, but—"

"Besides," he continued, *"they go back five years with the organization. They did the bank job freelance, or because they were working undercover."*

"Shit. Any description? Names? Anything?"

"Big, white, youngish, tattoos on the arms, most often called by a kind of group nickname."

"Group nickname? You're kidding."

"You said that once already," he reminded me.

"Give me the nickname, Wright."

"Okay, but it's not going to do you much good."

"Give."

"Leather and Lace."

"You're kid—I mean, say what?"

"Exactly. So it doesn't mean anything to you, either?" he asked.

"Well, it's a title of a song—a kind of wimpy, adenoidal kind of thing by Stevie Nicks and Tom Petty, I think. Other than that, it seems like exactly the kind of stupid code phrase we often make up."

"Thank you very much."

"You know what I mean."

"Yeah, I guess I do. Anyway, the scene up here is bloody and ugly, and I think you're going to be reporting the same thing from down there."

"Well," I told him, *"I'm certainly in the mood to kill somebody. After I shoot Rover, I mean."*

"Imagine how the taxpayers feel up here," Wright said. *"We've got the big boys robbing each other. Their hired guns robbing the city. The banks getting repaid*

by the insurance companies. And the insurance companies raising their rates to cover it. Meanwhile some clowns are running for city elections. Naturally half of them promise to clean up the city, while the other half accuse the rest of having ties to organized crime. F. J. is working for several factions, tailing candidates right and left."

"What's he doing," I asked, "working for both parties under different names?"

"You got it. He's got a couple of front organizations working for him, but he's still shorthanded. And he's about to be even more shorthanded."

"What do you mean?" I said.

"I'm quitting," Wright said matter-of-factly. "I'm coming down there."

"Really?"

"Really. Got to join the president of my new agency."

It took me a second for this to sink in. "You mean," I said, "it came through?"

"Yup. It's official. We are now Dauntless Investigations, Inc."

"Oh, not that terrible pun."

"I had to put down something," he said. "Besides, it'll make the media boys happy. You can have a more refined name later."

"Okay, Wright. And thank you."

"Pleasure. See you soon."

"Looking forward to it."

"Bye."

"Bye."

I hung up the phone with a nagging thought. If we were now officially in our own firm, we've got to stop wasting money on such long calls. I set about getting my life in order: my stomach settled, my transportation fixed, my body clean, my clothes mended. I almost got Rover up and running, too, but not quite fast enough for me to follow Langer as he raced back through the

*village, heading up the mountain in the opposite
direction from which we had come. He was followed
several minutes later by some clown wearing leather
and riding a motorcycle.*

*"This is weird," I said to no one in particular. The
whole thing was getting out of hand. There was no way
for me to follow them. And I wasn't looking forward to
another few nights on that precarious trail. If Mr.
Leather killed Mr. Langer, fine. If the other way
around, okay. Either way I would go after the money.
Didn't matter who had it, I'd get it. And then I'd
announce the results to the press. Correction: we—
Wright and I—would announce it to the press.*

*I finished the makeshift repairs to Rover, continued
on the road away from the mountain, reached civiliza-
tion, flew back to the port city, and waited for Wright. It
was there that we figured out how to get all the players
to show up in the same place at the same time.*

Twenty-one

TWO MORE LEATHER freaks attacked us while we were walking to where I hid the car.

I remember thinking that this was stupid. I had enough cash and coke in the fucking automobile to buy off an entire army, but here we are on foot while two bozos on motorcycles try to run us down. Besides, the whole setup was screwed. Why am I out here? Why get stuck with cash in the first place? Jesus, I should have taken it to Switzerland. Or left it on the boat. Or something besides trying to lug half of it around with the girl, the guns, and the dope.

We heard the motorcycles before we saw them. Then we saw the dust cloud rolling toward us, and suddenly the two bikes appeared over a little hilly part of the road. I threw the cases to the ground and began digging out the Uzi.

"What are you doing?" she asked me.

I got the weapon and swung it around to face the direction from which the roaring cycles were coming. I said, "I just don't see those two as tourists."

She looked at them, looked back at me, then at them again. She started to say something when a flash of red-orange-white sparked in front of one of the cycles, followed by a whoosh right by us and a shattering explosion some thirty yards past.

"Come on!" I yelled, and grabbed her arm, pulling her off the road and into a shallow ditch. The whoosh came by again, with the explosion much nearer this time. A dull throbbing pain hit my head from the inside. From the shock wave, I thought. Funny how you remember some things from the Army.

"Aren't you going to shoot back?" she yelled.

"They've got to be closer," I shouted back. We both had trouble hearing. The ringing sound in my ears seemed to pulsate throughout my skull.

They made a big mistake. They should have pulled up, taken careful aim, and finished us off from outside my range. The missiles they were using could have killed us just by coming within five yards of our makeshift foxhole. Instead, they had to ride in like modern-day gladiators or jousters or whatever, firing with one hand and steering their high-powered overhead-cam stallions with the other.

"A little closer, assholes," I said quietly. My voice was very far away. "More, more . . ." I stood up in a hunched-over stance and swept the two leather-clad figures once, twice, three times. One bike exploded almost immediately. The other rider tried to veer away from our position, but his bike flipped up and over as the engine roared even louder, then faded away to nothing. I didn't even think to shoot him, he was so pretty as he sailed across the sky, silhouetted against the cocaine-white clouds. He plopped to earth and didn't move.

"Let's get out of here," I said.

"Who are they?" she said.

"Friends of your friend," I snapped back.

"Will you stop with that?"

"No."

"You need to do some lines," she said. "Put the freeze on, you'll feel better."

"Shut up."

She shut up. Good. She was learning I was in control. She was right about the coke, though. Some lines would be good. Get the senses working right. Those suckbrain cowhide dinks were a downer. Now they were where they belonged. They were down, I thought, and I laughed out loud as we walked on toward the car. She dragged the bags along after me. I knew now that I was never destined to be down. I deserved to be up, up high. Very high. We got to the car and removed the covering of brush and the tarp that had been over the coke in the trunk. We got out a bag of the snow and laid out an entire picket fence of the stuff on the vinyl seats. We took turns at the white pickets until they were all gone. It felt good.

Suddenly she stiffened and got out of the car.

"What's happening?" I said.

"I hear something. An engine."

"Knock it off," I told her.

"No, listen," she said. "It sounds like a motorcycle engine."

"I said to knock—" I began angrily, getting out of the car. Then I heard it too. Someone had started a motorcycle not too far away and was revving the engine. We looked at each other, then off in the direction of the sound.

"Maybe he didn't die," she said. Then the engine noise stopped.

"But the motor did," I said, and laughed. She was silent, so I stopped and said, "What's the matter? Don't you get it? The motor died. It's funny." I laughed again. It really was very, very funny. I slapped her to see if she thought it was funny. She finally got it

after a while, and she laughed with me, although she
didn't seem to laugh quite as loud as she usually did.
We heard the cycle start, rev up, sputter and die a
couple of times, way off in the distance. I could make
the sound come very close if I really tried, right inside
my head, right between my eyes back under the skin. I
didn't like the noise there, so I made it go away far out
across the foothills. That's where we should be. High
in the mountains. That was very funny, too, so I
laughed again. Then I said, "C'mon, let's get going."
We got in the car and took off toward the same
mountain we had come down a couple days before.
Just me, her, and a ridiculous cargo of paper and dust
that people died and killed to possess. Now *that* was
funny. I punched the accelerator, and the car did its
clunky best to zoom us down the dust pit they called a
road. Shit, this is another downer. I told her to get me
some more blow.

"Now?" she said. "I mean, while you're driving?"

"Why the hell not?"

"Is it okay? To drive like that?"

"Who the fuck am I going to hit out here? C'mon,
get the stuff out. Put it on the mirror in your purse."

"I don't have a mirror in my purse," she said.

"Fuckin' A," I said angrily at her. I grabbed the
rearview mirror and struggled with it for several
seconds. The damn thing wouldn't budge, so I hauled
off and punched it again and again.

"Stop it, stop it!" she shouted.

"The fucking thing won't come off," I said. The car
was going up and down the soft-packed embankments
on both sides of the lane. We went *whump-whump-
whump* each time, and the steering was getting loose
because it was easier to swing the car into these little S
curves than it was just to go straight. The mirror
cracked, then the plastic holder splintered, and I had

the glass in my hand. "Here," I said, handing it to her. "Now put some lines on that and give me your straw."

"God, please don't run off the road while you're snorting it, okay?"

"Okay. But just as a special favor to you."

We sashayed all over the place, tires rumbling, fenders bouncing off the brush, sending enormous, billowing walls of dust soaring into the air behind us as I leaned over and took the fine white freeze into my nostrils, and then into the blood vessels in my nasal cavity. I felt the kid looking over at me and said to her, "What's wrong with you, honey?"

"Nothing," she replied sullenly.

"Nothing, my ass. You've been acting funny for a long time now."

"I've been acting funny? What about you?" she said in that whiny little way she sometimes uses.

"Oh, shit," I said, "this is just what I need. Jesus, now we're going for a downer. Why the fuck do you do this?"

"I'm sorry. I didn't mean to." She changed her tone and spoke quickly and quietly. "You want more coke? I can get it ready. Or we can just talk. Tell me what you're going to do when we get back to the boat."

I looked over at her and decided that I didn't want her around anymore. She looked hard and used up. Shit, why couldn't she have taken better care of herself? Worn-out and weak before she was eighteen.

"You know," I said slowly, "I don't need you any longer. I'm strong. You're nothing. I can make it through anything. You haven't got what it takes."

"What are you talking about?" she said, screwing her face up into an expression of distaste.

"See?" I said. "That's what I mean. Look at yourself." I picked up the rearview mirror from the seat and handed it to her. "You've got big worry lines all across your forehead. It's the beginning of the end for you now, baby, and I don't intend sticking around for the finish."

"You're crazy."

"You think I can't get any woman I want? Then you're the one who's crazy." We were nearing the base of the mountain. I was actually looking forward to taking the car through it again, pushing the speed through the curves, taking it faster than anybody thought possible, faster than anybody could go. For a moment I considered taking her along, watching her squirm and grab on to the seat as we leaned into the big turns, seeing her scream as we bounced into the cliff walls. But there was something I wanted to have her say, something I wanted to hear from her, and when I heard it, then I could think about fun.

"You brought that first leather guy up to the room, didn't you? You wanted him to kill me so you two could go find the car, go back to the boat, get all the money, get all the coke, get it all for yourselves. I'll bet you even planned how to kill him after you had it all. You think that this arrangement with the Russians is finished, so you're looking to get out. But it's not finished. If they don't want to stay at just the right level, then I can find some other country that wants to do it right. Keep every shipment down to the right size and we'll go on forever. Make a million every two months . . . instead of getting too much heat after trying for sixty million in six months. See? I've got it all worked out. So you blew it. Didn't you? Didn't you? Admit it. You tried to get rid of me, didn't you?"

"Go to hell," she said.

"Tell me the truth, baby. Tell me! Say it!" I shouted at her. It felt good to keep on screaming the same words over and over and over at her, letting the anger pour out. It tightened up every muscle and cord in my body, my veins filling, the surface temperature of my skin rising.

She shouted, "Yes, you shit! Yes, I did it to you, you fucking pig. Do you think I liked screwing you and getting you used to the sick sex? I did it just to see if I could find out how it all worked, where all the money was. You dickface, you've been poisoned and you don't even know it!" Her anger died.

"Poisoned? What the hell are you talking about?"

"With the coke," she said quietly. "You're a junkie on coke. You can't live without it. Your nose is starting to cave into your face. Your brain is starting to rot away. You can't even decide to go to the bathroom without taking a few lines."

"You're pronouncing things better than you used to," I said.

"You think I'm just this stupid little girl from the Midwest, don't you? That's what you wanted. Some dumb little jailbait to fool around with. Well, you'll see how dumb when you try to get your money out of Switzerland."

"The hell you saying now?"

"You'll see."

"You're full of shit."

"You'll see," she said again.

"You're bluffing."

She just smiled. The change from her screaming of a minute before was complete. Goddamn, the back and forth and up and down of everybody lately was enough to drive you . . . *insane?* Goddamm it! Now she had me fucking with my own mind. The little bitch. Clever. Yes, that I'll give her.

I said, "So, what do you think will happen now?" We were still moving along at a pretty good clip, going up, up, toward the rock faces and sheer drops and switchbacks and boulders.

She said, "You need me for a little while, just to get your Swiss accounts. I made a deal with the Russians, and the money you think was going to your numbers was really going somewhere else. After we get back to the boat I'll take a million in cash and give you the Swiss account numbers, or I'll just leave with the numbers. Up to you. My plan didn't really work out, but we didn't do too badly, either of us."

"Uh-huh," I said. I wondered if she really had talked to the Russians. She probably had time to do it, but would they have gone for it? Shit, they'd go for anything if they thought it would help them and screw up the Americans. And that twerp Svetlov—Jesus, he'd have come in his pants just looking at her in one of her outfits. That guy'd do whatever she asked.

"So," she said, turning to me, "don't you think you'd better turn around and go back to kill the other cyclist?"

"What for?"

"Well, he'll be between us and where we want to go."

"I don't know where you're going," I said, "but I'm going back to the boat."

"Not over the mountain?"

"Why not?"

"They've probably got it blocked off back at the camp," she said.

"So what. I've got this." I reached down to pick up the Uzi.

"They might have half a dozen men with those," she pointed out.

"I doubt it. We've been gone too long. They'll think we died up there. And even if they're waiting, they'll be bored, tired, off-guard. I'll take 'em out, easy."

"I don't know . . ." she said.

"That's it exactly," I told her. "You just don't know. You don't know anything." I slowed down, which was easy, since we were going up a pretty good grade by now. Without looking at the road, I swung the car around to head back down the hill. I kept my eyes on her face. She smiled a little at the turnaround, as if to say, "I told you so." She just didn't get the picture about my change of direction. I let the car roll by sliding it into neutral. Gravity worked on us for a minute before we got up a good head of steam, and then I said what I'd been planning to say ever since she had held the gun on me back in the hotel: "Get out."

"What did you say?"

"Get out. Get out of the car."

"Out here? Forget it. If you don't want to take me back, drop me off in the village."

"I'm dropping you off here, baby. Get the fuck out of the car."

"Look—" she began.

"Getthefuckoutofthefuckingcar!" I screamed at her. Shit, that felt great.

"All right!" she shouted back. "Pull over."

I nudged the wheel and brought the car over to the side of the road, now whizzing by at about forty miles an hour. "There," I said. "I've pulled over. Now get out."

"Stop the car," she said.

"You don't get it, do you?" I said. "I haven't got time for you anymore. I don't want you in my life. I don't want you in my thoughts. And I don't want you in the car. Get out."

"You're crazy."

"Out!"

"Hey, come on. Be real."

"Oh, I'm real, baby. I'm very real." I brought my feet up off the floorboard, swung them around up onto her seat, and—

"Look out!"

—slammed them into her. She yelled and tried to

pound at me with her fists. It was pathetic. I could grind her into dog food trapped where she was. I pounded her again while she screamed. We rolled down the hill, faster all the time. Up to fifty. Sixty. Freewheeling and scooting back and forth on the packed dirt roadway. She was writhing around, trying to escape into the backseat. She almost made it, too, in which case the fun would have ended with my putting a few dozen rounds into her with the gun in my hand. But I sank back just enough in my seat to raise my right foot high enough to crack her a good one in the head, and she slumped down for a couple seconds, dazed by the blow. I put the gun down and leaned past her to open the door. She came alive right then, and I had nails clawing at my eyes and teeth sinking into my arm.

We also had a car that was almost out of control. I fought with the steering wheel about as much as I fought with the demon in the passenger seat. The gun was wedged between me and my seat, and we both had the idea of going for it at about the same time. It's probably what made it possible for me to finally boot her ass out of there. I pulled back from her and the gun, got both hands on the wheel, and twisted back with my legs just as she got the gun out from between my body and the back of the driver's seat. Since she had to take the time to turn it around so that the muzzle was aimed at me instead of her, I had enough time to plant both of my size nines into her gut. The passenger-side door wasn't completely open—it had caught with the first latch after I had twisted the handle. Still, the force of her body crashing against it was enough to pop it loose, and she suddenly wasn't beside me any longer.

I nearly took the car right over the side at that point. Steering hard and pumping the brake, I got control, slowed to a stop, and broke out laughing right in the middle of the road. Still chuckling, I turned around again and headed back up the mountain. She was just a heap of clothing by the side of the embankment.

Spending the nights up on the mountain was a lot harder this time. The bitch had forgotten to pack food, water, or blankets.

I lit a nice little fire. And laughed and laughed at the sight of the green pieces of paper turning red, then into black ash and straggles of ugly smoke.

Twenty-two

I met Wright at the airport and we did our best to break
each other's ribs with our first hug. It felt good to have
two armfuls of solid man.

"God, I missed you," I told him.

"I liked that too," he said.

"We'll have to do it again in a little while."

"You got it."

We did the luggage bit, then drove to the hotel,
talking a mile a minute (me) and an acre an hour
(Wright).

"How did F. J. take your leaving?" I asked.

"Hard. Like hit in the gut."

"I'm sorry about that."

"Me too. Is it always this hot here?"

"Hotter, sometimes," I said. "But it can freeze your
buns off up in the mountains."

"How are your CIA pals?"

"Haven't seen them. I can't imagine what they're
doing, unless they decided to go after Langer."

"I don't think they can," Wright said.

"Why not?"

"Don't know, really. I got F. J. out in the open by a fountain—you know, plenty of ambient noise—and we went into it pretty hot 'n' heavy. He still won't admit who's spooking him, but at least he admits it's happening and that it's happening pretty high up in government circles."

"High up?" I said. "Like where?"

"Like the White House."

"Bullshit."

"Hey, I like the guy, too, mostly. It's nice that we're not wimps anymore. But that doesn't mean he has anything to do with this. Some White House official could have put in a request to leave Langer alone for the time being, the orders being carried out just a little too diligently for our tastes."

"Possible, I suppose," I admitted.

"One theory has it that there was some good reason to leave Langer untouched but that the reason has long since disappeared. Or been forgotten."

"But—" I started to say.

"And," he went on, "some other important business came up, and the order has never been countermanded."

"Knowing how government agencies work," I said, "this is sounding like a plausibler and plausibler theory," using a favored twisting of Lewis Carroll's "curiouser and curiouser" from *Alice in Wonderland*, the book that seems to describe this case more and more.

"Yup," Wright said with a sigh. " 'Fraid so. Although there's another theory making the rounds."

"Such as?"

"Well, let me preface it by admitting that this theory has already entered the realm of public acceptance, having shown up on an episode of *Miami Vice*."

"Shit, Wright," I said in mock horror, "you're not quoting eighties folk wisdom now, are you?"

"Well, yes and no. I just wanted to get that out of the way so you'd be sure to look at this theory in the worst possible light. Be the most critical, so to speak."

"Why?"

"Tell you in a minute," he said. "Ready for the theory?"

"Shoot."

"Okay, here it is. Balance of payments. Repayment of loans. International high finance . . ."

He paused, so I said, "That's it?"

"Oh, there are lots of details, but that about sums it up. This country owes a whopping amount of cash to some of our federally insured lending institutions. They can't pay off the interest, much less the principal. They do, however, happen to have the coca plant. So they sell cocaine to all the nose-hungry yuppies and showbiz types up in the good ole U.S. of A., and presto—money to repay their debt."

"To subscribe to this theory," I pointed out, "you've got to have somebody looking the other way."

"Absolutely."

"Shit, Wright, that puts the government sitting on its ass watching a bunch of people send their lives down a sinkhole just so Bank of America can get paid off by some corrupt government."

"It do sort of look that way, don't it?"

"You saying you believe it?"

"Well"—he sighed again—"as you so aptly put it, 'plausibler and plausibler.'"

"I'm going to have to think about that one."

"Go ahead. Doesn't much matter which theory you buy into. The fact is that nobody governmental—and nobody personal—seems to be doing much of anything to Mr. Daniel Langer."

That struck home. I was suddenly sad about the

whole affair. Wright looked over at me and said,
"Traffic's not that bad—why the long face?"

"Oh, just because."

"Uh-huh," he said, and went back to looking at the
road. "That the hotel?" he asked.

"What? Oh. That's it."

I drove to a parking space, unmarked, as were most
parking spots in the country, as far as I could tell. We
registered and got us and the bags up to his room.

"Nice," I said. "A whole suite?"

"You bet," Wright said. "I settled a pretty big case, so
I figured I could blow it here."

"So this isn't being done on company funds?"

"Nope. Our fledgling company can't afford it. Yet.
After we settle this Langer thing, I have a feeling we'll
be fighting off the clients."

"Maybe," I said, and turned away to look out the
second-story window.

"Problem? Something about Langer? Natalie?"

"I blew it. I should have gone after him. He drove
right by me. If I had my gun out, I could have shot
him."

"Tell me what happened this time."

I told him. The whole toady mess.

"Sounds like you did the only thing you could do if
your car was out."

"Yeah, but I let him slip away again. Dammit,
Wright, what's so fucking hard about going after a guy
and getting him? Why can't I do a simple thing like
that? Why?"

"Knock that off, Nat. What were you going to
do—run after him up the mountain?"

"I could have gone after him once Rover was fixed."

"And how long did that take?"

"Two days."

"And how long does it take to drive through the
mountain trail?"

"Three days."

"Great," Wright said. "So if you'd gone up after him, you'd still be up there one more day and he might be anywhere."

"Well, yeah, but—"

"And what did you do when you got here?"

"Checked the boat and the camp."

"Right. And any sign of Langer?"

"Not yet."

"Right. So he's still up in the mountains. Probably trying to figure out if it's safe down here."

"The guy on the cycle might have taken him out. Or he could have doubled back again and gone out the other way."

"Natalie, he's got a coke business right here, plus a whole hell of a lot of money hidden away somewhere. Do you think he's going to leave all that? No, if the guy on the motorcycle didn't hit him, he'll be back eventually."

"Well," I said, "what if that did happen? What if Langer's dead?"

"Then we'll just go get the rest of the money and/or bust the coke operation. Either way we can still go back to the States and announce what happened. It'd be better with Langer, but we'll get some local publicity even without him. And if the government tie-in with this case is in any way connected with the White House, we may still get national coverage. And you know what? If we could find just half the money, we could forget about the publicity and still do quite nicely with the insurance settlement. Ten percent of fifteen million is one point five mil. Enough to start a pretty amazing high-tech tec business, wouldn't you say?"

"Yeah, I guess you're right."

"You know it. Now, smile."

I smiled, sort of.

"Eech," he said.

"What?"

"Call that a smile? This is a smile."

He did his terrible Kirk Douglas impression: half
grimace, half bug eyes. It usually made me smile
because Wright was the last man on earth I'd suspect
capable of making stupid faces. This time it wouldn't
work. It wouldn't work. I kept on telling myself that
until . . . it just bubbled up from where it had been
hiding, deep down inside, waiting for an excuse to
escape, to burst out with a rush of tension-releasing
laughter. Let's face it: I cracked up. I caught a glimpse
of Wright through my half-closed eyes. He looked
pleased at the reaction he'd received, yet faintly puzzled, too, because I was approaching a major case of
the jollies, where practically everything produces laughter. There had been too much tension for much too
long, and now I was making up for it—body going
limp while still quaking from chuckles, collapsing on
the bed, giggling like an eight-year-old, just reveling in
the pure pleasure of it all. Wright must have sensed my
enjoyment had a serious therapeutic effect, because he
let me go on at some length without any snide comments. After I stopped shaking, he came over and
crawled up next to me on the bed.

He said, "How you doing?"

"Fine." Giggle.

"Good, good. That was a long time coming."

"Sure was." Half a giggle.

*"I know something else that's been a long time
coming."*

"What?" No giggle.

"Us."

"Us?" I said. "What us? You and me, us?"

"We's the ones," he said.

The kiss had indeed been a long time coming. It was
a long time staying too. Only our faces touched. He

was hunched up on his elbows, I think, and my arms were still holding my slightly aching ribs. But I no longer was aware of ribs. There was only internal excitement, heat, blue sparks, smoothness, caring. Stuff like that. Stuff like you feel on your first kiss with a boy you really like. Only I hadn't had that feeling for fifteen years. Odd to experience it again with an older man. An older man! That's how I thought of Wright! But we're about the same age. No, I'm a schoolgirl again—that's the only explanation for it. In a minute I became adult once more as we slowly, pleasurably brought arms, legs, bodies, and everything into the picture. We hugged a long time, kissed with enough intensity to create new stars in the sky, and gave the gift of loving to each other in as good and clean and nice and downright upright sexy an affair as I've ever known. Everything was beautifully balanced. He was just tender enough to make his strength a joy for me to experience. We moved together in rhythms that no one has ever used before. If love can be a noun and a verb at the same time, we managed that incredible, sensual, sharing feat.

Afterward we lay on our backs, watching the room turn from late afternoon to twilight glow—him flat out, one leg bent at the knee, foot scrunched up under him; me on my side, nestled into his hip and ribs and shoulder. I lightly ran my fingers over his body, up and down, up and down, slowly. I don't know what it did to him, but it sent chills through me from throat to knee.

We whispered and talked in half sentences, not really making any sense at first, just getting the emotional meanings across to each other: I like, I care, I feel, I love.

Gradually the sentences started becoming more normal, and the regular, logical sense of things returned to our conversation. Our voices took on a more *usual tone, although I noticed that both of us were speaking with voices that were deeper and more husky than before. I also noticed that we got sidetracked very easily.*

"So, we're going to go to work on Mr. Langer together?" I asked him.

"I think that's the plan," he said. "It's about time our side did some of the scoring."

"Speaking of scoring," I said. See what I mean about getting sidetracked?

"Yeah," he said with a smile. "You're some score, all right. You know, I could have won a hundred dollars on this."

"What?"

"One of the guys at work was willing to bet a C-note that he'd be the first to get to you."

"Bullshit," I said. "There are only wimps at work."

"Thanks a hell of a lot."

"Besides you, silly."

"That's better."

"Who was making the bet?"

"You don't want to know," Wright said.

"Oh, come on."

"Nope. It's for your own good."

I punched him in the arm.

"Ouch. You got the muscle just right on that one."

"Good. Like another shot?"

"No, no. I give. I'll tell. It was Pat."

"Pat? He's a fat slob, for chrissake."

"Hey," Wright said with mock seriousness, "there has yet to be found in nature something as powerful as the male ego when coupled with delusions of grandeur. When he looks in the mirror, he doesn't see a fat slob. He sees John Wayne."

"Jesus," I muttered.

"Him too."

I thought about it for a moment, then said, "So, did you bet him?"

"No."

"No?"

"I didn't think it was right. Since I wanted to, I thought it wasn't right to make a bet about it. Might make me try to force it. Then, even if I won, I might lose. Better to let it happen naturally, if it was going to happen."

"It happened."

"It did, didn't it?" he said with a smile.

"Yes," I said, smiling back. Something about the conversation stuck in my mind. It hit me all of a sudden, and I said, "Do you realize how many sexual connotations we have had in this little chat?"

"What do you mean?"

"Well, we've had scoring, get to you, and your unfinished sentence, 'I wanted to . . . ' All of which mean sex. Or lovemaking. It's sex for other people. We made love."

"Agreed."

"Lots of sayings about it, aren't there?"

"You mean, like 'the beast with two backs' and sayings like that?" he said.

"Yeah. And the dance with no steps."

"Making it."

"Screwing."

"Okay, if you're going to go that route, there's also fucking."

"Right, and getting in between the sheets."

We continued for a couple of minutes, giggling like school kids.

"Come on. Your turn."

"I'm all out."

"Unacceptable. Never heard that one."

"Very funny."

"Still your turn."

"No, really," he said. *"I don't think I know any more. Honest."*

"You mean, I won?"

"Looks like it."

"You let me win, didn't you?"

"No, Natalie," he said, smiling. *"I don't know any more sexual terms. We've named them all."*

"Every single solitary sexual term?"

"Every term to describe sex in English has been spoken in this bedroom in the last two minutes."

"Wrong, Detective Breath."

"Go ahead, then, Miss Sexual Innuendo. Name three more terms and you could win what's behind door number three."

"I'd rather have what's under this blanket."

"This blanket here?"

"That's the one."

"Right. Blanket number one."

"Of course, it's a small blanket."

"Hey."

"But it was a big blanket when it counted."

"And we'll count it again real soon."

"Ooo, I hope so."

"So, how 'bout it? Three more terms."

"Right. Okay." I took a deep breath and let him have it. *"Hanky-panky, nookie, slap-and-tickle."*

"Very good. I—"

"Going all the way, shacking up, getting some tush, roll in the hay."

"Well, that's—"

"Scratching the itch, jelly-roll, ground rations, jazz, balling, getting a piece, quickie, nooner, poontang, undercover activities."

"Enough already. You—"

"Having your ashes hauled, getting your banana

peeled, jump your bones, homework, pom-pom, cuzzy, play around, futz around, frig."

"Jesus, Nat."

"Pretty good, huh?"

"I didn't know you went to Catholic School."

"I didn't, silly. I just . . . made a study of unusual wordings of a certain activity that occupies the human mind more than it occupies the human body."

"Well," he said lazily, "we'll have to work on bringing the ratio of action to thought back up."

"We'll work on bringing something back up."

"Naughty lady, that's what I've got here."

"Thank you," I told him, most properly. We lay there in silence for a nice long while. Long enough for some semblance of seriousness to come back to us.

"You know," he said at last, "we do have a kind of weird case here."

"Langer, you mean?"

"Yes," he said, "I don't mean us. We're *really* weird, not *kind* of weird."

"We sure are," I agreed.

"Langer," he went on, "the CIA, the motorcycle boys, the Russians, the Canadians, the way money is flowing—or is not flowing. I keep telling myself that there's thirty million dollars floating around somewhere and that we should be able to figure out where it is."

"I know where some of it is," I said. "Unless Langer's moved it to a Swiss bank vault or something."

"What do you mean?"

I told him about the figures I'd read from the CIA's analysis of Langer's boat. About how the indications of mass and density didn't look right for the centerboard. That something was hidden in the centerboard.

"The centerboard?" Wright said. "Come on, Nat. That's the first place anybody would look."

"Hey," I said back to him, "consider who we're dealing with here."

"Okay, it's true they don't sound too bright, but they certainly must have looked at the bottom of the ship below decks. If there was a way to open up the centerboard, they'd have seen it."

"All I know is what I read on those reports," I said, "and that centerboard has something inside that's not supposed to be there."

"Well, let's go find out."

"How?"

"Let's take a look at that centerboard. From what you told me, everybody seems to be going on and off that boat."

"Wright, they're not going to let us on it."

"Maybe not, but they'd let two investigators from the World Health Organization climb aboard."

"WHO?"

"Right," said Wright. "WHO. Your quarantine caper will work just as well down here. We'll get Fend to send some bogus WHO cables talking about some potential epidemic or something—"

"AIDS is a hot topic right now," I broke in.

"Yeah, AIDS will do just fine, and then you and I will present ourselves as the American experts in the WHO, and as such, we'll just have to board that boat. After all, didn't it come down here from that wicked city of San Francisco?"

"So, when do we put this stunning plan into action?"

"Let's call Fend right now."

Twenty-three

THE GUYS THEY left guarding the camp up above
Chimbote were worthless. I rolled right into the place,
snorting up a cloud or two of the pure stuff, strung out
like Texas barbed wire and twice as tough, floating
inside the car, gliding out the door, feet barely touching the ground, swinging the evil, burping automatic
gun around to cut those two stupid ugly geeks into
little pieces of blood and bone. No flesh left, I thought.
Eaten away forever by the bullets. Great fun, watching
the bodies twitch and dance as they went spattering
into the dust.

"Assholes," I said. "Didja think you could get me
by just hanging around here? Is that what you thought,
you stinking slimeheads?" Their souls did not reply. I
fired every round left in the Uzi, at the bodies, at the
buildings, in the air. "God, that's loud," I said.

I climbed up into the main building. Somebody had
cleaned up since the last time I had been in here, but
they didn't bother to make things very neat. It made

no difference because I was going to sleep for about a day and a half, then move the whole operation to Lima. Live in one of the tourist hotels with plenty of protection and lots of flunkies to do the dirty work of the business. My big mistake was in trying to manage the whole thing myself. Stupid. Like taking the cash and coke in the car. Get it the hell over to the banks where it belongs. Let the respectable people use their energy to guard it, raise interest on it, invest it. My basic problem was in not believing the reality of the millions in the Swiss accounts. Like the cash I've got here is the only reality of my success. Bullshit. If I put the money into the establishment's banks, I'll get the backing of the establishment.

Yeah, I'll get the whole thing working right in a couple of days. Now for some sleep. I found the messy bed, swept the dusty blankets off onto the floor, and collapsed, facedown, on the mattress pad.

Damn. I was too tired to fall asleep. I kept shifting my body around, trying to find a position in which the muscles would let go, allowing me to drift off into some much-needed rest. It must be the lack of downers. The kid kept them, and now I only had the hop-up effects of the coke working on me. Christ, at this rate I might as well get up, head into town, and begin setting up things the way I wanted. That did it: I fell into a fitful doze.

The dream came back. Flying over rooftops, watching flames burst out the tops of buildings, ash-black smoke roiling upward, coming closer, closer, then enveloping my face, cutting off my air, blinding me, sending me falling toward the crackling roar of the flame-sheets as pieces of human debris shot out of the darkness to strike my body, my face, my mouth, just as the tips of the liquid fire storm seared my skin, making it crack, split, burn, bubble, and—

"Wake up."

Jesus! My whole body convulsed and I was awake. My mouth was like ashes, and my skin was full of sweat.

"That's better."

"Wha? Hunh!" I jumped at the sound of his voice, again at the muffled sound of my own voice, and yet again at the sight of him.

"You and me's going to have a little talk. Right?" he said.

"Who the fuck are you?" I heard myself say.

"Don't make no difference," he said. "Let's talk about the coke and the money."

The guy was at the foot of my storm-tossed bed. I had an eerie feeling of déjà vu. A man, dressed in leather clothes, standing in my bedroom. Jesus, it had happened before.

"We did this already," I mumbled to him.

"I asked you about the coke and the money."

"No, you didn't."

He had the gun out faster than I thought possible. "I want to know about the stuff," he said, "or I'm going to try out this thing on various parts of your body."

I had déjà vu again. The guy in the warehouse! Jesus, ever since I started this thing, people were pointing guns and making threats. I just gotta get me a good organization, with protection built into the plan. But right now I had an immediate problem with this guy and his very ugly 7.65-mm Beretta.

"Did you hear me?" he said, his voice turning as ugly as his weapon. "I'm going to put one of these into one of your feet. Maybe shoot a couple of toes clean off. If you live, you'll never stand up without a cane."

Time for the scared bit again. "Yeah! I—I heard you. It's just, uh, don't shoot, man. I'll tell you anything you want."

He liked the sound of that. I know because his voice went back to the smooth, jive talk tones he used before. "That's more like it. Now, what did you do with the thirty million?"

"Well, half of it is under the surface of the ocean," I said. Which was true, if not entirely accurate.

"And the other half?"

"Uh, you're not going to believe this," I said.

"Try me."

"Don't react badly to this, but it's out in the car." I said it as matter-of-factly as I knew how, but I still saw his jaw tighten. If his trigger finger did the same, things would be getting messy. "Careful," I said, "don't shoot. I'll show you if you want."

"This is bullshit," he said.

"No, really."

"Come off it. Nobody's going to drive around in the Andes in that stupid car with fifteen million bucks in it."

"Maybe it was dumb. I mean, I felt pretty stupid about it a couple of times. But maybe that's why it worked. You know? Nobody expected it." Got to get him thinking about it. Got to get my feet up and under me. I shifted on the bed, groaning as if my whole body were in pain. I sucked air through clenched teeth. A nice dramatic effect, I thought.

"What's with you?" he asked.

I liked that. Sympathy. Just what I needed. "Did you see the bodies outside?"

"Yeah. Disgusting."

"I shot them because those little buggers cracked me a couple of times with their gun butts. I think"— hissing in air again—"they broke some ribs." I made with the aches and pains again, managing to pull my legs up farther while slumping my torso to the side.

"Tough," he said, but didn't seem to mean it. "We'll come back to the money in a minute. What about the coke?"

"Well, the whole operation is done in one of the

valleys a few miles from here. I don't have much to do with that part of it. I'm strictly finance and overseas distribution."

"How's it work?"

"Easy. Driver to a drop point in Lima. Embassy flunky takes it inside. Diplomatic pouch to Canada. Canada to the U.S. by rail. Then regular dealers from there on out."

"And the payment?"

"Straight to Switzerland. And, of course, a percentage to the embassy boys."

"So a new man could just take over the whole thing down here?"

I hadn't thought of that. I better give him something to think about so he didn't just start blasting away. "Well," I told him, "the Russians may not like it if someone they don't know comes into the picture."

"From what you say, they'll never miss you."

"Well, I deal with them socially, and we touch base on the business end of things. Hell, just before the big shoot-out up here, they were trying to expand the operation into other parts of the world."

"You call two greasers a big shoot-out?"

"Oh, not these two," I said. "We had about thirty people shot up here not too long ago." I moaned and got my feet a little more under me.

"I think I'll take my chances with the reds," he said, smiling. "Now, let's go back to the money."

"What about it? It's yours, man. Take it. Just don't shoot." More groans. Feet an inch or two closer to my launching point.

"Where the fuck is it?"

"I told you, man. It's out in the car. Jesus, I'll show you, like I said. I know how stupid it sounds, but there's fifteen million dollars in the trunk, in the seats, under the floorboards, and in packets fastened up under the fenders and engine compartment of that car. That piece of junk out there is the most expensive compact car in the history of the world."

He paused, considering it. Now would have been a great time to make a move, but he was still down at the end of the bed. Too far away. I had to get him closer.

"Come on," he said. "Let's go take a look at your car."

"Okay," I said. I started to lean forward, preparing to get up from the bed, but then I made my body go stiff and let out a scream.

"The fuck?" he said, grabbing his gun with both hands, ready to fire.

"Oh shit, oh Jesus," I said, really laying it on thick. "Shit, I can't move. God, it hurts." My face was distorted with pain.

He just stared at me for a moment, slowly coming out of the crouch he had automatically assumed when my scream startled him. Then he said, slowly, putting an edge into his voice, "Maybe you didn't hear me. I said, let's go look at your car. Now, asshole."

"I'm trying to. Oh, Jesus!" I rocked forward, then stiffened straight up, grabbing my sides with both arms. I half screamed this time, as if really trying to bear up under the pain, got my feet under me on the bed, pushed up a little, then let myself overbalance and fall over to lean against the headboard. As I hit the wooden support I gave out with a minor convulsion and sucked lots more air through my teeth.

"Listen," he said, coming around the end of the bed, "if you think I'm leaving you in here while I go out to that car, you're crazy. Now, I don't give a shit about your ribs. You're getting up out of there, pain or no pain."

He reached down to stick the gun in my face and grab the front of my shirt with his other hand. Ahhh, perfect. I swung both arms outward from my sides, one knocking the gun off-target, the other slapping him across the face. At the same instant I was pushing off the bed with both legs, putting my shoulder into his neck, giving it a good snap. He made a major mistake at this point—I mean, besides falling for my act with the sore ribs. He thought his best bet was to use the gun. So he tried fighting me off in order to bring the gun back far enough to get off a shot. But since I was right on top of him, my arm over his, I just kept it trapped there, out behind me where he couldn't do much damage. I knew I wouldn't be able to maintain this position, but while he was momentarily shaken from taking a shoulder right under the jaw, I concentrated on putting a fist on his chin.

The way to find the button: Hit on the end of the chin, slightly to one side. Oddly enough, it's best if your fist is traveling in a slightly downward arc. That's a mistake lots of bar fighters make, trying to drive their fists up into their opponent's face. I got the button on the second attempt. There was that sweet feeling of knuckles and wrist and forearm all working together as one perfect lever, a beautifully oiled extension of upper arm, shoulder, and torso. I saw his eyes glaze after the lower jaw click-clacked up against the other skull parts, sending a jarring, blackout-inducing message to the brain. Like in many boxing matches, the knockout took effect after his last muscular action had started, so he went on struggling for a second, during which I hit him once more. The last blow just sent him to the floor faster than gravity would have done.

I removed the gun from him, frisked his limp body, and came up empty. I pulled the soiled sheet from the rumpled bedding and went to soak it in the shower. I took some time to coax the water to flow. Lots of hissing and spitting and rumbling of the pipes. While I was fooling with the taps it occurred to me that

Leather Boy might get to waking up, so I took a peek
at him, and sure enough, I had to tap his noggin again.
Finally I got the sheet soaked through and through
and wrapped it around him good and tight. Now I
could let him wake up.

Which he did. He went through the standard
struggles—yells, pleading, and the like. I smiled and
went to get some breakfast and the first freeze of the
day. When I came back to him, I found he had been
able to roll across the floor but couldn't loosen the
sheet. The two belts I had used to fasten the sheet
probably had something to do with it.

"You look like a mummy," I said to him.

"Fuck you."

I reached down and pinched his cheeks. "Such a
nice boy." I said. "Such a nice, nice boy." I gave him
an extra-hard pinch on each "nice." He tried to roll
away from me. I smiled and moved closer to him.
"Aww, don't turn away, nice boy." Another pinch.

"Stop it," he snarled, and tried to bite me.

"Don't be a bad boy," I said, slapping his face on
the *bad*. He rolled into me, probably hoping he could
bring me down to where he could bite something vital.
"Ohhhh," I said, "that's a very, very bad boy." I
kicked him on each *very*.

"You asshole," he yelled.

"A very, very, *very* bad boy. Now lie still, unless you
want me to explain your behavior some more."

"You're crazy," he whispered.

"Crazy? No, I don't think so." Was I crazy? Why
did he say that? I thought about it for a moment or
two. What's the matter with everyone these days
anyway? Fuck them! I was fine. It's these creeps who
are screwed up. This guy was just like the girl, trying
to mess me around in the head with crazy talk. But I
could show this one who's in total control, just like I
showed the girl. I smiled and looked down at him.

"Wh-what are you going to do?" he said.

"Talk."

"Talk?"

"That's right," I said. "We're going to converse. I'm going to ask you questions. You're going to answer. When I don't like the answers, I'm going to punish you. Do you understand?"

He understood. We had a nice long chat. I found out that he was Lace, or Ace, of Leather and Lace, the other two being Stu "Leather" Throckton and Andy something. The geek was actually proud of having a nickname in the underworld. That's how far he'd come, you see, all the way to being part of a muscle trio who maybe made a couple of hundred for knocking heads or scaring some suburbanites who had gotten behind on their payments to the bookmaker.

I also found out that he was the "brains" of the bunch, as he was the only one who knew that Greschke was behind them in their attempt to find me. Greschke, the only one of the Frisco bigwigs I never did get to see. Seems the old guy was in on it from the beginning.

I also found out a little something about the detectives who were following me. The guy was named Wright. Big. Smart. Worked with some high-tech, newfangled security firm. Also worked free-lance. He was with a girl, or the girl was here first. The girl wasn't so big. But built. Also smart. Able to handle herself too. She took some heavy muscle whom Falkes had hired and put him in the hospital. And there was talk that she was the one who broke the fingers of that dinkhead Mexican muscle, Humphrey or Humpback or whatever the fuck Tinkertoy name they had down here. For just a split second I wondered about the girl—the runaway. Could she have been this female detective? But that was . . . crazy. No way could that have been true. Stupid even to consider it.

We had run out of things to say to each other. I had no more questions. He had no more answers. The silence seemed to build up and also heat up. The room got very . . . tense. You could hear the water dripping from the faucet in the other room where I had soaked the sheet. My finely trussed-up leather-clad friend was squirming slightly down there on the floor.

"Uh," he said after a couple more minutes of twitching and sliding.

"What?" I said. I expected some elaborate ruse from him to try to sucker me into a compromising position.

"I have to go to the bathroom," he said.

When I got through laughing, I said, "Go ahead. You don't think I'd sleep in those sheets after you'd been in 'em, do you?" I laughed some more.

"It ain't funny, man," he complained.

But that only made me laugh louder. Eventually I settled down and considered his plight. And mine. I was on my way to setting up the kind of organization I should have had in the first place. He didn't fit into the plan. I said to him, "You'd feel better if I relieved you of your, ah, burden?"

"I'd sure appreciate it, man."

"Uh-huh," I said. I tried out his Beretta. It worked just fine.

Twenty-four

The bay was choppy and the air cool as Wright and I climbed aboard Langer's boat, accompanied by the fat, dim-witted harbormaster and three policemen.

"No need to waste your time or that of your men," Wright said, back at the dock. Time, however, was one thing these guys could easily afford to waste. They wanted to come along. We then tried talking up the horrors of AIDS, thinking they'd be put off. No dice. They didn't look exactly pleased about the situation, but they weren't about to stay behind and let us go aboard alone.

We all stood uneasily on the aft deck of the ship, wondering what to do. The breeze made lapels flap and ties flutter. It was at that point that Wright pulled his capper.

"This is where we'll take your blood when we're through with our search of the boat."

"Blood?" came the startled reply of one of the policemen. "Take our blood?"

"That's right," Wright said easily, throwing open a

small case containing a hypodermic needle and syringe. "Oh, don't worry," *he said, smiling,* "I have plenty of needles." *With that he flipped out a plastic packet containing about two dozen individually wrapped needles.*

"I do not understand," *the man said, clearly bothered by this turn of events. His friends, some of whom were not happy about this venture anyway, looked apprehensive.*

Wright and I quickly hammered home our point: If you go on the tour of the boat, you get the vampire treatment. Only we put it a bit more diplomatically than that, as befits two upstanding members of the World Health Organization. After conferring—well, muttering would be a better word—among themselves, it was decided that they would remain in the aft section of the boat while we went and gathered our evidence.

On this last point we were a bit unsure of ourselves. Just what, exactly, were we supposed to be gathering? The AIDS story worked fine so far, but since it is transmitted via blood or semen, what would we show as our evidence?

"Don't worry about it," *Wright had said when I raised the subject.* "Everybody's so scared of this thing, they'll believe anything an official tells them. We could grab a toothbrush, a box of tissues, and a couple of record albums, and they'd go along with it."

"Record albums?" *I said.*

"The important thing," *he went on,* "is that we look sharp, be suspicious of everything, and be very, very boring when we talk to anyone."

"Record albums?"

"We'll say that laboratory analysis of the dead skin cells that we remove from the toothbrush will be 'very significant.'"

"Record albums?"

"Stop saying that," he said. "Then we'll discuss the 'latent germinal remains' on the tissue box, which will 'point us toward legitimate conclusions' in this area."

"And the record albums?"

"I'm getting to that, dammit. The record albums, uh, will, um . . ."

"I'm with you so far."

"Okay, I've got it. The plastic grooves trap oils from the hands, and that will 'prove invaluable in formulating a scientific profile of the users of the boat.'"

"Uh-huh."

"Come on, Nat," he said. "It'll work fine."

"Depends on how stupid they are."

"No, it depends on how brilliantly we deliver our lines. With the proper playing of our parts, we will cause them to suspend disbelief."

So here we were on the boat, poking around pseudoscientifically. Or I was, anyway. Wright made his way below decks to get at the centerboard. I went around the rooms slowly, making notes on a clipboard and gathering samples of this and that, which I duly noted, labeled, and stored in small plastic bags. By accident I came across one of the CIA bugs when I was fooling around with the cabinet to the wireless set. I glanced back at the men who were standing morosely on the rear deck, but they were not paying me any attention (I like to believe that's because they couldn't see into the cabin due to the light shining on the glass). I glanced back down at the bug. Should I? I shrugged. And then I took it, labeled it ("air-sensing device"), and put it into one of my little bags.

After what seemed like a long time, Wright appeared at the cabin door. He hissed at me; I moved slowly over to him and looked a question. He pointed down, and indicated I was to follow. Here's where things could get tricky. We couldn't both be out of sight for too long *because we didn't know if or how long the men would wait. And we couldn't talk unless we didn't mind having the CIA pick up what we said.*

Wright led me into the darkness below decks. The centerboard assembly was recognizable only as a dim outline. Wright switched on a couple of torches and quickly opened the barely concealed false top to the assembly. He motioned for me to take a peek. I saw a couple of rows of what appeared to be videotapes. Wright picked one up, turned the cover toward the light, and showed me the crude, rude photo reproduction of an overweight woman in some sort of sexual ecstasy with what appeared to be the head of a buffalo.

Before I could react, Wright quickly removed most of the tapes, inserted a piece of wire into the "floor" of this secret compartment, and hooked something within. The bottom of the compartment sprung upward about two inches. Wright motioned me to look from a certain angle as he slowly lifted open this compartment within a compartment. At first I could see only darkness. Then a shaft of light struck green engraving. I looked closer and saw portraits and the names Franklin, McKinley, and Cleveland. These august individuals, as I'm sure you know, adorn the fronts of the U.S. hundred, five-hundred, and thousand-dollar bills. I was looking at cash. Oodles of it.

Wright was still not opening the compartment more than a few inches. I looked up at him and he pointed at a corner of the opening. Barely perceptible in the half-light was a thin wire embedded in the wall. I watched as Wright used a fingernail to scoop up part of the wall. Then he did it again on the bottom of compartment, next to the stacks of cash. I noticed he was very careful to alternate hands, and each sample was given to me to place in separate plastic bags.

He carefully closed the entire assembly, replacing the porn videos first. We made our way up through the ship and rejoined the group of puzzled and irritable men on the aft deck.

"Through?" one of them said, not bothering to disguise his hopefulness.

"Through," said Wright. We made as if to leave. They didn't move.

"What about your blood tests?" the man asked us.

"We did that already," Wright said to him smoothly. "When we were inside," he added, pointing over his shoulder at the main cabin.

"Really? Excuse me, but we did not notice you doing any taking of blood."

Wright stared at the man and never blinked. He said slowly, "Are you impugning the veracity of my statement?"

"I do not understand."

"Are you questioning my methodology?"

"I am questioning you about your blood test."

"Do you have laboratory facilities with you?" Wright asked contemptuously.

"What?"

"I didn't think so. Which means you will not mind our taking our evidence, along with our blood samples, back to our own facilities." And with that Wright swept the plastic bags, the notes, and the two vials of blood past the suspicious eyes of the official. "Now that we have settled that issue," Wright went on, "may we repair to the dock?" He had blood!

"Yes, yes, of course," the man said, clearly defeated.

"Thank you," Wright said dryly.

On the way back I caught Wright's eye at one point when his back was to the men. Without moving any other part of his body, Wright gave me a slow, lazy, almost lascivious wink. I glanced away quickly, as it was difficult to keep from going into the jollies again.

We left the little group of dour men at the dock and made our way to the hotel. I held my fingers to my lips,

*and we made the trip in silence, even up the elevator,
down the hall, and into the room. I brought out our
"evidence" and showed the bug to Wright. He nodded
and tilted his head toward the other room. I left the bug
and followed him.*

"You bringin' bugs into our rooms, girl," he said.

"I know," I said, hanging my head. "I'm sorry."

"The nerve," he said.

"It'll never happen again."

"Well, I should hope not."

*We looked into each other's eyes and smiled at our
mock serious dialogue. "What was that?" I said.
"Some forties movie or a supermarket romance
novel?"*

*"Oh, the flick, I think," Wright said. "So tell me
about the bug. You get it on the boat?"*

"You bet."

"You think it's still receiving at the other end?"

*"I don't know, but we're not really that far from the
harbor. I don't know if we want to use it, but I couldn't
resist. If you don't want to do anything with it, I'll just
give them the whistle and then we can toss it out."*

"The whistle?"

*"You know," I said, "blast a horn or something right
up close to the thing. It'll make them turn off their
volume buttons."*

"Tear 'em off, you mean."

"Whatever."

*"I've got a better idea. You know how the hotel
restaurant plays that terrible Muzak shit all the time?
Let's stick the bug up in the ceiling next to one of the
speakers."*

"Sounds good to me. No pun intended."

"Okay, we'll do it after lunch."

*"Great. Now, what was wired into the box holding
the cash? Another bug?"*

"I wish it was," Wright said. "No, it's a detonator."

"There's a bomb on the ship?"

"'Fraid so. We can have that plastique analyzed if you like, but I think we'll find it's one of the binary explosives."

"Like Triex?"

"Yeah. Or Quadrex, or one of the others." Wright looked pensive for a moment, then said, "We could arrange a little experiment with the samples I scraped out of there. At least I think we could."

"Like what?" I said. I didn't like the sound of this. The last time Wright got pensive, a certain individual back in San Francisco just suddenly disappeared. It seems that nobody much missed this certain individual, least of all the local citizens who had been receiving lots of pressure from this individual, pressure in the form of having their pets slaughtered, their homes and cars vandalized, and their families threatened. But still, it was uncanny that, after it developed that no legal action could be taken against this individual, Wright became very pensive (one of his friends was among the citizens feeling the pressure), and then the individual just up and vanished and suddenly Wright was no longer pensive at all. He was, well, content probably would be the word. Thoughtful but content. So when Wright was now looking pensive and more than a little thoughtful, and he was on the subject of explosives, you can see that this could spell danger for somebody. Binary explosives were particularly neat and nasty things. Comprised of two parts, each of which was perfectly harmless on its own, the two, when brought together, formed a potent force for blowing things into oblivion.

"Look, Wright-man," I said, "let's just hang on to the samples for the time being. We can try putting them together later on if we're forced into it. Okay?"

"Yeah, okay."

"I take it that you can't get the money out unless you defuse the bomb?"

"That's just it," he said. "I don't know. It sort of looks like you could open it up good and wide as long as you didn't snap that wire."

"But 'sort of' is a little too close for comfort when you've got binary explosive in there."

"You got that right," he said. "Still, it sure looked like someone had opened it up by putting something against that upper panel. Something that would prevent the edge of the false bottom from slicing into the hidden wire."

"False bottom, hidden wire, compartment within a compartment. Jesus," I said.

"Yeah, I know. Kind of describes the whole case, doesn't it?"

"Yes," I said. "It does, indeed."

"I wonder," Wright went on, "if I could defuse that thing."

"Come on. You don't know anything about explosives, do you?"

"Well . . ."

"Do you?" I insisted.

"Ah, in a word, no."

"Okay, then."

"But now's a good time to learn."

"Excuse me, but wouldn't it be better to learn in theory first, then put theory into practice?"

"Aw, Natalie, that's the old-fashioned way. Here we've got the perfect opportunity to combine theory and practice. It could be a big breakthrough for investigative science."

"Sure. An explosive breakthrough."

"Right. We could get a bang out of it."

"That's weak, Wright. Very weak."

"Sorry."

"*You're forgiven.*" Suddenly I was tired of the banter, tired of the scams, tired of the case. "*Wright? Let's get out of here.*"

"*Lunch? Time to plant the bug?*"

"*We can do that, if you want. No, what I mean is, let's grab some sandwiches and just get out of the city for a while. Maybe drive up into the mountains. Just get away for a couple of hours.*"

"*A picnic? Okay, why not?*" he said. "*You order up the grub. I'm going to change my shirt, stick the bug in the restaurant speaker, and grab some beers. Meet you at the car in half an hour.*"

The view of the city was unreal. It looked too close to us, too sparkling clean. I felt we could just step down to the harbor from a mile up. Of course, the beer probably helped some, but there was no denying the spectacular scenic wonders.

"*Pretty,*" Wright said.

"*That doesn't begin to cover it, darling,*" I said.

"*Do I sense a bit of sarcasm?*"

"*Very perceptive.*"

"*Bitch.*"

"*And that doesn't begin to cover it, either,*" I said with a smile.

"*Oh? Oh, okay. Bitch goddess—how's that?*"

"*Drink your beer.*"

We drank and munched and drank and watched seabirds float on the updraft, dancing in front of us. At one point Wright tore off a piece of bread and tossed it out and up. One of the birds gently banked, swooped, lunged deftly, and took the tidbit right in its beak. Two dips of the head, two gulps, and the bread was in the bird's belly with barely a flap of its wing. We both broke into applause.

"*All right!*"

"*That was great. Do it again.*"

"No, your turn," he said.

"Okay, here." I threw two pieces at once, and we were treated to the same aerial display, only this time involving several birds.

"Whoa, they're going to fight over the scraps," I said.

"Sort of like people," Wright said.

"And life itself." I fell back into my former mood. "Shit."

"What?"

"Oh, it's just all fucked."

"What is, Nat? Life?"

"Yeah. Life. This business. Everything. You know that what we're doing here isn't going to make any difference? You know that, don't you?"

"I know that," he said quietly.

"Well, that's screwed."

"I suppose so."

"Doesn't that bother you?" I said.

"Yes. It bothers me. It bothers me that no matter what we do, we'll never stop the coke traffic. We might shut down this particular bunch of people, but others will take their place." He paused a moment and looked right into my eyes. "But I'm going to get that son of a bitch. And embarrass the Russians. And change the locals. Because it's all I can do right now. And if I find something else to do, I'll move into that, whatever it is. Because it's all we've got."

I just looked at him for a while. For anybody that would have been quite a speech. For Wright it was a manifesto. "I love you," I said quietly.

He looked shocked. "I thought that was just a word we used, Natalie."

"I guess it has been," I said. "For too long it was just a word."

"I love you, Natalie. Always have. In case you didn't know."

We hugged as if to crush bones. It felt damn fine. We rolled over on our blanket, and for just one split second we thought to chance a public action of a very private affair; but modesty prevailed. We lay there, breathing hard and not noticing it. I had ended up on top, and I just relaxed all over. It was so nice to feel the solid muscle and sinew of this big man's body stretching out under me. I could have gone to sleep, but—

"You get a bit heavy with all your deadweight on my hotel keys," Wright said.

"Wright! Talk about spoiling a mood."

"Well, how do you think my hip feels about this great mood, girl?"

"How's that?" I said, sliding to one side.

"Better."

"And that?"

"Fine."

"And this?"

"Hey!"

"Umm," I said. "All man."

"Careful, woman, or I'll have to grab me some of your good stuff."

"Promises, promises."

He did grab me then, but it wasn't what you think; we enjoyed one of those solid kisses, the kind that combine with a bear hug and seem to put you inside each other. God, it was so incredibly perfect to have passion and love and lust and giving and taking all wrapped up in one package. We just lay there for a good long while, looking at the clouds. White against neon-blue skies, with a sun that threatened to burn through it all, made pleasant by cool breezes drifting up the mountainside.

"You know what they call this place?" I said.

"Chimbote?"

"No, I mean Peru. It's called the Empire of the Sun."

"Oh," he said.

"Try not to be overly impressed, dear."

"Sorry. Empire of the Sun. Wow. Poetry, sheer poetry. Tell me more, Miss Information, tell me more."

"I'll get you for this."

"Oh, I hope so."

"But, really, Wright, this is pretty special land here. You know, these mountains reach all the way to the start of the Amazon jungle. Or rather, the Amazon reaches the Andes."

"Weeeeellllll," he said, stretching, "I saw that on the map, but it didn't really register, I guess."

"And the Andes are connected with our Rocky Mountains, did you know that?"

"You made that up."

"No, silly boy. If you'd read your tourist-information guide in your hotel room, you'd know these things."

"And just when, dear sexy lady, have I had time to read in my hotel room?"

"Good point," I said, smiling.

"All right, then. Pray continue with your facts, Miss Information."

"Stop calling me Misinformation."

"Ow," he said.

"What happened?" I said.

"Nothing, yet. But whenever you use that tone, you punch me in the arm."

"Smartass," I said, and punched him in the arm.

"See?" he said.

I smiled some more. I was doing a lot of smiling since Wright arrived. I rolled over and rested my chin on my hands, elbows digging into the blanket. "You know, Wright, most field operations don't have profit potential like this one."

"Don't I know it."

"I guess you do. You make more money with your

attorney work than through the gumshoe stuff. Why do you do it?"

"Because it pays so well."

"What? No, I meant, why do you do fieldwork?"

"Oh. Because. I like it."

"If we recover the money and put it into our agency—"

"Your agency," he said. *"You have the headaches of running it, not me."*

"We'll see," I said. *"If we recover the money and put it into the agency, it's going to wind up as computerized and corporate-oriented as F. J.'s. You know that, don't you?"*

Wright sighed and said, "I suppose I do."

"Do you think it'll be all right? I mean, me running things in the office?"

"Yes, I do." He sat up in one fluid movement. *"You're fine out in the field, Nat, but you're better at handling people and getting good work out of them than anybody I've ever seen. And you like digging with the computer. I've seen you at it. You act all in awe of Fend and some of the keyboard jockeys, but when you go at it yourself, you're pretty damn good."*

"Well, thanks, but—"

"Besides," he continued, *"there'll always be some field stuff you can do, just to keep your hand in."*

"Sure, but don't—"

"Hell, we can even do some field stuff together if you like. You're a good partner." He grinned and added, *"In more ways than one."*

"Okay, but what about the seminars and all that shit?"

"Damn. I was hoping you'd forget about that."

"No way, Jose."

"You don't like that gig, either?"

"Hate it."

"So hire someone else to do it."

"Like a public-relations guy?"

"Or gal. More women in P.R. these days."

"Well, I'll have enough convincing to do about my being a woman without the problem of a gal P.R. rep. No," I said, slowly batting my eyelashes, *"I believe what I need is a strong, virile, handsome man to appear on behalf of my agency. A rugged guy but with plenty of brains. A former Rhodes scholar, perhaps, and someone who—"*

"Forget it."

"Oh, come on, Wright. It couldn't be any worse than dealing with your lawyers."

"Yes, it could. God, I never thought I'd say that."

We looked at clouds some more. Were these the same clouds from a few minutes ago but in new shapes? Or were they completely new clouds, the others having scooted off to another part of the sky? We couldn't tell, and the visible vapor was mute on the subject.

"Wright?" I said after a while.

"Mmrf?" he said.

"Do you think everything that happens is supposed to happen?"

"You mean, as in predestination? No."

"Neither do I," I said. *"At least I don't think I do."*

"Sometimes," he said, *"I believe a supreme being started all of this in motion. But I also sometimes think we're an experiment that has gone wrong. Or that that supreme being has lost interest."*

"Maybe we just can't see the whole picture. We may not know what the experiment is supposed to prove."

"Could be, Nat. In any case, I don't think there's a master plan for our actions. The random happenings of things sometimes look like someone planned them, so people call it 'the hand of fate' or something like that."

"Or providence."

"Or divine intervention."

"Kismet."

"Oh, not word games again."

"Yup," I said. "Come on, your turn."

"Happenstance."

"Deus ex machina."

"Wait. That's 'God by machine,' which is man-made. That proves my point."

"Oh. Right. Uh, chance."

"No, we don't have to continue now that you've missed one."

"Yes, we do. Come on, Wright. I said 'chance.'"

"Remember in The Gay Divorcee where Fred Astaire is going to say to Ginger Rogers, 'Chance is the fool's name for fate'?"

"You're changing the subject."

"You're right. And how that funny little Italian man kept running around saying the code phrase wrong?"

"I remember," I said. "He says, 'Fate is a foolish thing to take chances with' to one woman, who looks at him and says, 'so are you.'"

"Right. And he also says, 'Fate is a foolish thing— take a chance.' Well, that's my philosophy of life. Fate is a foolish thing. You can't count on it. You just have to try to make your own fate. You have to take a chance."

"Like you did with that bulletproof vest?"

"Well, sort of. Although I was thinking more of the big picture, as you call it. Big moves. Like our coming down here, for instance."

"It was a bit chancy, wasn't it?"

"A bit iffy, yes."

"So what are we going to make of this chance?" I asked him.

"Well, let's nail that sucker Langer and mop up the rest of the jokers in this thing."

"That's what we've been trying to do."

"Sure, but with a fairly legal procedure, so we could get the publicity. Let's just take out Langer. Then we can get everybody else."

"How's that?" I said.

"With Langer gone, we'll have the one thing that'll bring everyone running. The operation itself. Why, we could even pretend not to know what's on that boat and, as duly unelected non-representatives of the World Health Organization, we could auction it off. That would probably get lots of interesting bids."

"One thing, Wright."

"What's that, cute one?"

"Are we selling the boat and its entire contents?"

"Of course."

"I mean, as it now stands, or lies, or lays, or whatever boats do. The whole works?"

"Sure. Why not?"

"Well, there is a bomb on board."

"No!" he said, his mouth dropping open. "Not really. Gosh, that would make it considerably more valuable, wouldn't it?"

"Just be sure of one thing, wise guy."

"And that would be?"

"Sell the boat to the bad guys. When it goes boom, we don't want to murdalize some innocent tuna fisherman."

"Oh, we'll get it in the right hands, all right. That's the fun of it: seeing it go boom to all the proper parties." He paused, cocked his head to one side, then said, "I haven't heard 'murdalize' since junior high school."

"That's a good one, isn't it? Like creamacrush and stone-whip."

"You made those up, Natalie."

"I did not. I'll bet you know ones that are just as

stupid and just as real."

He looked off at the horizon and was silent.

"Well, don't you?" I asked.

Wright turned and said, " 'Boom' is good enough for me."

Twenty-five

I DON'T KNOW what's the matter with people anymore. Jesus, you'd think it'd be obvious that things would go better if they just *listened* to what I want.

Jesus. That's not so hard, is it?

Take the runaway, for instance. She had it easy with me. All the freeze she wanted. All the money she needed. Shit, she could buy everything. And nearly did, the little bitch. As for the sex, that was her idea. If she had wanted to stop for a while, or go slower, that would've been okay. I could've gotten the other women myself. Or Manuel or Jorge or Humberto could've done it. No, Humberto's in the hospital. And Manuel's dead. But that's not the fucking point here. The point is, somebody would've been around to take care of all the shit I need. She wouldn't have had to lift a finger once we got back off the mountain. Everything always works out when you've got money.

So I didn't go to Lima. So what if I stayed here in this Chim-bott place? I live like a king. The runaway was too stupid to deserve this. Too stupid to go on living. But that's all behind me. Now I'm on my way to something great. Fun. Relaxation. Girls. No more of that shithead stuff, like trying to manage a greedy bunch of greaseballs. Let Carlos take care of that. Me, I'll just lay on the protection and take my life of ease. Shit, we got this sucker up to nearly half a million a month right now. That crack or rock, as some of 'em called it, was just great. Brings the price down per hit. Gets a whole bunch of new users. Gets 'em hooked faster. Uses up more of the coke in the long run. Like I said, great. We use the Russians just like before, plus now we got some new deal going down with the Mexicans. And also, I've not been lying when I said "the organization" wants something done a certain way. Because now there really is an organization.

Carlos has a relative who is helping us arrange things with the U.S. Foreign Trade Office. I can't believe it. We're about to get federal protection on our scam. That Carlos has well-connected relatives. Actually Carlos has about a hundred and fifty relatives, most of 'em on the payroll by now. They're helpful for a fee. But this latest bit is outstanding. The feds—on my side! Something about aiding Third World debt financing. Which is crap talk. I know it all comes down to the old profit motive. Uncle Sam wants his taste of the green, even if it comes from the white stuff. I think the red, white, and blue plus yellow fringe should have green dollar signs instead of stars. Don't you? Carlos agrees. Carlos agrees with everything I say lately.

I think the killings up at the camp, and the end of the runaway, too, convinced Carlos and his friends and buddies and relatives and cronies and hired guns that I have some serious juice behind me. I think the turning point came right after I came down from the mountain and walked right into the city, calm as you

please. I had some major freeze inside, and I was as
big as a brick house and twice as strong. I saw fear on
his face. And something else too. Amazement. He was
amazed that I wasn't amazed at what had happened.

"So many killings," he said to me, puzzled.

"Yeah," I said. "Too bad the plastic bags we use for
the freeze aren't big enough to use as body bags." I
laughed at his discomfort.

"This is a scary thing," he said.

"I'm shaking in my boots. Come on, we've got work
to do."

"You are not scared?"

"Of what? Fuck-ups deserve to die."

"But your woman, she is also killed," he said,
clearly puzzled.

"She sure is." I was agreeable.

"You aren't sad at this?"

"Nah," I said. Cool. Cold, even. Smooth. "Hey, she
had it coming. She got greedy, just like the others." I
smiled at him. Saw him smile back, like he was in on
the joke. Saw his smile turn to stone when I laughed
too long and too meaningfully. I gave him a great big
hearty one with lots of teeth, then I stopped suddenly
and went back to punching numbers on a calculator.
Real cool. Like the feeling you get from putting the
freeze on really good.

I did miss the bitch a bit, though. She was a good
piece to use with the freeze. So when I saw the white
chick in the hotel bar, I had the urge. This one was a
looker. Great face, mainly nice around the lips. Legs
that went on forever. Looked like a sweet ass and hips.
Not too big, not too small. I wasn't sure about her
front at first. Her chest was a little hidden by a loose
blouse that had a couple of frills or flounces or
whatever they're called, but when she twisted around
in her chair to catch the bartender's eye, I saw the ripe

fullness of her as the material pulled in against the breasts. Funny how on whores they're tits, and on a woman you're trying to get they're breasts. Also funny how some women will do anything to get theirs to be bigger or look bigger, and those who've really got something will sometimes try to hide it with frilly, loose blouses.

I wondered about her for a couple of seconds. Shit, go for it. Nothing to lose. I went over to the bar and paid for the drink she just ordered, plus the rest of her tab. I told the guy behind the bar that I'd deliver the lady's fresh drink. He gave me the same big shit-eating grin I got from all the locals who were getting a taste of the payroll.

I walked up to her and set the glass down. "Allow me," I said. Then, before she could say anything, I looked back at the barman and gestured that I wanted the old glass removed. He snapped his fingers, and an old guy in a red waiter's jacket broke all known speed records getting her small table cleaned.

"You don't look like the hotel manager," she said, looking up at me.

"I'm not. I'm the guy who's buying you a drink. Two drinks. Or however many. I picked up your tab. Mind if I sit down?"

"Not if you use a chair," she said.

I saw what she meant. She was at a table for two but without a second chair. I stepped over to another table, grabbed one of the big wood-and-leather seaters, and hoisted it overhead as I walked back. That was the great thing about using the freeze. You were a lot stronger with it than without it.

"There we go," I said, plunking it down opposite her. I put myself into it, settling back, feeling good. Got to find out if she's alone. Might as well be direct. Use the right tone, and the direct approach disarms 'em more than if you try to finesse your way. "Who are you, what are you doing down here, and who are you with?"

"Oh, my. Well, my name's Cheri, and I'm here on a kind of scouting mission. Alone . . . uh, I'm here alone. I'm not with anyone."

"What are you scouting for?"

"Habits, customs, locations, and, well, everything. It's all for a professor—Professor Baker—and he's doing a research paper on the economy and the society and things down here. I just do the preliminary report on the cities and villages he might be interested in. I did it a couple of times before when I was in college, and he got in touch with me again now that he has this new grant. A grant of money, you know?"

"So what does he pay you to stop your life and do this stuff? Does he make it worth your while?"

"Oh, he does. I don't think the grant people know how easy it is." She glanced around as if afraid of being watched by grant people lurking in every corner. "Anyway," she went on, "when my divorce came through, I didn't really have that much to keep me in Tulsa."

"Oklahoma?"

"You betcha. You know another Tulsa?"

"You don't sound like you're from Oklahoma," I said. This was going fine, just keeping her talking about herself. They like that.

"Oh, I'm not from Tulsa originally. My husband worked there on some sort of electric-valve construction process or something. It was pretty boring, really. I'm from Northern California. Have you heard of Eureka? Eureka, California? Most people know about the scientist shouting 'Eureka,' but they don't know about the town. It's a paper-mill town. We've got logs, loggers, lumberjacks, log-hauling trucks, logging barges, logs, logs, and more logs. Boy, I just don't know. Going back to Mom and the logs would be okay, I guess, but I want to do this trip first. You know?"

"Yes," I said, nodding wisely, "I understand. You make it easy to understand."

"Really? Gosh, I don't think I do, not usually."

"No, I feel I can just see that town of yours." I could, too. The way she went on about logs, I could tell what was on her mind. She wanted something long, firm, and straight. This was perfect. Beautiful lady. Unattached. Probably hungry for it after her divorce. Went to college but not too bright. Seemed to have a thing for lumberjacks. Big, burly guys. As she talked, I slowly straightened up in my chair and tensed the muscles in my shoulders and neck. You can add about fifteen pounds to your appearance if you do it right, and it really makes your muscle tone stand out. At her next pause in the life story of Cheri, I said, "So, I take it that your husband was blind."

"Pardon?"

"Sure," I said, getting set to lay it on thick. "No guy is going to give up a woman as beautiful as you are without a fight or a big effort to change any problems he has. Like being boring. So I figure he must not have looked in your direction too often, which, as I can tell you right now, is impossible. So the guy must have been blind."

"Well, thanks, but no, he wasn't. He was blind emotionally, though. But I'm not really beautiful."

She was fishing. This was going to be easy. Just bait the hook and lay it out nice 'n' easy. I flexed my muscles and saw the admiration in her eyes. I leaned forward a couple of inches and said, "It's true that you've got your flaws."

"I do?"

"Sure," I said. "Your face is too perfect. Makes a man stop and lose his train of thought. Having no flaws is flaw number one." I saw her thinking this over. She was still puzzled over this gambit. "Then there's your legs," I continued. "Again, perfectly shaped, and very long. Makes a guy's knees weak. I mean, what am I supposed to do, sitting here with your legs right there across from me? Social convention says I can't touch, pinch, or even openly admire them. But it's not my fault that you are beautiful. And very sexy. No, I'd call that your fault. Fault number two." I smiled, just to show her this was partly playful. She was eating it up. "Then there's your body," I said as I rose to leave. "Excuse me a second, I'm going to get a Perrier. Do you want anything?"

"What? Oh, no. No, I'm fine."

You sure are, I thought, walking away. They didn't have Perrier, but they had soda and plenty of limes, so I settled for that. No sense cutting the effect of the freeze right now. Once I got her upstairs, I could drink and blow at the same time. I looked back at her in the mirror behind the bar. She had taken out a small compact and was fiddling with her hair. It was a dye job, just a little too reddish-blond to be real, but she'd be a knockout with any color, and the way she had it fixed was just . . . well, perfect. Some of my line was true.

Her little mirror was put away by the time I got back. I kept muscles flexed as I lowered into the chair. Easy, fluid, like an athlete. I let the silence roll out between us like a wall. Would she break through it?

"You were saying, before, that, um, well, what is wrong with me?" she said.

Jesus. She didn't want to use the word *body*. Could she be prudish? With a body like that?

"What do you mean," I said, " 'wrong with you'?"

"You were listing my faults, and you said something about my body. Well, what about my body, I want to hear how you turn *this* one into a compliment."

"Uh-oh, you're on to me." I smiled some more. Real sincere. She took a sip from her drink, put the glass down, but kept her hand on it, playing with it lightly. Like she was stroking it, I thought. Good. She can say *body* and make suggestive motions. Her eyes kept moving from mine, darting looks at my neck and shoulders. The muscled look was definitely working. I gave her a small, slow head roll, just gently flexing and stretching those tendons. Then I said, "It's the only part of you that you're not confident about. You wear things that cover up your body. That blouse, for instance. You picked it to hide behind. You have a beautiful body, beautiful breasts, but you worry about it. You look at pictures of models in *Vogue,* and you think you're built wrong. So you disguise the beauty you've got because you think that's the right thing to do." I shook my head back and forth once, slowly. "Big mistake," I told her. "Men don't like *Vogue* models."

"They don't?" she said.

"Nope. Well, real men don't. A man wants a woman to be all woman, you know? Proud of what she's got. Happy about it. Sensual, feeling, and alive." Go easy now. Not too fast. "You know," I said confidentially, "I think I know what you go through. I'll bet that when you're in a sexual situation, you can't help wondering if the man truly knows what a jewel you are." I like that. Jewel. Yeah, that was good. "I'll bet you've never had someone who . . ." I let the thought hang in the air.

"Go ahead," she said.

"Someone who made your whole body feel appreciated. I mean, truly loved. Adored, even." This was good stuff. *Truly* was a better word than *really.* I saw she got a faraway look. She was thinking about lovemaking. Some affair that had been good but which had ended badly, sadly.

"I—I don't know," she said.

"It's a matter of appreciation," I told her simply. "When you're with someone who appreciates you, everything is better."

"Yes," she said.

"Yes," I echoed. Her eyes were very far away now. She was getting turned on from my voice. I could tell. And I was getting hot too. But then I knew the things I was going to do to that body. I'd appreciate her body, all right. I'd appreciate the hell out of it. The trick now would be getting her to come up to my room instead of her inviting me to hers. I had the bindings, the equipment, the soundproofed floor. I waited until she looked into my eyes, held her gaze, and gave her a smile. A subtle smile, knowing, but a little—how'd they call it—world-weary. Yeah, that was it, world-weary. That always got to 'em. It's very romantic. With the smile still in place I said, "Too bad about social conventions, isn't it?"

"What?" she said.

"Like I said before, ladies and gentlemen aren't supposed to meet and discover an attraction for each other and act on that fact, not right away. Social convention says you're not supposed to find out that you both were missing each other, although you didn't know it, and then do something about it right at that moment."

"I guess that's true," she said slowly.

I kept looking into her eyes. She was getting dreamy. I wished I could take another blow, a good one. Get the freeze right up into the brain. Got to get on with this scene. Either way, I'd soon be upstairs with the freeze. I said, "I would very much like to experience love with you. I believe it would be something very beautiful." I paused a second. This was where she could make a sign. Lean forward or reach for my hand, say something, look hopeful, something.

She didn't move. Okay, time to move on. "But," I said with a sigh, "society says we shouldn't do this beautiful thing. Not right away. And heaven forbid we should go against society." I went into another slow, sinewy head roll. Let her think about missing out on feeling the muscle. Including the main muscle. I could see her thinking about it, hot for it, but shy, holding back.

Up to this point I hadn't told her anything about myself. I remembered how the bartender had barely acknowledged her request for a second drink, so I snapped my fingers at him and pointed at our table. A new round appeared in about fifteen seconds. She looked surprised.

"Good service here, don't you think?" I said.

"What did you do, bribe him?"

"Call it whatever you want. I pay for good service. It's like with my boat. If I want something done on it, I expect the finest, fastest service, but I expect to pay top dollar." She seemed interested in the boat, so I chatted about it. Then I told her about my place up in the hills, used to belong to one of the country's leaders. And I told her about my staff of servants, how everybody talks about the servant problem, but if you pay well, you get good results. And I told her about having the entire top two floors of this hotel. "You should see the view of the harbor," I said, not making anything of it. Just a friendly invite from a friendly guy.

"Well," she said, "maybe I could stop by to see that. You know, a little later on, in about an hour? I've got to send a wire to the professor. I was supposed to tell him about some weather records and stuff like that, but I didn't get them from the people down here, and I've got to let him know it may take a couple more days. Things can sometimes move slowly down here no matter what you do."

"Tell your professor you'll have your information in time to send it first thing Monday."

"But today's Saturday."

"So?"

"So that means I'd have people here actually working on the weekend. In this government? Ha."

"I can arrange it. I have influence with this so-called government."

"Really? You could do that?"

"Yes." Good, the money and power was what it took to get her. It was good because I didn't want to use the coke to get her interested. You never know how people will react. She seemed like she could be talked into it, but only after I got her upstairs. Then again, maybe not; I mean, consider: Eureka and Tulsa. Jesus. "So," I said, "will you come up a little later, to look at my view?" I'd show her a view, all right.

"I think so," she said.

"Great. Here's what you do. You take this." I handed her my key to the elevator. "It's for the penthouse express. You know where the hotel's regular elevators are?" She nodded yes. "Just go on past them, around that large pillar. It looks like there's no more lobby behind there, but there's one more elevator."

"I know," she said. "I looked around there when I first arrived."

She was inquisitive. Good, because that would make it easier to get her to put her wrists out where I could snap on the bindings. This was going to be fun.

"Okay," I told her. "That last elevator doesn't have a call button. Just use this key in the lock that's set into the wall. That way you won't have to ask at the desk for them to call upstairs. Much more discreet this way. A lady should always have things planned out for her that way, don't you think?"

"Yes, I do," she said.

"Good." I stood up. She slowly arranged purse and sunglasses and key, then got to her feet. God, she was beautiful. The only thing that seemed a bit out of place was that hairdo. Looked like a wig. Suddenly she was brushing her body against me.

"See you again soon," she whispered, and slid on past me toward the door.

"Umm" was all I could say as I watched her go. Her physical action caught me completely off-guard. Made me laugh. I'd been talking carefully for what seemed to be hours, trying to convince her I thought she was beautiful, desirable, sexy, and here she managed to say the same type of thing back to me with one movement of her body.

I went to the desk, got them to contact security to let me up, and told them I was expecting a visitor sometime in the next two hours.

"A woman," I said. "Alone."

"How will I know her?" the security guy wanted to know.

"Two things."

"Yes."

"First, she's beautiful."

"They always are."

"Yeah," I said. "Just lucky that way, aren't I?"

"Oh, it is much more than luck."

"Yeah. Anyway, the second thing is, she's got a key."

I went up, put on the freeze, changed clothes, and looked around for the best place to put the wrist bindings, so I'd be able to easily snap 'em on her before she knew what was happening.

Twenty-six

*I saw Langer as he came into the bar. I straightened a
little more in my chair, crossed my legs, hiking the hem
just a bit higher. In this show I was the lure. He was
sitting down, glancing around the room. Spotted me.
Good. Uncross the legs, then cross them the other way.
Pretend to be concerned with a section of the nylons up
about mid-thigh. Swing the legs out, slide the skirt up,
look down intently, and rub fingers along the smooth
fabric. Okay, swing the legs back under the table.
Wright always said my legs were my best feature, but
that was until he'd seen the rest. Now I wouldn't let him
forget his earlier comment.*

*Stop it. Don't think about Wright. You're here to
hook Langer. Just look your best, and make sure you're
alone until he comes over. If not here, then at the
restaurant tonight. Or here tomorrow afternoon. Or
down on the dock. One place or another, if you show
him enough skin and you're always unaccompanied,
he'll come over.*

I was just about done with the first iced mineral water, so I turned around and signaled the bartender to bring me another. As I turned back I noticed Langer was still looking over in this direction. Damn, is the wig slipping? I know I checked it about fifty times before, but when I turn my head too fast, it feels like it's not turning all the way with me. Can't get used to the feel of it.

"Allow me."

Langer was standing beside me, setting down a drink. He turned to look for the waiter, who appeared and removed the empty glass.

"Funny, but you don't look much like a hotel manager," I told him.

"I'm not. I'm the guy who's buying you a drink." Then a small laugh. "Two drinks." Laugh. "Or however many. I picked up your tab." He sniffed. Probably from the cocaine. "Uh, mind if I sit down?"

"Not if you use a chair." He saw that my table was one chair short. He went to get one, and instead of pulling it over, he lifted it over his head. Very impressive except for the sweat stains under his arms.

"There we go," he said, practically dropping it opposite me. Then the little laugh, followed by a sniff. "Who are ya, what're ya doing down here, and who're ya with?" Sniff.

Subtle. Real subtle. Ah, well, time for the dumb-bimbo routine. "Oh, my," I said, and gave him the name of Cheri, plus the yarn about doing research for a professor at one of the Stateside universities. Then I fed him the divorce story, and the mother back in Eureka, California, just waiting for me to come home to her.

"You make it so easy to understand," he said condescendingly.

God, I hate that. Might as well give him the dipshit routine. I said, "Really? Gosh, I don't think I do that, *not usually.''* God, I hate playing dumb. And this wig is making my head feel about three feet thick.

"No," he said, sniffing, *"I feel I can just see that town of yours."* Then he laughed. And sniffed. And began doing something strange with his neck and shoulders. Like he was trying to do an impression of a cobra. I thought he was having a reaction to the coke, maybe an overdose or a fit. But he kept doing it even as he talked. *"So,"* he said, still sniffing, *"I take it your husband was blind."*

Oh, not that one. *"Pardon?"* I said, playing along. Sure enough, he went into how no guy could take his eyes off me, no one could leave me, etc., and so the guy who divorced me must be blind. Oh, well, got to play along. *"Well, thanks, but no, he was just blind emotionally."* Might as well encourage him. The sooner he gets around to asking me out on the boat or up to his room, the better. I said, *"Besides, I'm not really beautiful."* That made him smile. I wondered at how he was going to lay out the compliments.

"It's true," he said, *"that you've got your flaws."*

Oh, no, first the blind bit, now the reverse flaws. And there he goes with the neck again. I tried not to look too disgusted. Remember, this is a way to gain insight into the lower-class criminal mind. It's a research project of your own. Okay, go along with the flaws gambit. I gave him the answer he wanted, and he went into his big description of my body. I tried to act amused and impressed. It wasn't easy. At one point he excused himself to go to the bar. He had paused at what he thought was a good point, leaving me hanging and hoping for a continuation of the compliments. Actually I was quite relieved to be alone for a couple of seconds. I took out my compact and checked to see if the wig was on straight. Once during his monologue, I had let my head rest against my hand. I could swear the wig

*slipped an inch, sliding sideways on my dome. No, it
looks okay. The style is hideous, of course, but it was
getting to the point where I could be recognized in these
parts, so the disguise was a necessity.*

He came back from the bar and just about freaked
me out with the way he got into his chair. Like some
television comic doing a slow-motion slapstick joke
about people with body casts. Then he just sat there
with a grin that can only be described as asinine. I
hated to do it, but I had to remind him of what he was
talking about or we'd still be sitting there. His eyes lit
up in triumph. He was actually waiting for me to ask
for it. As he began talking about me once again, I
thought about breaking my promise to Wright. I promised that I wouldn't shoot him right out in the open, but
this was getting to me. When he rolled his head around
in a parody of an exercise movement, I thought I was
going to burst out laughing. I widened my eyes, trying
to hold back what was close to becoming a case of
hysterics.

The whole sordid seduction scene dragged on and on
until he brought up the old saw about how society
doesn't approve of love at first sight. That's when I lost
any feeling for the humor of the situation. And when I
lost my anger. And when, to tell the truth, I lost almost
any feeling for anything. In other words, I got bored. I
made the standard responses, kept forcing my eyes
wide as though I were fascinated, and somehow en-
dured it. He switched from my body and beauty to his
money. That was a little more interesting, but I knew
he was likely to talk only of his possessions, not of how
he made his profits or of where he was putting the
dough. Then, suddenly, there it was: "You should see
the view of the harbor." He said it perfectly straight. No
leering, no laughing, no sniff—

I spoke too soon. He sniffed. But the point is, he was
finally offering to let me come up to his penthouse. All

right, now we're getting somewhere. I shyly agreed to show up in a little while.

"Great," he said. Sniff. "Here's whatcha do. Ya take this." He handed me a key. "It's for the penthouse express." He wiggled his fingers, putting quote marks around his little saying. "You know where the hotel's regular elevators are?" I nodded yes. *Since you couldn't get to any of the rooms except by breaking down the fire doors to the stairs or by going up one of the elevators, it would be quite amazing if I hadn't managed to discover the elevators by now.* "Just go past them," he said, "around that large pillar. It looks like there's no more lobby back there, but there's one more elevator." He said it smugly, like he was pulling off a fast one.

"I know," I found myself telling him. "I looked around there when I first arrived." *Damn. Don't make it sound like you notice too much. He's likely to smell a cop.*

He finished giving me my needless instructions for using his precious elevator and stood up. I got my glasses and purse together and stood up next to him. *Shit, he was staring at the wig. I couldn't get away fast enough, so I did the only thing possible to spoil his view. I moved closer to him. Right up against him.* I said in a half whisper, "See you again soon," and brushed past him, into the sunlight streaming in the front doors of the place. *I knew he couldn't get a good view of the wig with that light shining in his eyes.*

I wondered if I'd be able to tell Wright we were about to score, or if I'd just have to go up there without backup.

Twenty-seven

THE DOORBELL RANG. Could that be her? I knew that security wouldn't let anybody from the outside come up, but it might have been one of the men—Carlos, maybe. Or one of the hotel servants. I opened the door.

"Hello," she said.

"Helll-lo," I said back. She looked great. It seemed as if she had changed to a shorter skirt. Great. I'd always liked mini-skirts. I gave her a big smile, happy she was early, although it caught me by surprise and left me with a pile of pure stuff right out in plain sight.

"May I come in?" she said.

"Absolutely." I stepped back out of the doorway. "Sorry for staring like that. It's just that you look fabulous." I shut the door and threw the bolt.

"Thanks," she said, "but I think I've got a run in my stocking. See?"

She lifted her hem to reveal a small snag and a whole lot of upper thigh and lower hip. "Be still, my heart," I told her, using a cornball line that some old

girlfriend told me was romantic when we heard it in
an old movie.

"It can be arranged," she said.

The fuck does that mean? Oh, that our sex is going
to be a killer session. Okay. "Right," I agreed. Women
are funny sometimes. "Let's go into the living room,"
I said. "The view is great in there."

"All right."

"You can see my boat down in the harbor."

"Really?"

"Sure. Here, I'll show you." I stood behind her,
right in front of the large window. Moved in real close.
Put my left arm around her waist. Brought my right
arm over her right shoulder, sticking it out in front of
her, using it to sight along. "See where my finger is
pointing?" I said. "It should be right at the end of the
breakwater."

"Wait," she said, shifting her head and pulling my
arm a bit to the left. "Okay, there."

"Now, we come back this way and a little to the
right, past that brown-and-white boat, past the small
sailboat, to the one with the tall masts. That's the
one."

"Wow. You sail that big boat? That's very impressive. You'll have to show me sometime."

"Well, I like to use the engines, mostly. It has very
powerful engines."

"I'll bet," she said.

What the hell. Forget about it. She doesn't know
what she's saying. Get her over to the bookshelves.
The wrist bindings were just behind a large vase that
was sitting on a waist-high shelf just in front of the
stacks of books. It shouldn't be too hard to get her to
admire the flower arrangement in the vase. If I get her
over there, she can put down her purse and reach out
to adjust the flowers. I'll ask for her woman's touch

with the flowers. That'll do it. When she sticks her hands out, all I have to do is bring the bindings up and onto her wrists. They had an automatic click-lock mechanism—like handcuffs, in a way. I could snap 'em on in about one second. I'd been getting lots of practice lately.

The feeling was inside me, spreading. Thinking about making her body helpless, stripping her down, using her the way I liked. The sweet-sick weakness was in my gut, my throat, my legs. I nearly lost control of one knee as I guided her over toward the vase. She agreed to help with the flowers, to put down her purse. My heart was beating fast, helped by the freeze, but really going like a stripper's nightclub drummer because of the pictures in my head—pictures of her struggling against the bindings and ropes. She said something about my losing my balance for a second, but I waved it off. Then we were at the vase and she was making cooing sounds over the buds and leaves. She was swinging the purse strap off her shoulder, setting the purse aside, reaching up to the vase, hands not as high as I would have liked—what was she doing touching the vase instead of the flowers? Doesn't matter, I'm going to get her, anyway. The rushing in my head was deafening as I snatched up the bindings and brought them around the vase and up to her wrists.

A blur of movement. Her hands were gone. I was tugged by the wrists, losing my balance, falling down, at the edge of the shelving, look out for it, twist aside, glancing blow, roll on the floor.

Suddenly the sound in my ears went away. My heartbeat was going like crazy, but everything else was quiet. My wrists still had her fingers on them. But that was impossible; she was standing there, again holding her purse. My wrists had the bindings on them.

"The fuck is going on?" I said.

"Is that how you get your women ready?" she said. "Very suave, I must say. What's next? Chains? Ropes? Whips? A collar and leash? I'll bet you've got a room around here with all sorts of equipment. I think I'd like to see it, but first I want to get out of a piece of my equipment." She took off her hairdo. So it was a wig. Without it she looked familiar. In San Francisco! The one who had screwed Falkes.

"You," I said.

"Me?"

"You're the female dick."

"You got it, toots."

I started to get up. She had the gun out so fast, I didn't even get to blink. "What do you want?" I said.

"You can get up, but do it very slowly," she said, backing out of range of being rushed.

I got up slowly. "Look," I said, "we can work this out."

"Oh, I hope so. First let's find your playroom."

"What?"

"You heard me. Is it back that way?" she said, angling her gun toward the hall door. It was then that I saw the gun had a silencer. Not that it was really needed up here. I don't think anyone would hear a shot up here, with or without a silencer. I tried bluffing my way out of it, telling her everything in the room was monitored. No dice.

"In your little nest? I don't think so. Which way to your playroom?"

I tried stalling her, telling her what a great detective she must be to have put all the pieces together. She didn't buy it.

"Bullshit. It was just pure, dumb, blind luck. And I only did it because I wanted—" She stopped.

"The money?" I asked. "The coke?" No reaction. "You can have it. Hell, we could get the fuck outa here together, you and me. You and me and about twenty-five million bucks."

"Twenty-five million," she said, and sighed.

"Yeah, that's how much I've got here. And there's more coming in. It's a sweet setup."

"I'm sure it is," she said. "Let's continue this conversation in your playroom."

"Look," I started again.

"Move!"

I didn't have much choice. I went toward the door, slowly. When I got through it, that would be the time to move fast. Slip around the doorjamb, get the wall between me and the gun, grab something—anything —to hit her as she came into the room after me. Or get the door shut and locked if she just stood outside. Either way I'd have a chance to turn this thing around. When I was three feet from the door, she spoke.

"Hold it. Get down on your hands and knees."

"What?"

"You heard me. Move it!"

I was going to try talking her out of it, but she cocked the gun. The click seemed awfully loud. I went down to the floor. Could I still get up enough speed to make it? If I could put one foot against the door frame and use it to push off like a runner coming out of the starting block, I might just do it.

This was stupid, shuffling forward like a baby. Nothing for it but to slide along. Okay, just place the ball of the foot right in the center of the frame—no slipping off, now—turn the corner, slowly, and— push! I shot forward into the room, still in a crouch but with my head up to see a possible weapon. There, on the table, a big ashtray, solid and heavy. Grab it, spin, and—

"Nice try," she said.

She was in the room, backed away from me, about three feet on the far side of the entryway, well out of arm's reach. About all I could do was throw the ashtray at her. I noticed that she reached out to hold the door, ready to swing it in front of her like a shield.

"You would be dead before the ashtray got halfway over here," she said. "And I don't think I'd be hurt too badly even if I didn't have the door to block it. So, you want to put that down? That's a good boy. Now move, slowly, into the center of the room. Very good. All right, how's about you explaining how some of this equipment works. Tie yourself up to something and demonstrate for me."

"Hey, come on," I said. "This stuff is mainly for show. It's like sets in the movies. Atmosphere, you know."

"Sure. You just wanted to fasten a little atmosphere to my wrists."

"They're toys," I told her. "Look, I can get out of 'em." I reached the hidden slit in the leather, pried it back, found the release lever, turned it a hundred and eighty degrees, pulled it with my fingers, and off popped that binding. "See?"

"Oh, sure," she said. "That would be real easy to do while your hands were tied apart, even if you actually told your victims how to do it. Move over to that wall, slime."

"Aw, shit," I said. "You don't understand. I don't use this stuff to hurt people. You think I want anyone to get hurt in here?"

"Move."

"Come on, we can work this out."

"Would you like me to describe the kind of damage a shell from this gun can cause?" she said. "These bullets have a lot of what is known as stopping power. Why, I'll bet I could shoot your legs clean off with no more than two shots in each leg. Shall we give it a try?"

I moved over to the wall. Got to get her to listen. "What do you want? You want money? I can get you money. Lots of it. There's twenty-five million on my boat. It's yours."

"I know," she said.

"No, you can't get it. Not without me. It's rigged to explode."

"I know," she said.

"I can show you how to disarm it."

"I'll get it disarmed without you, thanks. Take one of those cords and fasten it to your right wrist."

Fuck, there had to be something else. That's when I saw the radio frequency detonator. When the charge had been rigged, the detonator was explained to me. It could explode the boat from up to a mile and half away. It worked on a very simple action: move a slide-bar switch, hold it firm against the spring-load, and press down a recessed button. I picked it up while reaching for the cord. Blowing up the boat would be the last trick, so I tried other things. I offered her the coke that was ready for shipment. I offered her the coke operation itself. I told her about the Russians, saying, "You could make a big splash in the States. Think about the headline: PRIVATE EYE BREAKS UP RED DRUG RING."

"I can do all that without you, Langer. Fasten that fucking cord or I'm going to blow your fucking foot off."

"Shit, you stupid bitch! What the hell do you want?" I jumped as her gun went off, snapping the cord out of my hand.

"What I want is you, asshole. Now pick up another cord."

"Okay, that's it," I told her. "See this?" I held up the detonator and told her what it was.

"It can't be a detonator, Langer," she said.

"Otherwise you would have the charge in one place and the detonator here. Which means you couldn't explode anything no matter how hard you tried."

"Jesus! All right, it's not a detonator. Fuckin' A! Look, it sends a signal to the detonator on the boat. Just look at it, will you?" I showed her how it worked. "I activate this and everything goes bye-bye. All the money, gone."

There was a noise in the other room. Could it be Carlos? Or the boys from security? She quickly moved over to the far wall, where she could keep me and the door in her line of sight. We both were half crouching, waiting to see who or what it was. Suddenly a man's head popped in and out of the doorway in the approved field-agent style, giving us only a small, briefly glimpsed target. She seemed to relax.

"Come on in, Wright, if everything's A-okay," she said.

"Yeah, it's fine. Don't mind if I do," he said. He was a big guy. He took one step forward and remained there, blocking the doorway. "How are things with the little shit?"

"Interesting," she said. She looked at me and said, "Tell the man about your little toy."

I explained the activating device all over again, adding some details about the amount of explosive planted on the boat. He thought about it for a while, glancing from me to her. Then he did something strange. He angled himself in the doorway, half in and half out, leaning one way and looking the other. "You know," he said slowly, "if I stand right here, I can see the boat out in the harbor. And if I turn back, I can see what goes on in this room. With just a slight shift of my head, I can see what goes down, no matter where the action takes place."

She smiled and said, "Thanks, Wright."

"No problem, Nat."

"The fuck are you two talking about?" I said.

"Something you wouldn't understand, creepo," she said. "Moral decisions. Ethics. Judgments. And one other thing. It also means we're going to conduct a little experiment."

Twenty-eight

WHEN WE HEARD the noise in the other room, we both stiffened. I got over to the back wall where I could take out Langer or whoever appeared at the door. It seemed to take forever for something to happen.

Then Wright stuck his head in and out of the doorway, grabbing a fast peek at the layout without affording anyone much of a shot at him. I relaxed a little, figuring he wouldn't have checked out the room like that if he had a gun at his back. Still, I gave him the code, just to make sure.

"Come on in, Wright, if everything's A-okay."

"Yeah, it's fine," he said. "Don't mind if I do. How are things with the little shit?"

"Interesting." I looked at Langer and told him to explain his toy to Wright. The guy was so rattled, he didn't even think to ask how Wright had gotten in. I saw Wright dangle some keys in his hand. That meant there were some dead or very shaken-up security people lying around somewhere in the hotel.

Langer finished explaining how his signaling device

*worked, and Wright stood there thinking about it,
looking at me. Langer was whining and pleading and
threatening all at once. He wanted to live and was
willing to give us twenty-five million if we'd allow it. Or
nobody gets the money. I thought about the people
Langer had destroyed, and about all those who were in
the process of being destroyed by the coke or crack that
came from Langer. I thought about the little empire of
drugs, death, money, sex, and power he had created
down here. I also thought about the possibility of letting
him go, getting the money, then capturing him again.
Not bloody likely. And we couldn't hope to do anything
except kill him if we wanted some semblance of justice
to prevail—we wouldn't be able to get him out of the
country without shooting our way out.*

*Wright told me what he was thinking. "You know,"
he said, "I can see the boat from right here. And by
glancing back I can see what goes down in the room
here. So whatever action takes place, I'll have a good
view."*

*He was letting me make the call. Money or no
money, I could do what I thought best. I smiled at him
and told him thanks.*

"No problem, Nat."

*"The fuck are you two talkin' 'bout?" Langer
whined. He sniffed and choked out a sort of giggle.*

*"Something you wouldn't understand, creepo," I
said. I rattled off a few words that meant a lot to me in
the last few days. Words like* morality, judgment,
conscience. *Words that were probably just words to
him. "And one other thing," I added. "It also means
we're going to conduct a little experiment."*

*In my hand the gun made a sound like a fist
punching a pillow. A kind of plopping sound. The bullet
went into Langer's chest, pushing him back against the
wall. I waited for him to bounce, then made the gun go
plop again, this time nailing him in the forehead just*

above his left eyebrow. I couldn't wait for his body to stop twitching this time—his hands, even in death, were working the radio signaling device—so I emptied the clip at his fingers, hoping to knock the thing away from him. No, not his fingers, aim for the wrists. There, got him right on the binding. Plop-plop-plop-plop-plop-plop. Finished off the eight shots. Got his forearms twice and his wrists three times. Five out of six, only two of them pure luck. Not bad shooting, especially with the silencer on.

But it didn't matter. Out in the bay, the boat went boom. I stood there for a while. Drained, empty. Not feeling as bad as I'd feared.

"You might want to see this," Wright said quietly from the doorway.

"What?" I said dully, walking over to join him.

"Look who's trying to investigate the explosion."

He handed me a pair of field glasses he must have found on the shelves. I focused in on a small boat with two guys in business suits, flailing around the oil-slicked debris and rolling smoke on the water.

"How'd they get out there so fast?" I said.

"They were on the way out already."

"How do you know?"

"Because I invited them."

"You what?"

"Well," he said, "the message was signed by Langer, or looked to be signed by him. I wanted to find out if they were protecting him or his operation."

"And they just missed dying for it."

"Yup."

I watched CIA Agents Daniels and Anderson make fools of themselves in their dinghy. I put down the glasses and said, "I don't feel much like talking, Wright. Let's discuss this later, okay?"

"What's the matter?"

"What do you mean?" I said testily. "I just made a

speech about morality and ethics, and then I shot a man in cold blood. It doesn't add up right in my head right now. In fact, I think it sucks."

"For what it's worth, I think you made the right call. Besides, we already went over all this before. Killing him was the only way to end this little operation. And having the others go at the same time does the whole world a service."

"Others? What others?"

"Carlos was on the boat."

"Carlos the policeman? Langer's Carlos?"

"The same. Also two Russian embassy officials, three different muscle men, and a couple of local coke packagers."

"How?"

"I sent messages to everyone we suspected was in on it," Wright said. "Demanded a meeting. Said the deal's either going to be doubled or canceled, so get your ass over to the boat. 'Course, I didn't use my name on the messages."

"Were you going to blow up everybody?"

"Nat!" he protested. "I didn't know about the remote control."

"Sorry. So what was the plan?"

"Get them all in one place, contact the boat on the radio, and tell them Langer had run off with the money. See what happens. Record it. Notify the press. Whatever."

"But they might have known about the centerboard," I said.

"Then they'd probably also know about the bomb. And if not, well, then maybe I wouldn't have minded too much if they'd blown themselves up. But," he added, "I would have directed them out to sea a mile or so before telling them about the money. For all we knew, the explosives in there could have taken out half the harbor."

I couldn't take it all in. I mean, it registered on my brain, but I didn't seem to have any solid reactions to the information. "Shit, I'm tired," I said.

"How long will it take you to pack?" he asked.

"I don't know. Under normal circumstances, about twenty minutes. Today, about three or four hours, I guess."

"Then you'd better start now. The boat for Chiclayo leaves in four hours."

"Why are we going to Chiclayo?"

"Because that's where I was able to charter a plane."

"Charter a plane? What's wrong with the regular carriers?"

"When you're smuggling twenty-five million in cash, you need a special flight path."

"What the hell? You got the money too?"

"Yeah." He smiled. "I'm very proud of you for not mentioning the money, not once. You changed from wanting the cash to wanting to rid the world of Langer. But," he said, "since you were doing such a bang-up job of getting him, I thought I'd do my part to make the trip turn a profit."

"Goddammit, Wright," I said. "You could have been killed."

"And you could have been in pretty deep shit yourself, coming up here with no backup."

"I couldn't find you."

"And you didn't wait another half hour. Hey, girl, you came early to this party. I said I'd see you between two and two-thirty. It's two-thirty now."

He had me on that one. "Shit," I said.

"Yeah. I gotcha."

"Okay, okay," I said. "But it worked."

"So did my efforts out on the boat."

"Right."

"Damn right. Now, let's get the hell out of this town. I do believe we've created an international incident out

there." He nodded toward the harbor, where the smoke was still hanging over the twisted, splintered, and blackened remains of the ship.

On the way out of the hotel I kept nagging Wright about all the loose ends. What will happen to the local police, army, navy, and other government agencies? Where's Langer's runaway girlfriend? What about the CIA involvement? How does this affect the big boys left holding the empty money bags back in San Francisco? Little items like that.

"Forget it for now," Wright said. "The CIA thing we can handle from the city. Down here is down here. Out of our hands unless we want to stay. As for Doris/ Diana, what happens to the girlfriends of other coke dealers? They get used up. Or they burn out. They disappear. Forget her."

"Okay, so what about the Leather and Lace trio? What about them?"

"They either joined Langer's operation or started one of their own. Or they got taken suddenly dead one day while trying to join Langer's organization or start one of their own. Forget them too. The story ends here."

We took a boat out of the harbor, past the fading oil slick that was all that was left of Langer's craft. On our way to rendezvous with our plane, I told Wright that we didn't really accomplish much in the way of stemming the cocaine trade.

"You got that right," he said.

I went on as if I hadn't heard him; I guess I just wanted to get it said, get it out in the open, the better to deal with the futility I was feeling. "I mean," I said to him, "this is Peru. Not one of the real biggies. Now, Colombia, Bolivia, sure. They probably have a few dozen setups like Langer's, with each one ten times as big."

Wright looked impatient. "Nat," he said with a sigh.

"I know, we talked about it before. Christ, Wright, it bothers me. I shot somebody, you blew up a bunch more somebodies, and all for what? We didn't do anything, not really."

"Hey," Wright said, "how many coke deals have been busted at the source? By private parties? How many busts have caught embassy officials using the diplomatic pouch for smuggling? Hell, if we do nothing more than call attention to that, we'll be doing the world a big favor. And how many busts have managed to cast suspicion on the law-enforcement agencies who are supposed to be protecting us from geeks like Langer? The neatest thing about this is being able to make some waves about the official sanctioning of the dope traffic."

"Well, okay, I guess . . ."

"We pulled it off, Nat. It wasn't the all-time greatest bust, but it may have been the biggest in dollars. It may not have involved the most criminals, but we got who we were after, and we've focused attention on some scummy scenes. It's now up to the locals to clean it up. We did what we had to do. It had some skill, some luck, and some pure, raw cussedness, but however it worked, it worked. So take that and be satisfied with it."

"Yeah," I said, nodding. I relaxed a bit. "Yeah, okay, Mr. Wright." I smiled for the first time since pulling the trigger on Langer. Not too long ago, to be sure, but an eternity for the grin muscles at the sides of my mouth. They were happy at the exercise.

"Besides," Wright said, half smiling, "you want to talk about ethics, we've got a hell of a moral problem on our hands."

"We do?"

"Sure. Do we return the twenty-five million and collect the two-point-five-million reward? Or do we keep it all? Just like with Langer, everybody will assume it blew up in the explosion."

"You're not serious?"

"*Well, not really. I do, however, recommend that we take our two point five off the top before returning the cash. I don't feel like dealing with the insurance-company paperwork. But as for keeping all of it, nah. It's just that, well, you see, Nat, people in love will say the darnedest things when they are deprived of affection.*"

"*Deprived?*"

"*That's what I said.*"

"*Wright, this is too small a boat for that.*"

"*Come here.*"

"*Wright . . .*"

"*It's all right, we'll just hug. We can do more on the plane.*"

"*No, we can't.*"

"*Yes, we can. It's got a bed.*"

"*The plane?*"

"*Um-hmm.*"

"*What have you chartered?*"

"*It's used by dignitaries, touring rock stars, that sort of thing. Nothing but the best for us, I say.*"

"*Trying to spend our two point five as fast as possible?*"

"*Oh, did I forget to tell you? I also cleaned out the little safe that your CIA pals had installed at their place. They only had about twenty thousand. I figure we'll use it for our expenses. Seems only fair.*"

"*Wright, they'll have to account for that money.*"

"*They can pay it off out of their salaries.*"

"*They'll come after us.*"

"*And we'll blow the whistle on their involvement in Langer's operation.*"

"*So you're letting them off the hook for twenty thousand dollars?*"

"*That and one other little thing.*"

"*What's that?*" I said.

"*They have to go straight from now on.*"

"How will you monitor that?"

"Fend will help. With our backing, he'll build the best computer network the surveillance world has ever seen. Or not seen, I should say, since part of what he'll do will be to cover his tracks."

"Oh, Wright," I said, *"I'm tired of all this. I'm tired of the fieldwork, I'm tired of the computer side of it, and I never did like the seminars and shit like that."*

"It's only natural to feel down right now. When we get back, you'll feel better about everything. You're probably not going to want to do much fieldwork, and we'll hire some suits to do the seminars. But I know you're not going to give up the game. You like figuring out people and their motivations, what makes them tick. You like putting together pieces of the puzzle. You like the digging, the computer searches, the a priori and a posteriori reasoning. You're not going to run away from that."

"I guess you're right. I mean, correct."

"Sure," he said. *"It's in your nature."*

His tone had changed subtly. He had been serious before. Now, although he was trying to sound serious, he was leading up to some outrage. *"You want to tell me about my nature, Wright?"*

"All right, Nat. You are perfect for this job because, well, because basically you're a snoop."

"A snoop?"

"That's right. A snoop and a sneak. A voyeur."

"Voyeur!"

"That's it. A sneaky, snooping, voyeuristic spy. And a busybody."

"Oh, great, now I'm a busybody."

"Right. Snoop, sneak, voyeur, spy, busybody, Peeping Tom, eavesdropper, gossip monger—"

"That does it," I said. I punched him as hard as I could in the arm.

"Ow!"

"Goody," I said. But I had to smile. Wright had done it again. He made me care. About me, about him, about us. About everything. I had slipped back on some sort of mental cruise control, and his little word game brought me out of it.

"You pack quite a punch, lady."

"You deserved it."

"You enjoyed that too much," he said.

"The sensation was quite satisfying, thank you."

The sensations we shared on the plane were quite satisfying, too, thank you.